ELEVEN ELEVEN
plus eleven

A collection of short stories

by
Colin G. Harley

Grosvenor House
Publishing Limited

The right of Colin G. Harley to be identified as the author of this
work has been asserted in accordance with Section 78
of the Copyright, Designs and Patents Act 1988

The book cover is copyright to Inmagine Corp LLC

This book is published by
Grosvenor House Publishing Ltd
Link House
140 The Broadway, Tolworth, Surrey, KT6 7HT.
www.grosvenorhousepublishing.co.uk

A CIP record for this book
is available from the British Library

ISBN 978-1-78623-582-4

Contents

ELEVEN ELEVEN

ELEVEN ELEVEN

A London hotel, an evening spent with the love of my life and an event that would change our lives forever. I have a tale to tell that I cannot explain, I can only relate it to you, the reader, and allow you to draw your own conclusions.

It all began with my partner and I planning a night out in the big city. It was our custom, once in a while, to book into a London hotel, take in a show or a meal (or both) and generally relax and enjoy each other's company. Although we varied the hotels that we used, I had a particular penchant for Barleys, one of the oldest purpose-built hotels in London, dating back to mid-Victorian times. It is reputed to be the first hotel to have electric lighting and one of the first to be fitted with lifts. For me, it has old world charm with modern attributes and courteous, helpful staff.

We had decided upon an Italian meal and had opted for one of our favourite restaurants in the West End. The meal had been good with the food and wine excellent and the atmosphere, well the atmosphere was typically Italian – noisy, happy and friendly.

On returning to the hotel we had made our way straight back to the room, we were tired and whilst we were far short of being drunk, by the time the taxi dropped us off the chill night air had had the effect of bringing the alcohol to the surface. We both felt replete and relaxed.

Although we would normally have made love before going to sleep, it didn't matter to either of us if we waited until morning to indulge ourselves, so we lay on the bed, gradually taking off each other's clothes as we caressed, cuddled and kissed each other in our own typically loving, caring way.

As we enjoyed each other's bodies we gradually slipped away into a comfortable contented world of our own. As Francesca closed her eyes and snuggled into me, I reached over her and turned out the bedside light. I remember glancing at the digital alarm clock on the bedside table. It read eleven minutes past eleven. We drifted away into sleep.

I was in no way ready for what happened next; I could not have foretold the events that were about to unfold.

Waking up was initially a shock, turning into a deep sense of disbelief. The only way I can describe the feeling is to liken it to that feeling when you wake up in an unfamiliar room and, for a few seconds, sometimes long seconds, that feeling of disorientation and confusion washes over you as your mind searches to take things in and make sense of them.

My first impression was that this was not the room I went to sleep in and that everything in the room was different. As each of my senses came into play, they told me that something had changed, something was different, something was wrong.

Firstly, there was the layout of the room. Everything, with the exception of the bed, had gone. Instead of the television, built-in drawer unit with minibar, fitted wardrobes and the large mirror on the wall there were separate pieces of furniture. Each of them was quite tasteful in its way but quite dated in design. The room was lit by a single lamp hanging from the ceiling, which was on but seemed much dimmer than it should have been. The wallpaper and curtains were of a different design than I remembered, as was the carpet. Even the bed we were laying on had changed although its position in relation to the rest of the room had not.

In addition to the visual impact, the room seemed to smell different; it wasn't unpleasant in any way, just different. It was then that I noticed the fireplace with the bright red embers still glowing in the grate. Above it was a mantelpiece with an old clock upon it. I could make out that the hands were showing eleven minutes past eleven.

A thousand questions went around in my head. Was this a hoax, a joke being played on us by friends, a television game show stunt of some kind? Had we been drugged, moved or possibly kidnapped?

I looked at Francesca. As far as I could tell we were unharmed, free from any restrictions and dressed (or rather undressed) in the same manner as when we went to sleep. I decided to wake her, although I thought it best to do so carefully to prevent us both experiencing the same degree of shock. I did my best but in the event she voiced the same concerns with the same disbelief and confusion that had raced through my mind only a few moments before.

Once we had calmed each other down a little, we had to decide what to do next. We got up, dressed and carried out a detailed investigation of the room and its contents.

As far as we could tell, not having been in that situation before, everything was genuine. The furniture seemed authentic, not from a film set, and of a type that I can only describe as solid and functional. The chairs were matching and covered in a red and cream striped patterned cloth. The fixtures and fittings were real and in full working order with two electric lights, one hanging from the ceiling and one in the form of a tall standard lamp standing in the corner. There were two doors in the room, as there had been when we went to bed and in the same locations as before. Opening one revealed an adjoining bathroom complete with hot and cold running water, but with bathroom suite and fittings of the same dated appearance as apparent in the main bedroom.

After about five minutes discussion, during which we tried to make some sort of sense out of this bizarre situation we found ourselves in, we decided that we should leave the room and take a look around outside. We did, however, make the commitment to each other that we would stick close together and not become separated.

Just as we prepared to take this potentially great leap into the unknown, we heard an unfamiliar noise from outside in the street. Looking back it seems odd, but neither of us had considered looking out of the window. Francesca encouraged me to draw back the heavy, dark red curtains and take a look.

The first impression was of a well-lit street, not the strong bright light that we have become used to but a more gentle light that seemed to permeate rather than shine through a dull haze. The light, it could have been gaslight I suppose, was emanating from a series of lampposts that were spaced along the street. As I allowed my eyes to follow them along I realised the difference between what I was looking at and what I would have expected to see. There were no shops. I recalled that, instead of the neat row of houses along the street, there should have been a row of shops. As I pressed my head against the glass to get a better look I could make out that this was the same for as far along as I could see.

I called Francesca to come and join me. We both stood there, taking in the view that was before us. We turned to look at each other and agreed that neither of us could explain it.

If this was a hoax it was certainly very elaborate.

If we were surprised so far, what happened next really confused us. We heard an unfamiliar noise made by something in the street outside, apparently coming towards us. As the sound approached and became louder, we were astonished to see a two-wheeled horse-drawn carriage go gently clip-clopping by and disappear out of our sight and into the gloom. We drew back from the window, looked at each other in surprise and sat down on the bed. At first we were silent, trying so hard to comprehend, wanting so much to make sense of what we were seeing and hearing.

Gradually, our combined stunned silence wore off and we started to try and talk to each other. At first our conversation was disjointed and stuttering as we tried to confirm to each other what we had seen; then it developed into being more supportive as we attempted to prove to each other that we were not dreaming or going insane.

After confirming that we were indeed alive and, as far as we could judge, well, we spent a few minutes discussing what to do next.

We decided that we might as well leave the room and take a look outside the hotel. We assured ourselves by saying that we didn't need to go too far from the room. If the whole thing was a hoax we felt that the perpetrators would be found out rather quickly and if not, well, if not, we were not going to learn anything more about our situation by staying put. The one thing we did agree upon was that we would stay together at all costs; nothing was to be allowed to come between us or separate us in any way.

On approaching the door, I was pleased to see that there was a key in the lock. It hadn't dawned on me before but I realised that we couldn't have gone far if we had left an unlocked room behind us.

We stepped into the corridor, turning to lock the door as we went.

The first thing that we noticed was that the internal layout of the hotel was just as we remembered. We made our way along the corridor, up a short flight of stairs, past the lift and towards the long flight of stairs that connected all of the floors to the main lobby. The lighting along the way was adequate; the corridor was noticeably slightly darker than before but the light seemed softer and in some way gave a warmer appearance than the harsh white light we were used to. I stopped and took a closer look at one of the wall lights; it was a little ornate in design but clearly an early electric fitting and bulb.

It was then that we encountered our first people. Coming up the long staircase towards us was a couple. They did not see us and were clearly not aware that we were there.

Looking more closely whilst holding back a little and observing the couple as discreetly as possible, we could see that the woman appeared to be in a rather distressed state. She was stooping forward slightly as they came up the stairs; she appeared to be softly sobbing even though she was clearly trying to retain her self-control and dignity. The man had his arm around her shoulder and was doing his best to comfort her. He was looking at her intently and caringly. They were both oblivious to our presence.

We stopped at the top of the stairs, not sure quite what to do. We watched as they approached, gradually ascending the stairs towards us. When they reached the top step, the man looked up at us. He stopped and a somewhat quizzical look came over his face as our eyes met.

I was equally taken aback. I was looking at my double. As his partner looked up at me, I could see that she was also the very image of my partner Francesca. They were dressed differently, it's true, but the similarities in our facial features and overall build were unmistakable. The four of us stood and stared at each other for what seemed like several minutes; I am sure that the situation we found ourselves in was equally incongruous to each of us.

I was the first to speak; the first to break the silence. I asked if we could help in any way. Looking back, I must confess that I don't know why I said it; it just seemed to be the right thing to do at the time.

He responded by saying that since his wife was feeling a little distressed perhaps we would care to join them in their room for a drink.

Their room was similar in décor to the one in which we had awoken, although possibly a little larger. It seems a little ludicrous looking back on it, but the four of us seemed to naturally accept each other right from the start. It was odd, given that we had never met before, appeared to come from different times, were dressed differently and the only common factor between us was the undoubted similarities in our physical appearance.

The first thing that we did was to introduce ourselves to each other. That was when the second coincidence became apparent. Their names were Felicity and Charles, and ours being Francesca and Colin we shared common initials. As I recall surnames were never stated, although I suppose that they may have been a little surprised to find that we were not married.

The next stage in the proceedings was to organise refreshments. Unlike the minibars of today the room had a small but adequate bar stocked with a limited choice of drinks compared with the wide range we are used to today. Suffice it to say that brandy was the selected drink for each of us, although Francesca had to forego her usual Coke and settle for soda water.

To start with, and in an effort to make sense of the somewhat bizarre situation in which we found ourselves, I attempted to make conversation on general topics such as had they travelled far to get to the hotel and what did Charles do for a living. My aim was to break the ice, learn more about our situation and try and make some sense of things. It did not work. Felicity bowed her head and bravely stifled her tears with a short muffled sob.

Charles interjected and explained, quite openly, that they had recently had the dirty done on them in a deal over land. The land was to be used for the new railway and, because he had foolishly tried to save money by not engaging a solicitor of his own, the railway company owners had deceived them and they were now in danger of being made bankrupt. They had come to London to reason with their bank. They were in danger of losing everything and the manager of the bank had been less than supportive to them in their plight.

Charles went on to say that he had been advised that afternoon that an agreement had been put forward by the bank that if they gave up their land and their house, they could be provided with a small farm, complete with farmhouse, buildings and livestock. It was clear that they had been swindled out of their property but by accepting this offer they would, at least, not be made bankrupt and thus lose everything.

It transpired that they had been waiting for a messenger to come to the hotel that evening to advise them whether the railway company had agreed to settle on the bank's proposal. The messenger had arrived late at 11 o'clock with the final papers and once Charles had signed them the settlement had been finalised.

The enormity of what had happened and the impact of the eventual solution now having been reached had taken their toll on Felicity. Since she was so distressed by the whole process they had decided to retire to bed which was when they had chanced to meet us at the top of the stairs on their way back to their room.

I offered, without thinking how I could possibly deliver, my help in any way that I could.

Charles began his explanation. It transpired that he had spent the early part of his life in the army as an engineering officer. He had met Felicity, the love of his life, whilst stationed in Lincolnshire and decided to buy himself out and set up home there.

He found employment at a local engineering company and they had married and set up home together.

They had had some luck in that an aunt of Felicity had died and left her a small estate with some land and a rather run down farm managed by an elderly couple with no children. The aunt had been a spinster and had a soft spot for Felicity, who had done her best to care for her in her final years.

All was going reasonably well but Charles aspired to greater things and that was how he came to take a chance on the deal to sell off part of the land for the railway.

My mind drifted for a second as he was speaking and it jolted me back to my senses. I suppose that I had assumed either that I was engaged in some rather detailed and intense dream or that so many strange things had occurred in a relatively short space of time that my mind was totally taken up with receiving and assimilating all the new information it had taken in and had to deal with.

Here we were sitting in an hotel room, apparently from the past, discussing the problems of two people from another era who we didn't know and offering to help them in any way we could. How on earth could we understand their situation and what could we possibly do to help them? I decided that if this was 'real', even if I didn't understand it, I would need to know more if we were going to assist in any way at all.

My first task, I thought, would be to ascertain the period that they were from and, if possible, an accurate date.

Cautiously, you might even say nervously, I attempted to ask what they thought the date was. I couldn't think of a way to make the question sound sensible so, in the end, I just came out and asked it.

I wasn't prepared for the response that Charles made.

After his initial comment that it was an unusual question to ask, he politely told me that it was Friday the sixteenth of November. Initially, I thought that I had finally caught someone out and that the hoax was unmasked. When we had gone to bed it was Friday the seventeenth, he had clearly miscalculated and maybe now we could find out what was really going on.

It took my lovely sensible Francesca to ask the right question and get straight to the heart of the matter. She simply asked what year it was. Charles responded immediately, "1900, of course".

All was quiet for a few moments. I looked at Francesca and she looked at me. Neither of us knew what to say.

Felicity was the one to break the silence. She asked where we came from, our clothes were clearly not contemporary and it was strange that we appeared to be confused over the date.

I found it difficult to speak at this point and it was Francesca who decided that it would be best to try and explain our predicament. This was probably a good thing because she has always been the calm level-headed one in our relationship.

She proceeded to explain how our meeting had come to pass from our point of view. She told the story very gently and carefully, how we had gone to sleep at eleven minutes past eleven and woken up in these strange, and yet familiar, surroundings. She delayed the bombshell about our having come from the year 2000 until the very end, then it was their turn to sit and stare at each other.

Charles poured us all another drink.

They broke the silence. Each of them asked questions that made it clear that they did not believe us, him more so than her. Why were we here? Where had we come from? Was there some purpose behind our meeting? I suppose you would expect them to mistrust people after what they had been through.

Felicity had been quiet for a few minutes and then she made the most profound statement of all of those made that evening. She simply said that even if they couldn't understand, perhaps fate had played a hand and we had been sent to help them.

My logic was no better than hers, I was in no position to contradict her or argue with her thinking.

And so we set about the task of helping them.

We needed to understand more about their world and what it was like to live in those times. Although I suppose we all have our ideas about what things must have been like many years ago, neither of Francesca nor myself could ever be described as history buffs. I would venture to suggest that even if we were expert historians our knowledge would be general rather than detailed in terms of precisely what was going on in a specific time or place.

We gleaned that Charles, from his background of engineering in the army, understood military hardware and was used to adapting and improvising equipment. Therefore, it would be reasonable to assume that something of a mechanical nature may hold the key. I decided to confine my questions to areas that would enable us to learn more about the world that they lived in whilst concentrating on information that could provide some guidance for Charles to build on and develop.

We talked of many things that night, too many to recount here. I shall relate the main ones that I can recall that enabled me to come up with some ideas as to how to advise and guide them.

Charles felt that the future was in horse-drawn transport, although it was evident that steam-powered road and agricultural vehicles were being used but they were, for the most part, heavy and unreliable. Electric powered transportation was in use, but only for some of the railways and, in the big cities, trams.

My knowledge of recent history was insufficient to enable me to judge the status of the development of the automobile in 1900 and therefore I asked Charles to tell me. He said that petrol-driven carriages were around. They were expensive and only for the rich. Their reliability was improving, this being demonstrated by their owners annual run from London to Brighton. He said he could see no future in the new-fangled motor car.

I find it interesting that it took someone from the past to tell me that the first London to Brighton run was in 1896, we look upon it today as an annual outing for veteran and vintage cars, back then it was a demonstration of their reliability!

I attempted to steer Charles away from his thinking on the automobile and the future of horse-drawn transport. What I needed to do was identify some kind of expanding market that would suit his capabilities and experience. I needed to guide him towards an investment opportunity which they could take advantage of by utilising his skills and knowledge and thus make their fortune.

Given his background, I attempted to steer his thinking towards motor-driven vehicles such as motor cars, lorries and public transport. The manufacturing of agricultural or farm vehicles and equipment was also a possibility.

This last suggestion struck a chord with Felicity and she launched into idea after idea on what they could invest in, the main one being in steam powered lorries, buses and tractors.

Charles was not convinced, he said that her enthusiasm was commendable, but he was not so sure that this was the right course of action to take. I felt it necessary to step in and tell him that we knew that they were witnessing the demise of the horse as far as transportation was concerned; it was destined to become a novelty as far as the transport and agriculture industry is concerned.

Felicity continued to chip in with ideas of her own. The colour came back into her cheeks as her enthusiasm rose and the ideas seemingly burst forth from her mind. He may have been the practical engineer in their relationship, but she was clearly the entrepreneur. They became more enthusiastic and the comments and suggestions ebbed and flowed between them to the extent that they almost forgot that we were in the room with them. I now started to believe that all would be well with them, working as a team I felt that they could not fail to succeed and that, for them, the only way was up.

We expanded a little and told them a little more of things that we knew but they couldn't. We mentioned flying and travel around the world, how accessible places had become as a result. They promised to take heart, to persevere with the ideas that we had fostered within them and not give up.

After a while their thoughts returned to us, they were apologetic for ignoring us but at the same time were clearly elated from their plans for a new beginning.

They now directed their questions to us. Were we angels? Where had we come from? What were we doing there and by what means had we travelled, apparently through time itself?

We didn't have any answers, of course. We had no explanation to offer them. All we could do was try and tell them our story; it seemed absurd and impossible even as we said it. We could only repeat that, as far as we were concerned, we had gone to bed at eleven minutes past eleven on the seventeenth of November 2000 and awoken to find ourselves in the same place but at a different time, apparently a hundred years in the past. Reasons as to how or why were beyond us.

When it came down to it, they had little choice but to trust us and try – it could be their only chance. Maybe our coming was the plan of some higher entity, maybe fate or maybe some fault in time that put us together. How many times have you thought that someone was looking over your shoulder or that some inexplicable force had intervened to provide assistance?

How could they thank us enough for helping them? Just their thanks were enough. It would be sufficient for us to know that we had helped in some small way. We told them to go forward, believe in themselves and each other and to play to their strengths then we, in turn, believed that they could achieve their dreams.

They asked if there was anything they could do in return. At first we said no but then Francesca had an idea. She said that we would like to see and learn something of the world that they live in. It was Felicity's idea for them to lend us some clothes in order that we could go for a walk around without, hopefully, causing any confusion. We would look less conspicuous, certainly, than dressed as we were.

She went to the wardrobe and handed us each a set of clothes. In turn, we went into the bathroom and changed. They fitted us perfectly.

We decided to take a ride down in the old lift; after all it was supposed to be one of the oldest in London. What am I saying, of course, at that time it would have been one of the newest! It was slightly different to more modern versions in that it only had the one set of doors and you had to operate them yourself, but it was an electrically operated lift for all that.

We came out of the lift, turned left and through a set of double doors into the foyer. At our first glance it was much as we remembered, a relatively large open space with two large columns rising up to a high ornately sculpted ceiling. To our left was the base of the long staircase with the reception desk beyond, in front of us the double doors into the street and to our right the entrance to the bar. We consulted briefly and decided to opt for the bar first.

The doors to the bar were open. Francesca took my arm, giving a little reassuring squeeze as she did so and together we stepped one pace inside.

I sensed that nobody took any notice of me. When they saw Francesca, however, it was apparent that there was a noticeable decrease in the level of noise as, one by one, the customers in the bar turned to look towards us. Gradually, all became quiet.

I realised that whilst the men in the bar were drinking and smoking, as you might expect, the 'ladies' with them were dressed differently and were probably 'ladies of the night'. Francesca, dressed as she was in what I can only describe as Felicity's more discreet clothes, did appear to be somewhat out of place. I felt that we were therefore identified as interlopers and, as such, I decided that this was not the place for us to be. We turned, trying as much as we could to retain our dignity and composure, and left immediately.

Next we turned our attention the main hotel double doors into the street. We walked towards them and as we did so the two attendants, one on each side, bowed their heads slightly and pulled the doors open as we approached.

We looked past them and into the street beyond. The first thing that struck me was that the atmosphere outside was more hazy than in our day and it had a decidedly smoky odour about it. The smells of the city were noticeably different, although I was unable to identify any of them with any accuracy.

The building immediately opposite the hotel on the other side of the road was the underground station. It took me a minute or two to work out what initially seemed odd about it and then I realised. The name was different. What was Gloucester Road in our day was then called Brompton. (I have checked it since and discovered that it wasn't renamed Gloucester Road until 1907 when the Piccadilly Line was built.)

We watched as a two wheeled carriage drew up outside the hotel and a couple got out. The man had a brief exchange with the driver (I could not make out if he paid him) then he turned and helped his lady companion to the kerb. They came up the few steps towards us, we moved aside to allow them to pass and the man wished me good evening as the woman nodded her head to Francesca but said nothing. We responded in the same manner, simply because it seemed the right thing to do. They swept past us into the hotel and on towards the lifts, collecting what I presumed was their room key from the reception desk as they passed.

Something told us that it was unwise for us to go outside, nothing particular, just a feeling inside. It could have been a fear of the unknown or even a fear of us not being able to get back. We stood in the doorway for a few minutes, then I made some mumbled excuse to the doormen and we drew back.

Eventually, after noting that the big grandfather clock in the foyer was showing four o'clock, we returned to their room and changed back into our clothes. We bade our newfound friends a fond farewell with an embrace and a kiss. (Gestures that struck me afterwards that may have been unusual to them, but at the time we did naturally and without any second thought, just as family or close friends would do today).

Before we parted, Charles said that if I ever needed to contact him I could do so through his solicitor in London. He told me that his name was Robert Jenkinson of Chancery Lane.

We returned to our room and lay down on the bed together, side by side. We made a rather feeble attempt to talk over what had happened but the whole enormity of what had happened had tired us so much that we were gradually overtaken by the need to sleep.

Just before I finally succumbed, although I may have closed my eyes for what seemed only a few seconds, I recall now that I felt, just for an instant, that I could see the digital clock on the television again and that it was showing eleven minutes past eleven. But looking back I couldn't be sure and even now parts of the whole experience seem like a dream.

When we awoke it was to a bright new morning. A pencil-thin shaft of strong bright sunlight was spreading through a narrow gap in the curtains onto the wall above our bed. Looking around, it was evident that the room had returned to all that it should be with everything back in its rightful place. I could hear the noise and bustle of the traffic outside. The digital clock on the television indicated half past seven.

I wish, in a way, that I had had the foresight to slip into my pocket some small item as a memento that could have led me to believe that the strange events of the night before had not all been a dream. The problem with the dream theory is that as we discussed them it became clear that Francesca's recollections of events were exactly the same as mine and 'parallel dreaming' (as I shall call it) in such detail is something of which I have never heard. We have known almost as long as we have known each other that Francesca and I are blessed with psychic capabilities and have the ability to read each other's thoughts on occasions, but no occurrence or event passing between us was ever as detailed or extensive as this experience had been.

We took breakfast in our room; neither of us felt like mixing with other people and our conversation was likely to be considered rather peculiar if overheard.

We decided that a short course of retail therapy was called for to take our minds off the happenings of the night before so we opted to take a trip to Oxford Street and go shopping. We made our way down to the foyer.

As we reached the bottom of the curved flight of stairs and walked towards the main doors, we could see another couple about twenty paces in front of us.

A uniformed man, I believe the hall porter, stepped forward and pulled open the door for them. All of a sudden the memory of the previous night hit me, I had a mental picture of the two doormen opening the door the night before and the image in my mind made me stop dead in my tracks. The view through the door into the street outside was very different now and back to normal but the memory of the night before was strong and powerful.

As I stood there, transfixed, I was brought to my senses by someone politely saying, "Excuse me".

I turned and was faced by a smartly dressed rather young man. He asked if, by any chance, we were Colin and Francesca. Once we had confirmed this to him, he handed me a business card and explained that he was from a firm of solicitors in the City.

He said that he had been asked to request that we visit their offices and meet with one of the senior partners on the following Monday. He told us that he was not privy to the reason why, he was sent purely as a messenger. He could see that we were hesitant and he added that he was permitted to add, however, that he believed the visit would be advantageous to us.

We had intended to return home on the Sunday, but after a short period of consideration, decided to stay on for the remainder of the weekend and make the visit to the solicitor as requested. We confirmed this with the messenger and he departed. We then made the arrangements with the hotel receptionist to stay the extra nights before departing on our shopping trip.

On the Monday, as requested, we duly paid our visit to the offices of the solicitor. We had no idea of their precise location and so we opted to go by taxi. Upon arrival we made ourselves known to the receptionist. She, in turn, contacted the senior partner who came and welcomed us in person.

He took us into his office where coffee and biscuits awaited us. He asked us to sit down and make ourselves comfortable. He told us that he had a rather strange story to tell, but one that had become almost legendary over the years in professional circles.

The story, he said, starts many years ago before either of you were born. As such, it was inexplicable, but now events had come to pass just as they had been predicted.

He went on to say that they were acting on instructions that had been handed down to them, via a somewhat circuitous route, from a solicitor that had long since died, one Robert Jenkinson. The mention of the name caused me to take an audible sharp intake of breath; Francesca leaned towards me and reached out to squeeze my hand with hers.

He told us that it had been established that there had indeed been a highly respected solicitor by the name of Robert Jenkinson operating from an office in Chancery Lane between 1888 and 1925. The practice that he started was no longer in existence but that all of the files outstanding from his business had been transferred to a practice currently working out of offices in Old Street and then, in time and by circumstance to them.

He explained that he had a package for us that had always been of some intrigue to those few in the practice that knew about it. Why would become evident when we saw it.

He opened a cupboard and produced a package about the size of a shoebox, wrapped in brown paper, and tied with several bands of string such that it could not be opened without removing the string or cutting it. The string was then coated with sealing wax in three places with an imprint of a seal in each. Next to each seal were two sets of initials. The solicitor explained that this was common practice in Edwardian times to demonstrate and verify that the contents of a package had not been interfered with since the originator had placed the contents inside.

Accompanying the box was an envelope. He showed it to us, explaining that this was the item that had caused more discussion over the years than even the box itself. The writing on the envelope stated –

'This envelope and its accompanying package are only to be opened by persons who will identify themselves to you as Colin and Francesca. This event, if it occurs at all, will not take place until after the seventeenth day of November 2000. In the event that nobody comes forward within twelve months of this date, the box may be opened and the contents disposed of as the current holding solicitor thinks fit. Sealed this day, Tuesday the seventeenth day of November 1925 by I, Robert Jenkinson, on behalf of and in the presence of Charles and Felicity.'

"You will note that there is no surname used by the owners of the box," said the solicitor, "and we don't know why". It was only then that I realised that we had never exchanged surnames in our meeting with Felicity and Charles and, after all, we had thought to be a strange, albeit deep and somewhat confusing, dream.

The solicitor explained that there had been an accompanying envelope addressed to the solicitor which, when opened, directed them to go to the Barleys Hotel on the appointed date.

When the seals were broken and the box opened, there were found to be three items inside.

Firstly, a further envelope containing a letter explaining a little of what had happened since our meeting in the hotel. It provided an outline of how things had progressed and developed for them, how they had utilised their capabilities and resources to start a manufacturing company that initially concentrated on agricultural equipment and then moved on to produce specialised parts for the motor car and lorry industry. The company had gone from strength to strength under their ownership and guidance, so much so that larger companies were approaching them with a view to buying them out. If this happened they would make their fortune and be comfortably off for the rest of their lives.

Secondly, a small gold carriage clock set to eleven minutes past eleven with engraved with '*Francesca & Colin, A Very Special Time, Felicity and Charles*'.

Thirdly, a larger envelope containing sheets of paper which, on examination, the solicitor advised he could identify as official shares certificates. On closer examination we could see that the company name at the top of each of the certificates was **F&C Engineering of Lincolnshire**.

The solicitor offered to investigate the value of the certificates and advise us of the outcome. The other contents of the box, and indeed the box itself, we were welcome to take away.

It transpired that companies had changed hands several times over the years but, by careful planning ahead, each time Charles had managed to ensure that a caveat protecting the shares destined for us was invoked. By precise forward action on his part he had managed to maintain this condition, such that his original requirement had survived the years between. Thus Charles had ensured that our shares had to be honoured if his plan worked and they were, in the fullness of time, submitted for valuation.

When valued, the share certificates were found to be worth half a million pounds. We kept four as keepsakes, one each, two in memory of Felicity and Charles, and cashed in the rest.

Francesca always says that it is her belief that any generosity you show towards your fellow beings will always be repaid in the end.

There were no records to lead us to understand who Felicity and Charles really were, most of Robert Jenkinson's records having been destroyed in a fire resulting from bombing in the Second World War. We were told that it was only by some miracle that our box had been blown into the air and had landed some way down the street, away from the fire that ensued and eventually destroyed the building. Apparently it had been found by some honest passer-by who had handed it in to the police.

The carriage clock now sits on the sideboard at home, still set at eleven minutes past eleven. We have never attempted to wind it.

I suppose we could have gone further and attempted to find out if there had been any children or other relatives but after a lengthy period of thought and consideration, we decided not to delve any further and to leave our memories as they were. We were, in some ways, curious, but there was little to be gained and no advantage in terms of lending any explanation to what transpired that night.

Strange, though, to think that our box survived the years and all the things that could (and did) happen to it. Perhaps we should just put it down to fate – just like our meeting in the hotel really…

END

LATE TRAIN TO LIVERPOOL STREET

LATE TRAIN TO
LIVERPOOL STREET

"**D**on't fall asleep, must stay awake. Don't fall asleep, must stay awake." As much as I tried to prevent my eyes closing, I could feel the welcoming release of deep sleep starting to wash over me. Even my somewhat feeble attempts at focusing and concentrating my mind were starting to fail me as my thoughts began to blend in with the motion of the train.

"Don't fall asleep, must stay awake. Don't fall asleep, must stay awake." The rhythm of the sounds of the wheels on the track and the rocking to and fro were having a gently soporific effect. I suppose the motion must be distantly reminiscent of the cradle. Whatever the reason, my resistance was starting to crumble.

It was very important, however, that I did not succumb to the forces that gently edged me towards the precipice of sleep.

The train I was travelling on was a London Underground train, speeding its way towards Liverpool Street. If I gave in to temptation and fell asleep, I would miss my stop, miss my connection at the main line station above and finish up goodness knows where. It was vital that

I disembarked at Liverpool Street and made the change to the British Rail train. Then, and only then, could I rest for a while.

I had been working late in the office, as seemed to be the norm in those days. At that time I had a flat out in the wilds of Essex, at Kelvedon. There weren't too many trains I could catch at that time in the evening, but by leaving the office at the right time, and with the proper connections, I could catch the eight o'clock. I remember that it was around fifteen minutes to eight, so all being well there would be no difficulty in my catching my train. The date? I shall never forget it – 3 March 1982.

I was alone in the carriage, there was no other passenger to distract me. Nobody to look at, study, or think about. You can make up games about fellow travellers in your head. What they do for a living, where they are going, what their names are. I have always found it necessary, however, to take a certain degree of care when doing this. Being caught staring at, or even glancing at, strangers on tube trains, particularly late at night, may be misconstrued and can lead to unexpected and undesirable confrontation.

Momentarily, I allowed my eyes to close, my leaden eyelids finally being too heavy to resist. With all my willpower I forced them open again, but I knew I was fighting a losing battle. Just as I was about to give in completely, the clatter of the wheels as they rattled across points in the track jolted me back to some sort of consciousness.

And then the train began to slow.

When you have undertaken the same journey for the best part of seven and a half years you get to know instinctively the times and places where trains slow. Even though it is pitch black in the tunnel outside, the seasoned traveller develops almost a sixth sense as to where they are in relation to their subterranean journey. More to the point, you know where the anticipated normal slowing and stopping points are. Any unplanned or unscheduled stop means a potential source of delay and thus a possible missed connection. In my case on this particular day a delay at this point in my journey could, in turn, lead to an extra hour's wait for the next main line train at Liverpool Street.

Ah, the stresses and strains of commuting.

My level of concern increased as the train continued to slow. More to the point we were alone. We? As I said, I was alone in the carriage. It is odd how an inanimate object of glass, steel and aluminium can be awarded the apparent accolade of human companionship in times of growing mental pressure.

Looking out of the window into the darkness I was unable to identify any of the markings on the wall of the tunnel. Sometimes these could be a clue to the location of the train and thus, hopefully, the proximity of the next station.

The train slowed and came to a stop.

Outside I thought I could make out a platform but if it was so, it was very dimly lit and I could not make out any major distinguishing features that would enable me to identify it or any visible station identification sign.

And then something odd happened. The door closest to me in the carriage opened. There were four doors in each side of the carriage, but only the one nearest to me slid open.

I did not get up from my seat; wherever this was, it was not Liverpool Street.

After a few minutes, however, curiosity did get the better of me and, without getting up, I leaned across to try and peer round the internal glass panel and see out through the open door. Having no success, I once again sat back in my seat and waited.

The train did not move, there was no announcement from within the train or that I could hear from the station outside. I waited, getting more frustrated and wound up by the minute. I checked my watch. The thirty minutes I had allowed for my journey would be sufficient, providing we moved on soon and were not delayed here much longer.

Time passed; there was still no information, no movement, no activity of any kind. I checked my watch again. Oh no! Wouldn't you know it, what a time for my watch to stop! Now, not only did I not know where I was, I could not tell how long the delay or calculate the consequent effect on my onward journey home.

It is a strange thing but one which I believe is worthy of psychological analysis; the stress level for a commuter goes up and up all the time that there are delays until the point is reached where all hope of making an onward connection is lost. The individual then becomes resigned to the fact that the journey as previously planned cannot be completed and a feeling of mental relaxation occurs. It is feasible that the individual retains a high level of mental activity that requires to be sated somehow. Given the right circumstances, such as a long wait between mainline trains, there may be a consequent long period of spare time to be killed. I suppose that if this were not true, at least in part, then there would be no investment in so many shops, bars and food outlets in main line railway stations these days.

So this was the state of mind I found myself in – all wound up with nowhere to go!

It became apparent that just sitting there would do nothing to improve my current situation and it was patently obvious that no information was about to be forthcoming, so I stood up and went to the open door. I put my head out and looked up and down the platform. I could not make any real sense of what I could see; only that it was a very poorly lit station, dark, somewhat dank and that it smelled rather musty.

Going back to my seat to collect my briefcase (the hardened commuter leaves nothing behind) I resolved to go in search of information. Maybe I could find some member of staff who surely by now would be in a position to tell me what on earth was going on.

I took just one step onto the platform and one more towards the front of the train (with the idea of talking to the driver). As I did so, wouldn't you know it, the door closed. I turned to try and thrust my briefcase into the rapidly shrinking gap but I was too late. By the time my briefcase hit the door, it was shut. There was a hiss of air as the brakes released and the train moved off.

I watched, at first stunned and then angry as the train accelerated away, through the station and out of sight. I shouted at it, I swore at it but, of course, it did no good at all; in truth it didn't even make me feel any better.

So there I was, alone on the platform of a dark and somewhat musty unidentified underground station, feeling tired, angry and becoming noticeably increasingly colder.

In the gloom, which was worse than ever now that the train had gone, I peered along the platform, my eyes struggling to adapt to the light. At a distance which I judged to be about forty paces away, I could make out what appeared to be an exit. The light was better there, the glow emanating from this smaller tunnel serving to illuminate the immediate surrounding area.

As I made my way along the platform towards the light, I glanced at the tunnel wall nearest to me. I recognised the familiar station identification sign with its circle bisected by a horizontal bar, but I couldn't make out the name of the station. Apart from the absence of sufficient lighting, the sign also appeared to be rather grimy. I reached out my hand with the idea of cleaning off some of the dirt from the centre section.

As I did so, I thought I heard a noise coming from within the exit tunnel. This being the first indication of any activity since the train had stopped, I forgot the task in hand and moved briskly towards the source of the sound. Hopefully, I would be able to obtain some information as to what was going on.

I turned into the smaller tunnel, half expecting to see someone but there was nobody there. I followed the 'Way Out' signs until, some way along the tunnel, I came across the steel shutter doors of two lifts. I remember that they looked a bit old-fashioned with brass mechanical indicators rather than the more modern electric illuminated numbers or letters to show their position. According to these devices, both lifts were on the surface.

I pressed the lift call buttons several times, but to no avail. There was no sound, no indication of any kind to suggest that either lift was about to descend.

Giving this avenue up, I stood back from the lift doors and spotted a sign on the wall with an arrow pointing to the stairs. Of course, I thought, all underground stations with lifts had stairs, usually a spiral staircase, as an alternative route to the surface.

I didn't count them but I estimate I must have gone up about a hundred and fifty stairs when I came upon a sight that stopped me dead in my tracks, both in the physical and the mental sense.

The stairs stopped abruptly; my way being barred by a solid wall of concrete blocks. The blocks were properly laid, with mortar in-between and formed a solid horizontal barrier, like a ceiling. I went a couple of steps further and reached out to touch them. As I ran my hand along the edge of one of the blocks, a small piece came away in my hand, but apart from this loose sliver, the barrier was quite permanent and totally impenetrable.

Turning round, I made my way back to the bottom of the staircase. It was at about this time, as I descended, that I realised another thing that confused me. Although the electric lights on the stairway were not on, there was still sufficient light for me to see. Even in that strange situation in which I found myself, part way up a blocked stairway deep within the bowels of the earth under London, there was still just enough light for me to see ahead of me and make out some of the things around me.

By now I had returned to the base of the stairs. I stood still for a few seconds, thinking, contemplating my plight and wondering what to do next. Logically, I thought that my next move should be to find a linking tunnel through to the westbound track (I had come in on the eastbound), surely there would be an exit to the surface there. It was possible that I could find someone there to advise me or, in the worst case, even a train to take me back in the direction from which I had come. Alternatively, I could go back to the platform on which I had arrived and just wait for the next train to come.

As I stood considering these options I sensed that I was not alone. Turning, I saw a man standing behind me on the stairs down which I had come less than a minute earlier. Seeing him there caught me quite by surprise and I took a sharp intake of breath. How could he possibly have got there? He could not have got past me and I had just discovered that the stairs on which he was standing led nowhere.

We looked at each other for a few seconds before he spoke.

"Good day," he said politely in a voice which I would describe as fairly well spoken.

"Good evening," I replied with what I must admit was more than a slight tremor in my voice.

I turned and proceeded to walk along the tunnel, back towards the platform. I had no reason or desire to engage in conversation with this stranger, my priority was to find a way out of the station and then get home.

He followed me.

I had decided that the best option was to wait for another Liverpool Street bound train and so I sat down on a slatted wooden seat on the platform. The stranger came and sat down alongside me. Had he sat too close and 'invaded my space' as they say, I might have felt intimidated or, worst, alarmed, but he chose to sit a good arm's-length away.

A few minutes passed.

I started to think that I had maybe prejudged this fellow traveller who, after all was stuck in the same predicament as me. Possibly I had been a little terse, if not rude, in my response to his greeting. I resolved to enter into some light conversation; if nothing else it would help to pass the time.

I looked across at him, he had a fixed expression, staring across the platform and down towards the tracks. I would guess him to be around fifty years old, possibly mid to late forties. He was dressed in a brown suit, double-breasted, cut with wide lapels, a style which looked rather dated. To complement this he wore a white shirt with a plain brown knitted tie and sturdy brown brogue shoes. His face looked a little drawn with a pallid, pale complexion; he was well groomed with maybe a couple of day's stubble.

Without moving his shoulders, he raised his head slightly and turned to look at me. For the first time we made eye contact. In the gloom, with pupils wide open, his were dark and deep.

"How long have you been waiting?" I asked

"Longer than I care to remember," he replied dourly.

"Got far to go?"

"Oh yes, a great distance," he responded.

"Well I hope one comes along in a minute."

"It will not be of any use to me if even it does," he said.

In good true British fashion when we don't know what to say, I reverted to our favourite subject.

"The weather's not been too bad lately," I said. Even as I uttered the words they sounded bland and meaningless.

He said, "I have missed the weather," in a distant, almost wistful, way.

I wondered what I had done to deserve this and how much worse things could get. My situation had deteriorated even further. My companion was clearly of dubious mental prowess. As my less polite colleagues would say 'a sandwich short of a picnic' or 'the lights are on but there's no one at home'. I seem to be one of those people who naturally attract these poor unfortunates whether it be on the train, on the bus or when doing the shopping.

Thinking about it, I decided that my best course of action was to humour him, after all, I had no way of estimating the extent of his disability or, more to the point, what he may have done if I had upset him.

His next response, however, stunned me and shocked me into silence as my brain struggled to take it in.

I said, as casually as I could, "I'll be glad when I can get home and have my dinner, I'm famished."

He replied, "We have no need for food and drink here."

My mind raced through three parts of his statement in quick succession.

"… no need for food and drink…"– Why?

"… here…"– Where was here?

"We… "– Who could he possibly mean by 'We'?

I looked him squarely in both eyes. Now my body's adrenalin was definitely pumping. I was beginning to feel threatened and maybe even more than a little frightened.

He spoke quietly, as though reading my thoughts.

"You have no need to fear me. I realise that my words may be rather confusing to you, but I am in my own way trying to prepare you for what I have to say. Please hear me out."

I nodded my acquiescence. He then related his story which, as it unfolded, had me rooted to the spot.

"I would ask you to cast your mind back to the Second World War, to be precise, to 1944. I am sure that you are too young to remember personally but I trust that there are still sufficient people around who can recall their own experiences of those terrible times and that the historians have done their job as well.

I was a senior clerk working with the War Ministry. I had worked hard and reached a position of some responsibility. My job was mainly to monitor and record troop movements in order that the Army could keep pace with where everybody was. Although I held a similar position before the war, this had become, as I am sure you can understand, vitally important work in wartime, particularly since we had invaded France just a few days earlier.

My group of fourteen men and six girls were based at an office in Finsbury Circus, along with approximately two hundred other Ministry personnel.

One day, one fateful Friday, I was requested to hand-deliver a package to another office in Commercial Road. This, I thought, would be a relatively short and quite pleasant walk on a sunny summer's day. The actual date was 30 June 1944 but I suspect that it will be of no special significance to you."

He paused, presumably in case I wished to interject. I shook my head. He continued.

"At that time the Germans had recently introduced a new weapon into the war, the V1 Flying Bomb, although most people called it the Doodlebug. These pilotless planes had a sort of double fuselage, one above the other. We thought the top one to be the engine because it appeared to belch flame, consequently the bottom one must house the bomb. All the evidence showed that tremendous damage was caused when they came down.

There were lots of rumours about the flying bombs both within the Ministry and outside in the general public. These and other so-called 'secret weapons' were always a cause of great speculation. The engine made an eerie monotonous droning noise and the one thing that was certain was that when it cut out the bomb was heading for the ground. The short spell of silence before the explosion was the sound that everybody dreaded; it injected fear into the very hearts and souls of those beneath.

As I made my way to Commercial Road, in the sky above I heard the steady drone of a V1 engine just as I have described it. Others around me were looking up, trying to catch a glimpse of the approaching machine. Then horror of horrors, that terrible silence. Being out in the open street I suddenly felt exposed, vulnerable and very scared.

I looked around for a bolt hole, there were no purpose-built shelters close by. Then I spotted the open entrance to an underground station and I ran as fast as my legs would carry me towards it. I reached the top of the steps just as somebody screamed out 'It's coming' and I ran down so fast in my panic that I thought I would surely lose my footing and break my neck in the fall.

I cannot remember if I heard the actual explosion, but I know I made it to the spiral staircase and part of the way down it before everything in my world came to an abrupt stop.

Afterwards, there was a period, I don't know how long, when I had a sensation of hovering in the air, of floating. All was misty to me, like being in a cloud. Finally, there came a time when I found that I could walk around again but only within the confines of the station which, by then, had every entrance and exit blocked either by fallen debris or, in the case of the spiral staircase, walled up as you have seen it.

In time, again the length of which I am unable to specify, I met another and another until… ”

“Until what?” I interrupted.

“I am sorry, you still do not understand, how could you?”

He took a deep breath and exhaled slowly before continuing.

“We believe, and there were thirty-two of us, that the station suffered a direct hit. We were all killed and, for whatever reasons, our bodies were never found. We cannot comprehend why it is so, but we believe that our souls are trapped, interred here with our remains.”

“But that's barbaric!”I burst in. “Surely your bodies were recovered and given decent Christian burial.”

“We are not here to judge or condemn, that is our understanding and explanation of what took place.”

“You said that there were thirty-two of you – originally?” I said, questioning his statement earlier.

“That is the second part of what you must understand. There is a way out for me but I need your help.”

“Go ahead, please.” I said. I was very intrigued to hear what he was going to say.

"For what seemed like many years, although we have no real concept of time, we wandered the station. As I said, there were thirty-two of us, fourteen men and eighteen women, although one was only a lad of thirteen and two of the women were mere girls of fifteen.

We can see each other and converse. You can see others if you wish, but you will not be able to speak with them, nor them with you."

As he said this, looking over his shoulder I could see four or five shapes had appeared behind him in the shadows, coming towards us down the poorly-lit platform. I looked down and shook my head vigorously; this was becoming too much for me to take in. The discussion with him was difficult enough to cope with; I was certainly not prepared to meet any of his poor unfortunate brethren. The shapes turned back and melted away.

He continued with his explanation.

"One day, without any notice and much to our surprise, a train drew into the station once again. No train had been through since the time of the explosion, you see.

The train stopped, much as yours did, and only one door opened. A man alighted and stood alone on the platform. The train departed on its way.

That first encounter was very strange for both parties."

He paused, then continued with his tale.

"The man from the train stood stock still where he was and called out a name. When nothing happened, he called a second time and then a third. The name was that of James Jenkinson, one of our number. James duly stepped forward.

The visitor explained that he was a clergyman, the Reverend Albert Lesney by name, and that he had come in response to what he could only describe as a 'visitation' he had received whilst alone in his church very late one Sunday night. He was 'advised' that he was to catch a tube train bound for Liverpool Street late on the evening of 30 June. The train would pull into an unidentified station and by following the instructions he was given he would meet the said James Jenkinson.

After the meeting, he was to return to his church and pray for James's soul to be released from its earthly confinement. The year was 1956, twelve years to the day after the disaster occurred.

Three days after the Reverend's visit, James told us that he felt a change coming over him and that he was about to embark on a long journey. He was then surrounded by an aura of white light as he faded away and left us.

Before James went he told us that the clergyman had said that there would be others and that each of them would be paired with one of us. Since then his prophecy has come true and visitors have come and gone with similar results. That is, in all cases so far with the exception of one.

A lady came and met with one of the two girls, young Sadie. We do not know what went wrong but, whatever it was, Sadie did not leave us. I remember how devastated she was. There is always hope, however, for a second person, this time a man came and, to the joy of all of us after her disappointment, Sadie left us.

We are now down to twelve, six men and six women, and you, my friend, have come."

"What is it that you want me to do?" I asked.

"All I ask," he replied, "is that as happened in the Reverend's case you pay a visit to a church of your choice and offer a prayer that I, Frank Swethers, be released from this tomb in which my spirit is entrapped. As far as we are aware, that simple prayer will do. It is all that we have asked of the others that have come and it has worked in the past."

I was momentarily distracted by the distant sound of an approaching train.

"I would like to ask you a question," I said.

"Ask away," he responded.

"Why me?"

"That is something I cannot tell you because I really do not know. I presume that you and I are kindred spirits, that we share some sort of spiritual affinity. Only the Almighty can know the answer to your question. I do, however, have one further request of you."

The train burst through the mouth of the tunnel and thundered down the track towards us. The noise seemed even more deafening than usual as it shattered the previously hushed quiet of the station.

"What is it?"I shouted.

The train stopped and a door opened very near to where we were standing.

"I would like to know your name."

"Colin Honeywell."

"Good luck, Colin Honeywell."These were his last words as, with a hiss of air, the door closed and I could see him no more.

In the last fraction of a second as the door slammed tight I caught sight of the station identification sign, now illuminated by the bright lights of the train. The name that I read was London Wall.

The train departed.

I sat down, put my briefcase across my legs and my head in my hands. I massaged my eyes gently through closed eyelids.

Within what seemed just a few minutes the train started to slow down, I looked up – Liverpool Street. I checked my watch. There were five minutes to go to eight o'clock. If I moved swiftly through the tube station and up to the main line platforms I could still catch my train. Then I remembered that my watch had stopped. I looked again; the second hand was definitely moving. It didn't make sense but I didn't have time to worry about it. I quickly found my way to the usual platform; the train was there, waiting. I checked the destination board; all was well so I boarded the train.

We pulled out on time.

The journey was about an hour and I usually dozed off for part of the time, but not tonight. My head was in turmoil, full of thoughts of all that had happened just a short while earlier.

There were no further hold-ups and I got back to the flat at a reasonable time having stopped off on my drive home from the station to pick up a fish and chip supper.

I remember not sleeping very well that night, my mind repeatedly going over and over the events of the evening before, causing me to toss and turn in my search for a comfortable resting position.

By the early hours, I had come to the conclusion that my mind must be playing tricks on me. I convinced myself that it had all been a dream and that none of the occurrences relating to that mysterious tube station had ever taken place. I thought back to being on the tube train, to my attempts to fight off sleep as my eyes did their best to close and then rubbing them as they opened on the approach into Liverpool Street.

I read somewhere that the speed of thought is phenomenal, that we can dream an amazing amount in just a few seconds. Yes, it must have all been a dream.

Once I had explained to myself that this was indeed the case and subsequently all my questions had been answered, I fell into a deep sleep.

I woke in the morning not surprisingly feeling rather tired. Nevertheless, I went off to work in the usual way.

As I stated, the dream, for that is what I now perceived it to be, had occurred on my way home on the Wednesday evening. By lunchtime on Thursday I had dismissed all the events that had apparently taken place as the ramblings of my tired and weary mind.

Thursday, Friday and Saturday passed fairly uneventfully and then on Sunday came the discovery which was to change my whole perspective of the strange happenings on that homeward journey a few days before.

My custom was to walk down to the local pub and have a few lunchtime drinks with friends. I got myself ready, checked that the roast chicken for my lunch was cooking nicely, locked up the flat and started on my way. It was a little chilly so I had put on my lightweight topcoat that I sometimes wore to the office.

I walked down the lane, enjoying the countryside and taking deep breaths of fresh air that you couldn't get in the city. It was one of the reasons that I chose to live in the country, to escape the dirt, grime and unclean air of the metropolis.

The cold air snapped at my fingertips so I slipped my hands into the outside coat pockets. One of them touched upon something hard and rough. When I took it out for a better look, what I saw before me stopped me dead in my tracks.

The object I was holding in my hand was the piece of concrete from the walled-up stairway of the old tube station.

So was it true? Had it really happened after all? My mind was thrown into confusion and turmoil.

When I got to the pub the others had not yet arrived. I ordered myself a large scotch and took a gulp. It helped to calm my nerves a little. There was nothing I could do at the moment, no time to think through or consider what to do next.

I decided that the best thing in the short term was to do nothing. I would try and keep this lunchtime as normal as possible and then I could spend more time considering the courses of action open to me. Certainly bringing up the subject of what had happened to me on the Wednesday would have been a mistake; if I raised it in that company I would probably be a laughingstock.

I therefore did my best to push all thoughts of Frank Swethers and his friends to the back of my mind and engage in the general Sunday lunchtime pub banter.

Although the individual members varied a little, there were generally about ten of us that met regularly in the Prince of Wales. As we sat, discussing some matter of vital international importance like the degree of success of British football clubs in European competitions, it dawned on me that one of our number, Jim Hardy, could possibly be of assistance to me.

I remembered that Jim was a freelance reporter who regularly worked for major National newspapers. He would have access to all kinds of historical information and data.

Jim was not what I would describe as a friend or a close confidante, he was more of an acquaintance who had happened to tag along with our Sunday lunchtime group. If I was clever and handled it properly, however, I may be able to solicit his help without necessarily having to provide him with a complete and detailed account of my story.

I told him that I was gathering information for a book I was intending to write and that needed assistance in obtaining access to a good archive library such as that which may be held by a big newspaper. He told me that he had contacts within all the major national daily papers and that he would be only too willing to help me.

We arranged to meet for lunch on the following Thursday. As far as I was concerned, that was a good day for a meeting since it allowed me time in the early part of the week to carry out some research of my own.

Because of work commitments, I was unable to visit the library on Monday, but I rang to check that they held a newspaper archive. They confirmed that they had *The Times* on microfilm so I went down there on the Tuesday. It was only about a fifteen minute walk from the office.

A very helpful lady librarian explained to me how the system worked and brought me two spools of microfilm, one for each half of 1944.

I scoured the newspapers of the first and second July 1944 for any news of a bomb in the area of London Wall Underground Station, Finsbury Circus or Liverpool Street. Although there were reports of other bombs, there were no references at all to these three areas.

It did not take long for me to realise that the level of information available to the newspaper reader was very different in those dark days of wartime from what we would expect today. It was obvious that the reports I was reading were deliberately kept very vague. There was the element of propaganda that could be generated by the enemy if such events were published openly and in full, as well as the potential effect on morale in London, the capital city under fire.

There were reports in the paper of flying bombs hitting a children's hospital on1 July but the exact location and even the actual date of the incident were not given.

While I had the microfilm I took the opportunity to look at *The Times* for the day of the disaster, 30 June, and there I did find an article of some interest. It referred to discussions the day before in the House of Commons which specifically referred to flying bombs. Questions were asked requesting the issue, on a weekly basis, of figures relating to the casualties caused by these weapons. This was rejected because the release of details of particular incidents or locations could provide useful invaluable information to the enemy on their successes.

As I now believed the story told to me by Frank Swethers, or should I say the spirit of Frank Swethers, to be true, I found it difficult to comprehend that there was no mention of the disaster. Surely the direct hit of a bomb on a London tube station with the resulting deaths of thirty-two people and presumably many others injured would have been recorded in the national newspapers of the day.

It did cross my mind that reports of major events of this kind could be delayed in wartime by censorship rules and therefore I also checked the newspapers for the following three days, the third, fourth and fifth July (the second of July being a Sunday, *The Times* newspaper was not published). I found that they too carried no information regarding a major bomb incident in those areas of the city.

My conclusion, therefore, however surprising it may seem, was that no newspaper reports exist of the London Wall Underground Station disaster. It was becoming clear to me, however, that the control of information exercised during the War was such that many incidents could have gone unrecorded.

On the Thursday I met Jim for lunch at a pub in Fetter Lane, near Fleet Street. I followed through with my original plan and discussed with him what he thought to be the research for my book, my non-existent book.

I told him that the book was set in the World War Two period, in war-torn London, and that I needed information on secret weapons of the time such as the V1 Flying Bomb. I kept the description of my requirements very general in order not to encourage him to ask me any questions of too specific a nature. He was, after all a reporter and trained to 'sniff out' a story. I did not want him to suspect the real motive behind my asking, although in retrospect it was unlikely in the extreme that he could have any inkling of my true reasons.

I needed, I said, statistical information and dates, approximate numbers of V1 weapons aimed at the capital, the start and end dates of the use of the flying bombs and where they were launched from. I made sure that more specific points were also addressed, although hidden, such as anything relating to bombs that fell on the Finsbury Circus or Liverpool Street areas with direct reference to London Wall Underground Station, which is where my story was to be set. He did query the name of the station since we both realised that there was no current station of that name, but I said that I thought I had read about it in an old reference book and could he therefore do what he could to check it out.

He said that he would see what he could do and would call me in a few days. I was glad that he raised the question of how quickly he could obtain the information because I had not come up with a suitable excuse for broaching the subject of timing with him. I did say that I wished to resolve the whole matter as soon as possible but since he was doing me a favour, there was no way that I could exert any pressure on him to ensure his timely response.

Jim Hardy rang me on Saturday morning and said that he had obtained some information for me. He must have sensed my surprise at the speed of his response, but, as he said, the best way to deal with my request was 'quick and immediate', then it would not get forgotten. He did also mention, in passing, that he would like to borrow my socket set and hydraulic jack to do some work on his car; by way of he had helped me and the loan would be a favour in return.

He told me that he had been called in to the offices of two of the national dailies to discuss some work and whilst there he had asked his contacts in the research archives to help him out.

We arranged to meet in the pub on Sunday lunchtime and then go back to my flat where we could discuss his findings in detail in relative quiet. I offered him lunch but he said that he wanted to get away to go and visit his mother in the afternoon and he would eat there.

I could hardly wait for Sunday and hearing of the information that Jim had unearthed.

In fact, he turned up late at the pub on Sunday, either that or he turned up at the usual time but I was too keen to see him. Anyway, the arrangements went as planned and we ended up back at my flat. I made coffee for us both and he revealed to me what he had found out.

This, in his own words, is the information which he provided to me.

"What can I tell you about the V1? Well, the locals nicknamed it 'doodlebug' or 'buzz bomb'. It was the first attempt at a guided missile although once launched no control was possible from the ground. Flying and directional controls were crude by the standards of today, but the weapon was none the less very effective. With regard to size, it was twenty-one feet long with a wingspan of sixteen feet. It weighed around two tons which included half a ton of explosives. Flying speed was 400 miles per hour at a height of 25,000 feet.

"They were launched from ramps located along the Northern coast of France, Belgium, Holland and Germany. Once launched, they flew on until a preset device cut the fuel to the engine. At the same time, the elevator control was flipped fully down such that the machine went immediately into a nosedive earthwards. The machine plummeted down until, on impact, a detonator in the nose set off the high explosives. The damage caused by these weapons was enormous, being both extensive and widespread.

"As to numbers, it is estimated that between 13 June 1944 and 4 September 1944, 8,070 of them were launched at Southern England, with approximately 2,300 of these coming down in the London area.

The detail of precisely how many of these bombs actually fell and caused major damage and loss of life is now not possible to determine. Reports were restricted by Government control during the War. For propaganda reasons, a great deal of information was kept from the public at large. It is possible that the detailed knowledge of some major wartime disasters is withheld to this day.

With regard to the station that you mentioned, London Wall, I can find no reference to it either before or after the War. The street known as London Wall is situated in the Finsbury Circus area. Although there is no record of a tube station there, it is not impossible that there was a station in that location during the War. There were a lot of buildings in the area that were commandeered for War Ministry and military use and it is possible that a station was opened to provide a service to these offices. There were instances of this in wartime where the station was retained and is still in use today."

I asked him if he had any idea how much information from the War relating to bombing raids and the damage and loss of life caused by them may still be retained in Government records and archives. He said that he didn't know, but even if any such data existed, it still may not be considered 'in the public interest' to release it. He added that as the years have passed since the end of the War, information such as this has become less and less relevant, there are fewer and fewer people alive who were involved in or affected by the terrible events that took place.

I thanked Jim for his assistance and told him that his information would be invaluable to me as part of the research for my book.

In truth, I spent the rest of the day thinking over all the facets of this curious story, a story in which, whether by chance or otherwise, I had become a key player. I went through them in my mind over and over again.

I thought of the journey home, my meeting with the mysterious individual in the abandoned underground station, the curious story that he told, my initial scepticism and the discovery that changed my mind about the whole episode. In addition to these fundamental points was the lack of available verifiable information on what may or may not actually have happened all those years before.

Was it really feasible that the wartime authorities had deliberately suppressed the news of a major disaster in the heart of the capital because of the likely negative effect upon public morale? What could be the thinking behind the events of that fateful day in 1944 being withheld?

Eventually I came to the inevitable conclusion that it had all been true, that the tragedy had taken place and, for whatever reason or circumstance, those poor lost souls had been interred there in the wreckage and debris of the station. Undoubtedly they had perished in the carnage, some of them as they went about their normal business and some as they had sought refuge from the terror falling from the sky.

I made my personal commitment to the memory of Frank Swethers, my kindred spirit. I would endeavour to carry out his wishes as he had requested. If my perception was wrong, then I could see no harm in it, but if I was right, then hopefully I was in a position to be of some help to this man who I had never known but for whom I had developed a great deal of respect.

I therefore resolved to carry out his request in full, just as he had asked.

Once I had reached this conclusion, I only had to decide when and where. This, I felt, was not a decision to be rushed and so I slept on it.

The following day, as I travelled to work on the train, I realised that there was really no choice in the matter, it was blindingly obvious.

The ultimate symbol of war-ravaged London and its resilience and resistance to the airborne attacks by the enemy was, of course, St Paul's Cathedral in the City of London. Every book I had ever seen on the subject of wartime London contained at least one photograph of St Paul's, its great dome standing intact and defiant over scenes of destruction, surrounded by rubble and debris.

I had to earn a living and the office was very busy so the first opportunity I had to get away early was on the Wednesday. I managed to leave at a reasonable time and made my way to St Paul's. I recall that I arrived at about five o'clock.

I made my way up the wide stone steps and through the high wooden doors. There were a few people wandering around but the big groups of tourists were long gone at that time of day.

I would not describe myself as a great churchgoer, in fact I wouldn't describe myself as a churchgoer at all, so I wasn't really sure what my next step should be. For a few minutes I stood still and looked around, drinking in the majesty and splendour of that great place, it was truly breathtaking.

I thought that to go down the centre aisle could be considered a little irreverent, if not arrogant, on my part since this was the first time in years that I had set foot in any church, let alone a vast cathedral. I must admit to feeling rather nervous and self-conscious. I therefore chose to go down the right-hand side aisle and sit in a pew on the left, in the main body of the seating a few places in from the end.

I didn't know what wording I should use, I had not thought it through properly, so I made it up as I went along. It must have sounded decidedly clumsy but I think it went something like this...

"O Heavenly Father, I know that I must be considered a sinner in your eyes, I am such a rare and infrequent visitor to your house, but I do believe and I know that you can help. I ask not for myself but for the soul of your faithful servant, Frank Swethers, who, through no fault of his own is trapped in an earthly grave. I ask you, on his behalf and mine to do all in your power to release him and come to join you in heaven."

I don't know quite what I expected to happen but I suppose it is hardly surprising that nothing did. I certainly didn't feel any different. There was no reason why I should but I suppose I did think that these were rather strange circumstances and maybe I should have felt something.

I looked around. Nobody was bothering to give me a second glance. For a moment, I was undecided as to what to do next. The next thought was that maybe it hadn't worked or that I had got something wrong. It was still possible that it had all been a dream and I was making a fool of myself. Maybe it was a dream now.

I had come this far, however, and this was no time to give up on Frank.

I knelt down again, closed my eyes, clasped my hands together and repeated the prayer as if to make absolutely sure. The second time I tried to concentrate all the power of my heart and mind on the words that I whispered quietly to myself.

Again I felt no different, and so I decided that enough was enough and that it was time to for me to leave. I retraced my steps, back down the side aisle, towards the main doors.

As I crossed behind the pews and turned slightly to make my way towards the main door, something,

I don't know what, made me turn and look back in the direction of the altar.

What I saw made my lower jaw drop and my mouth gape open.

In the centre of the rows of pews, about ten rows down from where I was standing, stood a figure, I can only describe it as an apparition. It was instantly recognisable to me as Frank Swethers.

The vision was completely surrounded by a ring of bright light that I can only liken to an oval of intense multicolour incandescent starlight.

Frank raised his right hand to about head height and waved it gently. He smiled; it was the one and only time I saw him smile.

I smiled back and returned his gesture with a similar wave. As I did so, he and the aura that surrounded him gently faded away into nothingness.

I watched him go.

When there was nothing more to see, I came to my senses. There I was, standing in St Paul's Cathedral, waving at something, somebody, that only I could see. If any other onlookers had been able to witness what I had seen, they would surely not have been quietly going about their business, as they clearly were.

Nearby I spotted a couple of elderly ladies who were watching me intently. One of them leaned over slightly and whispered something to the other.

The nearer of the two then started to make a move towards me but as she approached, I realised that this was no place for me to dwell, not at the moment. They were obviously acting out of a genuine sense of concern for a fellow human being and, as such, I was sorry to snub them. As far as I was concerned, however, it was far more preferable to me to have two little old ladies think me ill, rude or crazy than to have to attempt to explain anything to anybody. I don't even know if I could have spoken then, after what had happened, even if I had tried.

As I left the Cathedral and walked slowly back down the steps to make my way home, I felt good inside. Not the feeling that comes from winning a game or beating an opponent, but the unsung unrewarded knowledge deep within that results from doing something, however big or small, for another. And all the sweeter for the recognition for having them acknowledge your unselfish good deed.

I felt good about Frank Swethers. I could tell nobody, who could possibly understand? But we knew, Frank and I, and that was good enough for me.

* * * * * *

I have waited for some years to tell my story. The primary reason for my delay came out of a feeling of respect for the dead and my feelings for the entrapped spirits of those poor souls.

I hope that, by now, all have been released from their torment and that the station is still and quiet, abandoned by both the living and the dead.

Of course, I could be wrong, maybe there are still those held there awaiting a spiritual partner to come and effect their release. Possibly there are other travellers who will have their journey to Liverpool Street interrupted.

I suppose it is just possible that under the city there could be other stations like London Wall...

END

WHEN I SNAP MY FINGERS

To whomsoever finds this document I commit to you its future disposition, for you are now the appointed custodian of the true and accurate confession of one John Granby.

The only restriction upon you is that you must not retain or withhold the tale within it. You must release its content and message to the world in any way at your disposal.

If this action brings about financial reward or gain then so be it and good luck to you!

John Granby
20 December 1986

WHEN I SNAP MY FINGERS

I was christened John Granby some eighty-four years ago in the fine old city of Lincoln. I know that my course is run and that I am about to die. It is this which leads me to commit to paper the tale which is about to unfold.

You see, this last document is by way of being a confession. Not that I feel that by making it I may in some way absolve myself in the eyes of my maker, it is too late for that, but that it will give me a sense of great satisfaction in my last few hours to know that this will be found and that then the world will learn of my secret. The secret that I have kept deep within me for fifty years and can now be released. Then I, John Granby, will be remembered and revered.

I will relate to you the story of how I committed the perfect crime and not only that, dear reader, the perfect murder.

Let me take you back to the 1930s. They were good times. At that time I was known by a second name. To the world I was known as Cluno, assistant to The Great Orsini, of whom you may have heard. Fifty years ago The Great Orsini was the only illusionist in the world who could name his price to work in any theatre in the land. The impresarios, theatrical agents and theatre owners were queuing at his door. The Great Orsini was at the height of his career. By that time, as I recall, we had been together for ten years, the three of us, Orsini, myself and the glamorous assistant of the act, Sarah, my wife.

We had met, quite by chance as it happens, when both he and I attended a series of auditions in Manchester at which each of us was trying to break into a better class of theatre circuit. The auditions did not go well for either of us and each of us having been unsuccessful in our endeavours, we both felt rejected and unsure of our future prospects.

We thus found ourselves drowning our sorrows in a local hostelry talking over our options as to where we could go from here. As the drink flowed one of us (I can't be sure who) raised the possibility of us merging our acts and try our hands together going forward. By the time we came to leave, the outline plans for the act were established and future meetings were agreed.

Orsini was the son of a music hall conjurer who had eked out a living in small town theatres with a fairly mundane and unadventurous act for many years. The advantage in those days was that a performer, once established, could play a circuit of smaller theatres and the act could remain largely unchanged from year to year. Thus the outlay was low both in terms of props and the staging required. The fees paid by the theatre owners, however, reflected this.

There is no doubt, however, that Orsini was something different. He had a gift, knowledge and understanding of the theatre magician and his art which few are privileged enough to possess. His appreciation of that which could command an audience's attention and subsequent amazement was second to none.

At that time our act was built around conjuring and sleight of hand tricks. I would assist Orsini during the act and on occasions when it was necessary for the audience to be somewhat distracted, Sarah would put in an appearance on stage. She was undoubtedly a very attractive woman, quite beautiful both in terms of face and figure with that indefinable quality that forces men to watch and admire. One look around the audience and they were hers for the asking, the men hoping for a glimpse from those fascinating eyes, the women jealous of her power and angry with their menfolk.

Then came the chance occurrence that was to bring about the breakthrough that changed our fortunes forever.

We had just completed a week appearing at a small theatre in Oxford and, since it was our policy to keep an eye on the competition for new ideas, we went to watch a rival act nearby one evening before moving on to our next venue.

The act was not particularly good and appeared to contain no surprises so we opted for an early night to get some much needed sleep. Just as we were about to leave, however, the performer produced an illusion that had the audience on the edge of their seats and Orsini's immediate and concentrated attention.

The magician had the customary member of the audience on stage and proceeded to count slowly backwards from ten whilst gently moving the fingers of one hand in front of the man's face. Much to our surprise, the man appeared to fall asleep and then, as the magician spoke softly to him and then snapped his fingers, he opened his eyes.

The magician explained that the man was in a condition of induced sleep and remained fully under his control. The act that followed had Orsini deep in concentration, intently watching every move, and the rest of the audience held transfixed, open-mouthed and somewhat bewildered.

The man was informed that he was to become a dog and that on the magician's command, followed by a snap of the fingers he would bark loudly. This barking was to continue until he was instructed to stop by the same method. The action as described was duly carried out and in the period between the two clicks the man proceeded to utter a loud barking sound, hang out his tongue and raise both arms to simulate the begging position of some small hound.

The act continued with the whole operation being repeated, firstly with the man as a duck, with much violent flapping of the arms and loud quacking, and then as a cow with the man alternately chewing the side of his mouth and uttering deep lowing sounds.

The audience had by now overcome their initial awed silent reaction and were laughing, cheering and jeering at the poor unfortunate victim as he made his way back to his seat.

As we left the theatre we consulted the billboard. On the lower part, across where the magician's name was stated, was a sticker proclaiming, **"With The New Hypnotical Power – Power Over The Mind"**.

We were, of course, convinced that it was all a put up job, the individual selected had to have been part of the act, a magician's assistant like myself. However, this new dimension could not be ignored; the effect upon the audience had been truly stunning; they would be talking about what they had witnessed for days to all and sundry. Any act that could have its fame spread by word of mouth throughout the general public was sure of a sound future with secure and regular bookings.

Apart from the time spent on stage together, Sarah and I did not see much of Orsini over the next few weeks. He spent all of his spare time visiting libraries and museums in whichever town or city we were appearing.

One afternoon he came to us and told us that he was now convinced that the act we had witnessed was not a trick and that he felt he could develop the necessary powers and abilities required for us to include a demonstration of hypnotism in our act. He told us he had spent a great deal of time over recent months gathering knowledge of the subject and he was now convinced that we could, together, make it work.

We discussed the matter fully and at great length, considering all the possibilities and facets of how this could be done.

It was agreed that we would not use a member of the audience in this part of the act. By stressing the point that only certain individuals are receptive to the influence of hypnotic power, we would be able to develop and control the overall effect of the performances. In addition, we felt that this may also help to engender a certain sense of security within the audience, after all, the unlucky victim chosen would not be one of them!

It is undoubtedly true that Orsini did develop and retain very considerable and intense powers in this respect and that I did prove to be very receptive and susceptible to his hypnotic influences. We were, therefore, very well matched. And this was no confidence trick, he could induce in me a trance-like state and neither could I resist him nor recall afterwards what had taken place.

After a very few performances the success of the new venture was assured, aided by Orsini's style and charisma, which seemed to blossom under this new challenge. We then took the decision to drop the rest of the act in favour of the hypnotism routine alone.

Within what seemed to be a very short space of time we were at the top of our profession; we were in great demand and could almost name our price to perform.

* * * * * *

It was about that time that I was first introduced to the professor. I cannot recall his name, Johnson or Jackson or something similar, it is not important. He expressed great interest in Orsini and his powers. He wanted our permission to carry out some sort of special tests in what he called 'controlled scientific conditions'. He was particularly interested in the ability of Orsini to make me do things that were substantially against my very nature.

The theorists apparently believed that, whilst to induce a hypnotic state in another individual was quite feasible, it was not possible to make the person under the influence undertake any action or activity which was outside their normal psyche. Indeed, all activities suggested or requested could only be performed if they were a natural extension of the personality of that individual. It was not possible to induce in any individual an action that they felt, morally, to be malevolent.

I must admit that the early discussions with the professor really intrigued me. You see, I had little or no idea of what actually took place during the act whilst I was under the influence of the great man and this approach could possibility present me with an opportunity to find out.

I should explain that I was portrayed in the act as a very mild-mannered and humble man. Although these traits were probably exaggerated for the purposes of the act, I suppose that this, in essence, is how I would have described myself.

From my position of complete oblivion whilst under Orsini's control I had, of course, never been able to see or follow the act. I was, therefore, interested to learn that the professor wished to film our performance as part of his studies.

Orsini readily agreed but I for my part must say that I was a little apprehensive at first. My curiosity did, however, get the better of me. The thought that I could come to know what actually took place during the act via the intervention of the professor and his talking motion pictures proved to be too much of a temptation so I capitulated and agreed.

The actual filming took three or four days and with processing and editing or whatever else they had to do, the final product was ready in about a month.

Once we were advised that all was complete, I contacted the professor and arranged for a special private viewing, ostensibly to put my seal of approval on the production, but not admitting to him that the majority of the content would be a revelation to me.

There is no doubt that the act was brilliant, both in concept and execution. The power that Orsini exerted over his ineffectual assistant, Cluno, was awesome to behold.

The early part, to a large extent, mirrored the act from which we had gained the original idea; I was made to do somewhat demeaning party tricks such as mimicking animals by reacting to simple 'trigger' words. I must say that I felt slightly uncomfortable at the idea of people laughing at me and my foolish antics.

Orsini then turned to the audience and expounded the theory put forward by others that a person under the influence of hypnotism could not carry out any act that was not within their nature. He, and only he, The Great Orsini, had the power to prove otherwise.

Following a demonstration of my normally placid and docile demeanour, he gradually added to the tension by making me commit increasingly more aggressive acts, some of these being directed towards inanimate objects, some towards him and some, for maximum effect, towards members of the audience. Even I was shocked at the change in me, both my personality and demeanour.

At the climax of the performance, Orsini had me coming at him with a sword in each hand, raised as if to come down and cut him through from top to toe. I was all aggression, with that glazed expression that one imagines psychopathic murderers have; I appeared totally fixed in purpose and totally unstoppable. Even watching these events on film and knowing him to be alive and well, my heart was beating as though my chest could not contain it.

At what seemed the last possible moment, Orsini snapped his fingers and I immediately became still. My appearance was that of a human statue, frozen in time for all to behold. Orsini turned calmly to the audience, held out his arms to accept their acclaim and bowed low. For a few seconds you could hear a pin drop and then they erupted, as one being, into rapturous applause.

For months after I lived in a world where nothing could dampen my feeling of elation. We were a success, I was a part of it, our future was secure and the things could only get better still. I was in the clouds, floating along, everything and everybody was good.

And then it happened, the event that was to change my life forever.

* * * * * *

Our success had brought us fame and fortune, Orsini and I had purchased country homes within a few miles of each other near Maidenhead.

It became customary for us to rehearse at home, that is, at each other's homes, the two of us and, of course, Sarah. On this particular occasion, Orsini was visiting us. We had taken lunch on the terrace and had moved into the living room because the weather looked a little uncertain. At his bidding I took a seat in a large comfortable armchair.

I cannot recall now whether it was necessary to hypnotise me or, as I suspected, that Orsini could by now put me into that trance-like state almost at will, but I realised afterwards that I had been in a very deep sleep.

For some reason, which is unknown to me to this day, I awoke. I awoke to find myself alone. It could, I suppose, have been the closing of a distant door, the click of a heel on the floor, or even the brush of the cat against some indeterminate object, but the truth of it is that some sound, which presumably emulated the sound of a snapping of fingers, brought me back into the consciousness of the living world.

For a few seconds that seemed like many minutes, I was transfixed, all was still and strange.

Hearing voices from elsewhere in the house, I went from the living room into the hall. As I stood listening for a short while, it was apparent that the distant sounds were coming from upstairs.

To this day I do not know why, but I did not call out. It would have been perfectly normal for me to do so. Somehow something told me not to. Instead I followed the sounds up the stairs, taking care to avoid the third step which had a preponderance to creak violently and noisily if one's weight was applied in the wrong place.

I came to a stop outside the bedroom door; mine and Sarah's bedroom door. The voices coming from inside were clearly of two people thoroughly enjoying each other's, company. They sounded very close to each other, speaking softly but oblivious to their surroundings and with much muffled laughter. They undoubtedly were completely unaware of my presence.

I was in a state of utter confusion, my mind raced, my heart was thumping. The door was slightly ajar, I did not want to look and yet I had to see for myself. I gently squeezed the doorknob and eased the door open by just a couple of inches.

All my worst fears were confirmed in an instant. There lay Sarah and Orsini in our bed together and, to them, nobody else in the world existed.

Waves of emotion poured over me; shock, then horror, anger, then tears. I backed away from the scene, stumbling, it was as though my legs would not support me. What was I to do next? What action to take? Confrontation, threats, physical attack, running away, just nothing at all; many options raced through my mind.

In the event, to my surprise, I found myself going back down the stairs. In my haste with my mind racing, I forgot the infamous third step on the way down the stairs. To me the sound that it made was as loud as the creaking of a rusty cathedral door.

I realised that this may have alerted Orsini to my presence so, by way of a distraction, I unceremoniously grabbed the family cat, Blanco and threw him somewhat ignominiously from his favourite place resting by the door directly to the foot of the stairs. I believe that I heard Orsini come out of the bedroom and onto the upstairs landing. My ruse had apparently worked since he returned to the bedroom to continue with his evil shenanigans.

Returning to the chair from which I had risen just a few minutes earlier, those fateful few minutes which had torn my life apart for ever, I thought over what course of action to take going forward.

I cursed that occurrence, whatever it was, by which the chance sound had been caused to bring me out of my trance. I felt at the time that I would have preferred to remain ignorant of their deception and thus not be suffering the spinning brain and leaden stomach. What is done, however, cannot be undone.

I learned that day that whatever shortcomings or failings I may have, my mind has the facility to consider, assess and plan at an amazing rate when under stress. Within what must have been only a few seconds, in my mind, my way forward was decided.

About half an hour later Orsini and Sarah returned. I heard them approaching so I adopted, as much as I could, the trance-like state and sat back in the armchair just as Orsini had left me. They entered the room and quite blatantly exchanged one short kiss in my presence. She then left before he came closer, stood in front of me and, with a flourish, snapped his fingers. On hearing this command, I made the pretence of waking up and returning to the real world.

I must admit to being pleased that Orsini made no attempt to continue with our rehearsal of the act, since I felt that it would be very difficult for me to deceive him into believing that I was still under his influence.

My mind was now set upon the course of action to be taken.

I vowed to learn as much, if not more, about the art of hypnotism than Orsini had in those early days. It would take time but I had the motivation and thus the dedication. I obtained all the reading matter that I could and studied hard the principles of hypnotism and power over the mind.

In my case, however, there was a difference, for I was attempting to achieve control over my own mind and not the minds of others. My aim was to give every appearance of being in a hypnotic trance whilst actually remaining in a fully conscious state.

After a while, as I remember a period of some two months, I felt that I had managed to attain a sufficient level of proficiency to try out my new skills.

I then visited the professor once again who, by now, had continued his work and extended the scope of his studies further. I learned much from him. In addition, I viewed the film again to refresh my memory. It was all part of the greater plan.

As an experiment, in order to test out my theories and measure my progress, I attempted to play out my part in the act whilst resisting the hypnotic influence. This proved to be the most difficult part of all. It meant testing myself against Orsini and resisting his steady voice and piercing eyes. I still recall how nervous and apprehensive I was the first time.

There came a time, however, when I knew that my resistance to him was growing and not only that, I was convinced that he had no inclination as to my new-found ability. I found that as I developed my skills I could resist him at will, my will. He was totally unaware of any differences between the times when I allowed him to take control and when I remained my own man.

There was one final piece necessary to complete my plan. I suggested to Orsini that when I had seen the film of the act I thought it may be even more impressive if, at the climax, I made as if to attack him with the swords rather than just walk towards him with them raised high as if to bring them down to cut him in two.

His inbuilt inflated ego led him to readily agree, he arrogantly stated that he felt that such an improvement would serve to increase the impact upon the audience. He even suggested that I take lessons in swordplay in order that I would be seen to handle the weapons correctly.

All was ready and I waited for my time to come.

Three months later found us booked to play in London to what would be a full house. It was important to me that my plan should be carried to its fruition in front of the maximum number of people, even if they were in no position to grasp the true significance of what they were to see. Also it was of paramount importance to me personally that the two key players were on stage with me.

The performance went well, as it always did, and the time soon came for the finale.

Orsini called for the attack. As I came across the stage, directly at him in my blind and apparently subconscious rage, our eyes met. At that instant in time I know he realised all but was powerless. The Great Orsini was powerless. He knew in that split second that this was my revenge.

I cut him down in a matter of seconds, from the number of times that the swords cut deep into his flesh there could be no doubt as to the outcome.

By the time the stagehands had rushed on to restrain me and the curtain had come down Orsini was dead. The theatre was in uproar, men and women alike fainted at the sight of his horribly mutilated body.

At the inquest I put on a good show of remorse and self-recrimination. I was, of course, deeply distraught and inconsolable following the sad loss of my partner and friend.

At the Coroner's Inquest a verdict of accidental death was recorded and no charges were ever brought. The basis for the judgement was that this being the most dangerous part of the act, Orsini had, for some unknown reason, failed to snap his fingers in sufficient time to prevent my advance. I could not be held responsible owing to my state of induced hypnotic trance which the learned professor had testified was perfectly genuine.

It is with some pride, therefore, that I state today that I can claim to have committed the perfect crime, indeed the perfect murder. For my part, however, I would say that justice was done and seen to be done.

You see, nobody realised then or has realised since that with the first upward stroke of the two swords I cut off both his thumbs.

END

THE FLESH-COLOURED ROSE

THE FLESH-COLOURED ROSE

I live in the country and I work in the big city, it's as simple as that and I like it that way. I don't expect everybody to understand how I feel, but then, why should they, it wouldn't suit some people. I have always loved the style of the English countryside in which I was born and raised and now that I have the opportunity and the funds, I have come back to live in the same village, to my roots, so to speak.

Anyway, enough of my philosophy of life, let me relate to you my story.

As I pen this, it is a cold dark winter's night and the wind is howling around the outside of my cottage. I am sitting by the open log fire, safe and warm, in my favourite armchair with a glass of my best brandy.

I bought this cottage four years ago from old Ben Dickinson. Ben had lived in the village for as long as anyone could remember. He was eighty-four when he left to go and live in a small self-contained flat which had been built on to the side of his daughters house some distance away. He was becoming a little infirm, or so his daughter and her husband thought, and probably getting to the stage where he was not looking after himself properly.

The cynics in the village had said that Ben's daughter was being selfish and did not relish the idea of paying regular visits see him, that her and her husband were thinking only of themselves. But, for my part, taking into consideration the long drive and the fact that he was going to be well looked after, who was in a position to criticise?

Although I had known that he lived in the cottage when I was growing up, as a child I had little contact with Ben. He was known to me as 'Mr Dickinson from Rose Cottage' and that was all. I was as polite (or as cheeky) as any other youngster to their elders, but by the time I was fourteen we had moved away and I suppose I forgot all about him. That is, until I heard about his impending move away from a friend in the village and decided to come back to view the cottage with the idea of buying it for myself.

I remember the meeting with old Ben very well. It was one of those discussions where you are not sure who is interviewing who. It is certainly true that I had a mind to purchase what he would see not just as a place to live but as his home of many years. I felt that he was not selling so much as checking me out as to my suitability as a prospective owner and resident.

There was little talk of money, he had been well advised as to the value of the cottage and I did not feel that I could enter into negotiation with the elder statesman of the village, it just would not have been right. Also, I felt that I wanted him to have sufficient funds to see out his days, however long that may turn out to be, in whatever way he thought fit.

During the course of our conversations he made a statement that at first sounded a little strange but stuck in my mind, and, as you will come to understand as my story unfolds, was to become more significant than I realised at the time.

He moved his face close to mine, looked me straight in the eyes and said, in a serious and sombre voice, "It is very important that you understand that you are the custodian of Rose Cottage rather than the owner. Look after the roses and they will look after you. This is the promise I made to my predecessor as you must promise to me. Look after and nurture the roses and they will bring you pleasure beyond your wildest dreams."

It seemed a small price to pay to clinch the deal and keep the old man happy so I played along and made him his promise as he asked.

When he took me out into the garden to show me around I was not quite sure what to expect. Were there to be tens, or even hundreds, of rose bushes for me to tend, to spend all my free time on?

He seemed to sense my apprehension.

"Don't worry." he said. "There are not a lot in terms of quantity, you see, but each bush is very special in its own way. Each has a secret embedded within it. You may live here for fifty years and yet not be privileged to know the secrets of them all.

He did not add anything to further explain or clarify his remarks and I did not know quite what to say or ask for fear of offending him in some way. Thus there the matter rested.

A slightly uneasy silence followed. Uneasy, I have to say, probably only on my side, Ben seemed perfectly content with his thoughts as he gazed somewhat wistfully into the distance.

I thought that I heard him mutter something quietly to himself, under his breath, so to speak, something about, "What goes around, comes around..." But it did not seem as though it was intended for my ears, rather as a private comment to himself.

I searched my mind for a question to break the deadlock and restart our conversation. After what was only a short while, but seemed like an age, I blurted out a question.

"Of all the roses in this magnificent garden, can I ask, do you have a personal favourite?"

After a few moments thought he responded.

"That is very difficult to say because each has its own special qualities, but I suppose if you persisted and pushed me into giving you an answer..."

He hesitated slightly and then beckoned to me with his hand.

"Come, follow me."

He led me to a central island in the garden where there were five rose bushes in a line. He pointed to the bush second from the left hand end as we stood looking at the row.

"I suppose if there is any rose in the garden that, for me, has an edge over the others in my affections it is this one."

He stroked one of its now leafless stems gently, almost lovingly, with one finger. I looked at his face and his eyes glazed over a little as some distant recollection drifted across his mind.

"When it flowers, the bloom is the deepest, richest red you could ever wish to see." he said.

I told him that I would be sure to look out for it next summer.

We made our way back into the cottage. I asked him if he was happy for me to be the next custodian, I was careful to use his term, of Rose Cottage. He responded positively, we said our goodbyes and I left.

The deal was done and dates agreed. Ben moved out to be with his family and one chilly evening in November I moved in.

The change of address brought along with it a daily fifty minute commute to the office but the first winter was fairly mild and I soon settled into the routine of the route and the drive. There was no doubt in my mind that it had all been worth it just for the sheer joy and relaxation of having my own place in such a beautiful setting.

I have lived here for four years now as I write this and I wouldn't change a thing for the world.

* * * * * *

When the first summer arrived, I was not prepared for the glorious explosion of colour that the roses brought to the garden. There were other flowers, of course, and they came and went with the seasons as flowers do, but the roses in full bloom were something very special to behold.

At that time, I suppose because I did not know much about them, I didn't really know what to expect. I was not ready for the sheer variety of colours. Some were strong and vibrant, others more pastel and subtle in nature. In addition, each rose seemed to have its own distinctive individual scent, some light and delicate and some more powerful and striking.

I watched for Bens favourite. I was not disappointed.

It flowered early in July. One by one the buds opened, each revealing a deep red rose with exquisitely shaped petals. Although it was strong in colour, the scent released was very subtle, almost imperceptible at first, but once taken in it seemed to possess the ability to linger on the senses. It was possible to detect it long after leaving the garden and returning inside.

It was about a week after the emergence of the first flower on Ben's favourite rose that I first noticed the problem.

I remember that it was a Sunday and I was taking an early morning walk around the garden, cup of coffee in hand.

Ben's rose, as I shall call it, looked very poorly. Each stem of the once proudly upright bush was drooping badly, the flowers limp and sagging with the heads pointing down towards the ground.

I looked around at the other immediately adjacent bushes. My first thought was that if there was some common cause then it would affect all of the bushes in the vicinity. If this were the case, then probably those in close proximity to Ben's rose would also exhibit some similar signs of distress.

In fact, each of the others looked fit and healthy; some were already stretching their petals wide to the warming rays of the new day's sun.

But not Ben's rose.

Next, I looked to see if there was any evidence of a specific reason why this rose bush alone was affected. I looked for any signs of an animal, human or otherwise, having been in the vicinity and then whether there was anything to indicate attack by any insect or fungus. I could find no immediately obvious reason for the very sorry state of the bush.

Later in the day I contacted a local nursery that luckily happened to specialise in roses, describing in as much detail as I could what had occurred and how I came to discover it. After about twenty minutes on the telephone with one of their experts, most of it spent discussing the symptoms, he told me that utilising this remote method of diagnosis it was not possible for him to determine what was wrong. It was then agreed that he would come and visit me on the Tuesday evening to see the problem for himself.

He duly turned up as arranged and carefully carried out his examination. He was very thorough, if a little intense, and spent a lot of time studying each of the different parts of the plant. His work was accompanied my much muttering to himself, a lot of scratching of his rather unkempt beard and constant reference to three well-thumbed books that he had brought with him.

At the end of his deliberations, he admitted to me that he was none the wiser as to what the cause may be and also that he could give me no guidance as to a cure. He did, however, collect samples of bark, leaves, petals and soil to take back for analysis in the nursery's laboratory.

On the Friday he called me at my office to advise me that, despite their preliminary tests, so far they had no idea as to the cause of the problem. They could only suggest that I left well alone and awaited the outcome, whatever that may be. In the event that the bush survived, would I be kind enough to let them know. It was plain that they thought that survival was an unlikely option.

I was away all day on the Saturday, so the next opportunity for me to take a look in the garden was Sunday morning. When I got to Ben's rose it was plain to me that it was dead. There was a thin layer of deep red petals around the bush, staining the ground like drops of blood. These were interspersed with leaves which once having been green and so full of life, were now black and dead.

I lightly touched the top of one of the stems. It broke away in my hand and fell to the ground. I picked it up and tried to bend it between my hands. Once, only a relatively short time ago, it would have been so supple and pliable but now, almost immediately, it snapped with a sharp little crack. It was dry, brittle and devoid of life. I threw the pieces on the ground and walked away disconsolately.

Quite by chance, on the following Tuesday morning I called in at the village Post Office. I recall that I did not have to go into work until lunchtime and so I took the opportunity to travel in a bit later and miss the traffic.

Mrs Frobisher, the postmistress, greeted me warmly and served me with my newspapers and a couple of books of stamps.

"Have you heard the news about Ben Dickinson, the old gentleman who used to live in Rose Cottage before you?" she said.

I replied that I hadn't, but that I was interested to know.

"Mrs Stevens, who does all the flowers in the church, heard from the vicar's wife that old Ben was taken ill ten days ago, on the Sunday she said it was. No matter what they did, the doctors couldn't save him. She said that they didn't know what was wrong with him, but I don't know about that. Anyway, the poor old chap only lasted a week. He passed away on Sunday. Sad isn't it?"

I went straight home. I suppose I was more than a little stunned by the news. I rang the office and told them that I had had some bad news, that I was feeling unwell and that I wouldn't be going in that day.

I went into the garden, took out the fork, and carefully removed Bens favourite rose bush from the plot of ground in which it rested.

I took it to a quiet corner of the garden where there was a small area which was not used. I carefully clipped the bush into slightly smaller and more manageable pieces. Next I took the spade and made a hole large enough and deep enough to lay all the pieces in and bury them.

To some, it may seem a nonsensical thing to do but before I filled the earth in to inter the now dead rose bush for ever, I held a brief ceremony of my own. Quietly, to myself, I said a short prayer of thanks to old Ben, in memory of what he had done for Rose Cottage and in appreciation of him entrusting the garden to me.

After completing the covering of soil, I marked the spot by first placing some stones on top and then painting them white.

One year later, almost to the day, the minor miracle happened.

Quite by chance, I went to look at the little shrine to old Ben, as I suppose I would describe it.

Pushing up through the centre of the now faded white stones, was a rose, a single tiny white rose, one bloom on a single stem.

I went down on my hands and knees and studied it closely and carefully. It was beautiful.

Somehow, old Ben's words drifted into my mind, "What goes around, comes around...."

After seeking advice from the nursery experts to ensure that it was safe to do so, I transplanted the new rose back to the vacant space where Bens rose had been and I have to say that it settled well and continues to flourish there to this day.

* * * * * *

Moving on, the main purpose of my story is to relate to you the events that took place in the warm sunny July of the third year, that is, some two and a half years after I moved in.

I had tended the roses just as I had said in my promise to old Ben.

At first I bought around ten reference books covering various specialised features of that particular plant; varieties, history, planting, growing, tending, pruning, etc. There was no aspect of the rose about which I did not read.

Like all things, however, there is no substitute for practical experience and I found that I had to enlist the help of some experts to assist me in the finer points of pruning and general plant care that are not in the textbooks. As time went by, I learned enough to continue by myself, safe in the knowledge that I could call in the cavalry if anything went disastrously wrong or I came up against a problem that I had not encountered before.

Although I lived very much on the back of Ben's many years of tender loving care, I was the grateful recipient of one or two complimentary remarks from other villagers regarding the garden at Rose Cottage.

The only slight cause of disappointment to me was that of all the colour that abounded as the roses came into bloom, with all the joy of the beauty that they displayed and the delicate scents that wafted into the air, there was one bush that I could not get to flower. No matter what I did, what book I read or advice I took, I could not get this one particular rose to come into bloom.

It was right under the bedroom window that once Ben, and now I, occupied. There were two other rose bushes, one on either side of it that flowered successfully each year. Indeed, they seemed to thrive. There was no obvious factor such as location, light or soil that affected it, but flower it did not.

Now, to come to that balmy warm summer evening in July. I recall it was a Saturday. I had had a fairly restful day, a short trip into town in the morning for a little shopping, followed by a few general odd jobs and tidying up at home.

I didn't go into the garden until late in the afternoon; I had decided to have a light al fresco meal of pasta with carbonara sauce and my favourite Italian Gavi di Gavi wine. While the pasta was cooking I went to arrange the garden furniture and lay the table.

I turned and walked towards the cottage and in doing so I passed the open bedroom window. The sight that befell my eyes stopped me in my tracks and forced me to stop and investigate.

There, beneath the window, was the rose bush that I thought to be barren and, for some inexplicable reason, incapable of flowering. Rising high and straight from the centre of the bush was a single tall long stem and on the top of this stem was a bud.

The bud was new and mostly green in colour, the colour of the outer covering, but just visible beneath was the lighter colour of petals waiting to break through. I looked carefully around the bush; there was only the one bud and no sign of any other.

I bent down to look more closely at the solitary bud, intrigued by the apparent spark of life from the previously dormant bush.

As I came within about a fingers length of the bud, something happened which caused me to jump and move my head back suddenly in surprise.

I swear that, for no apparent reason, the whole plant gently shuddered, causing the top, to which I was so close, to move, not violently but certainly with what I can only describe as a non-plant like motion. It was as though someone or something had knocked the base of the bush and the movement had cause a ripple effect right through it and out to its extremities.

I looked down to see whether I had inadvertently caused this motion or if a bird or animal had somehow touched the bush. There was no immediately obvious explanation for the sudden movement and so I leaned forward once again.

I hesitated slightly at about the distance at which the plants first apparently involuntary movement had occurred but nothing happened, of course, and so I moved nearer.

I suppose, looking back, it was a pointless act, but my intention was both to take a closer look and to try sniff the bud to get a hint of the likely scent.

As I did so, a second and most peculiar event took place.

Somehow my lips brushed against the unopened bud. As they did so, a strange tingling sensation ran from the point of contact in each direction along both top and bottom lip to the sides of my mouth and into my cheeks.

It was not so much an unpleasant sensation as very unexpected. It came as a surprise but did not seem painful or strike me as harmful, in fact, in a way I found it rather enjoyable. I can only liken it to one of those experiments you do as a boy where you feel the low electrical energy from a small battery on your tongue.

I backed away from the rosebud, not quickly as in the first instance but quizzically and wondering what on earth could have caused that very odd effect.

After some thought, I put the occurrence down to some natural phenomenon such as static electricity and vowed to keep an eye on the rose over the next few days. It generally took two or three days for a flower to emerge and open to its full extent; it would be interesting to watch and observe this late newcomer to the garden display.

I went on with my preparations, had a very pleasant meal in the warm evening sun and relaxed with my feet up in the garden watching the birds and the insects going about their business.

It was late into the evening, after the sun had dipped down below the hills, when I realised that the first of the bats had arrived, swooping and darting around the garden. Only then did I think about going to bed. Only then, when I picked up the empty wine bottle, did it become evident to me that I had finished off the entire contents on my own.

And so to bed.

As is the nature of English summers, it had been rather humid and I had taken to sleeping on top of the bed wearing just my underpants with the window wide open to catch any cooling breeze.

Whether it was due to the drink I don't know, but I went into a kind of half-sleep, not really one thing or the other, with my mind playing over various thoughts and ideas but not letting me drift off into a deep and restful slumber.

I was lying on my side, facing the window, trying to clear my head of all distractions when I heard the rustle of a heavy breeze moving through the garden. The curtains billowed and the force of the gust coming into the room was enough to push me over onto my back. My first thought was that this could be the first sign that a summer storm was about to blow up.

Although I was tired and sleepy, I summoned up enough energy to get up and close the window. The one thing I didn't need was to wake up in the morning with everything soaking wet, assuming that the rain, or possibly the thunder, didn't wake me up during the night.

Having done this, I went back to bed, once again taking up my favourite and most comfortable position, lying on my side.

The next thing that happened caused a reaction in me that I can only describe as delayed-action surprise. A short sharp gust of wind, similar to the first, pushed me onto my back again. It took a couple of seconds for my brain to remind me that this was impossible. My brain told me that it couldn't happen, but my senses told me that it had.

Whilst I was still trying to take it in, I felt the momentary touch of skin, a hand, albeit a soft and gentle hand, brushed against my shoulder. I moved slightly, not away from the touch so much as to make sure that it was not purely imagined. There was no sensation of force to restrict my movement in any way, if it was a hand there was no hint of restraint or increased pressure on me.

As my mind raced to try and cope with what was happening to me, I heard a voice, a soft and gentle voice, a female voice.

"All is well. All is as it should be."

For some reason the manner in which the words were spoken dispelled any fears that I may have had of being under any kind of threat. At the same time the words were coupled with a delicate fragrance which wafted gently into the air. Initial thoughts of attack or robbery simple melted away, somehow there was only reassurance.

I recognised the scent as that of a rose, but it was somehow distinctly different from any other rose with which I had ever come into contact; fragrant and all pervading, yet delicate and subtle.

The gentle touch of the hand moved around my body from one shoulder, down across my chest and to the other. Now I could feel a smooth hand resting on each shoulder. As she gently lowered her body towards me I felt her arms on mine and, a split second later, her naked breasts touched lightly on my chest. She did not press down on me but moved slowly from side to side, drawing little circles on my chest with her nipples, nipples that seemed to get firmer and harder with the smooth friction of skin on skin.

Now she came a little lower. I felt her lips at first brush against mine, as if searching for my mouth and then, once found, she uttered a quiet murmur and pressed them firmly against mine. As she did so, I felt the same electric sensation as I had earlier in the evening when I touched the rose. At the same instant, there was another release of the delectable fragrance.

All my senses danced at once.

I was not able to resist even if I had wanted to (which I didn't) and I raised my left hand to where I judged her left leg would be, to the outside of her thigh. I felt her tremble slightly as my hand brushed against her skin; amazing skin, soft and smooth, yet firm and taut to the touch. I caressed her leg gently, but with slightly more deliberation than the first contact and she let out a low murmuring sound.

I ran my hand from the outside of her thigh, up across her hips, past her waist and up to the side of her body where I let it come to rest. I held there, exerting a little light pressure but motionless and, at the same time, letting my thumb rub gently against the side of her breast.

I now knew that she was completely naked and this aroused me even more, I could feel the blood rushing to my loins.

She seemed to read my very thoughts. As I raised my head a little, she moved her head to one side and kissed the nape of my neck. The gentle nibbling that accompanied the kisses drove my mind wild.

She brought her head back to face me and once again pressed her lips against mine. This time we both opened our mouths at the same time and let our tongues touch and explore each other.

Her hand now slid down the length of my body, pushing down my pants and releasing my firm erect manhood into the cool scented air. The effect was immediate; it grew even more, like the sudden freeing of a tightly coiled spring.

With a swift deft movement from her, synchronised with a quick and eager response from me in moving my hips and legs, the pants were gone. The only way to feel the full unbounded pleasure of this experience was to be totally free.

She slid on top of me so that she had one leg between mine and I one leg between hers. If I close my eyes I can still recall in my mind the motion and the feel of her velvet skin sliding across my naked body.

In doing this, she could feel my fully erect manhood rubbing gently but firmly against the outside of her thigh. She could feel my leg against her, throbbing gently between her legs against the most sensitive part of her body as I flexed my thigh muscle aiming to produce the maximum effect for her.

We allowed ourselves time to slowly explore, investigate and enjoy each other's body. One of us would move slightly to experience the touch of a new point of contact and the other would respond.

Maybe I would run my fingers through her hair and then let my hand travel down her back, keeping a little pressure with my fingers on her spine. The hand would continue down to her bottom, where the fingers would slip between her buttocks and the hand would gently squeeze and knead her cheek which she would clench and release as a response.

At one point she lifted her body away from me, took my hands and cupped them to her breasts. As I held them and caressed them gently and yet firmly, all I could think was how beautifully shaped and firm they were. I adjusted my hands slightly so that her nipples were held between my outstretched fingers. She tilted her head back so that the breasts pushed forward, I could feel the nipples harden even more.

She leaned forward again but this time with one breast directly above my mouth. At first, I squeezed the nipple between my lips, not biting with teeth, you understand, it was purely skin to sensitive skin. Then I took as much of that gorgeous breast into my mouth and sucked gently, at the same time flicking the hard nipple with my tongue.

I remember moving away and muttering something about it being wrong or unkind to leave the other one out and repeating the whole glorious activity with the other breast. She responded with soft appreciative murmurs and gentle thrusting movements of her hips against mine.

By now, we were both moving against each with firmer, more intentioned, movements; as our pleasure increased, both of us let out short gasps of joy as each aroused the other, our bodies and minds becoming more and more entwined.

I motioned gently with my arm on her hip and she slid effortlessly on top of me. We lay there with our legs slightly apart for about a minute or two. She was sliding her body up and down me a little. She could feel me hard between her legs. The effect on me was electrifying. All that had gone before took me to heights I had never known, but this, this was now becoming altogether something else, something only dreams are made of.

All of the time that she moved on top of me we kissed each other passionately. We kissed as the feeling took us, on the lips, the neck, the shoulder, anywhere we could, each time with more fervour as our passion increased.

I ran my fingers through her hair, massaged her neck and then moved my hands down her back, making circles with the palms of my hands as I moved my hands down to her waist. I pulled her gently towards me before letting my hands travel on down to her velvet-skinned bottom. I caressed the firm cheeks a little and then squeezed them, at first pushing them together and then slightly apart.

As a response to this she slid her knees up alongside my body so that she was astride me. I didn't have to do anything, I slipped inside her quite naturally and effortlessly. It was as if we were perfectly matched together. She let out a short sigh of pleasure just at the point that she felt me slide within her.

We moved together now, slowly at first, with me pulling back so that only the very tip of me was inside her and then, without warning, suddenly thrusting my hips forward and pushing into her as far and as deep as I could go. I did this several times and on each occasion she let out a little yelp of joy which was accompanied by a groan of intense pleasure from me.

We moved more and more, deeper and deeper, faster and faster until we came together in an explosion of immense physical and mental emotion.

My mind raced as the multitude of feelings washed over me. I felt as if I was floating around in free space.

For a few minutes we lay there, locked together, held tight in each other's arms. There were just a few little involuntary pulses of movement from our bodies as we gradually began to relax and float back down to earth together.

Eventually, she gently slid off to one side and snuggled up close alongside me with one arm resting across my chest. I, in turn, put my arm around her shoulder and gently held her warm scented body close to mine.

I drifted off into a deep and restful sleep.

When I awoke, the feelings of utter completeness and deep contentment were still with me. The world was a happy place. Even if I had dreamed it all, it would still have been worth it all to feel the way I did at that moment.

I put my arm out across the bed. There was nobody beside me. I was completely alone. Bright rays of early morning sunlight streamed in through a gap in the curtains.

Whatever confusing thoughts came into my mind and played with my senses; the unmistakeable fragrance still lingered in the air; it still seemed to fill the room.

I felt the need to find her so I got up and put on my dressing gown. I searched the cottage room by room but, being unsuccessful, I found myself back in the bedroom looking out of the window overlooking the garden.

I had the compulsive urge to go outside; I don't know where the idea came from but what better way to take in the full joy of that glorious morning.

I left the bedroom, went through the dining room, into the kitchen, out of the back door and into the garden. I could feel the cool morning dew from the grass between my toes.

As I walked towards the area of the garden outside my bedroom window, I could see the rose, the beautiful single rose.

No more was it the tight green bud of yesterday, a sleeping beauty waiting to be awoken. It was now fully open, a proud and radiant flower with exquisite shape and perfect petals. The most distinctive thing about it, however, was the colour. The only way I can describe it in my meagre ineffective way is that it was as the delicate flesh colour of a young woman's skin.

As I bent down to cup the bloom in my hands, I sensed that it released a tiny amount of the same beautiful scent that now filled my bedroom. It seemed to bend a little towards me, as if to greet me.

I kissed it gently with my lips and whispered, "Thank You".

******

And so, as I sit here by the open fire relating my tale to you, I am reminded of the phrase that old Ben used of which I am only now just beginning to understand the true significance.

"… pleasure beyond your wildest dreams…"

I can tell you that there has been no repeat of the events of that night and no reappearance of the flesh-coloured rose.

But I live in hope…

END

THE BOY WHO COULD FLY

THE BOY WHO COULD FLY

"I can fly! I can fly!" The thoughts pounding in Tommy's head as he soared high above the town made him want to shout out loud. They had all told him that it couldn't be done but now he had shown that they were wrong. Just you wait, when they saw him, high up there in the sky, they would be so surprised!

It was funny really, but he couldn't really remember how it was that he actually came to fly in the first place. He remembered lots of things, he knew lots of things, after all, his mum was always telling him how bright he was, but he just couldn't remember, no matter how hard he tried how he came to fly.

Perhaps that was just how things are when you are nearly seven, maybe you can't remember everything anymore, maybe your head just isn't big enough, maybe your brain runs out of space and some things have to be forgotten to make room for new ones.

He closed his eyes and tried as hard as he could. And then, slowly at first, it started to come back to him.

He remembered sitting in the front room with Josh, his older brother, and watching a video while their

Mum did the ironing in the other room. Josh was very grown up; well he would be, wouldn't he, being nearly fourteen.

They had sat and watched the Astroman video together.

Astroman was one of Tommy's heroes. Tommy knew all there was to know about Astroman. Tommy knew that when Astroman was only five, he had woken up one morning with a strange tingling feeling in his fingers and toes. By the end of the day he had discovered that, by concentrating very hard, he could rise a little off the ground and just about manage to hover there for a few minutes.

Within only a few weeks, with a lot of hard work, concentration and practice, the young Astroman found that he could move around just off the ground whenever he wished. Then the time had come for him to go higher. He had gone to the open window of his bedroom, stood there for a few minutes collecting his thoughts, concentrating his power and looking far into the distance.

When he felt it was right, he had launched himself fearlessly into the sky. The music in the video broke into the Astroman theme that Tommy knew so well. Astroman flew high into the sky, as high as any bird, as fast as any plane. He could swoop and soar at will.

Astroman used his power of flight to help the good and defeat all the bad and evil people and things that he came across. Astroman was Tommy's hero.

Then one morning when he woke up with the rays of sunlight streaming through the gap between the curtains, Tommy awoke with a funny tingling feeling in his hands and his feet. It was as though he couldn't really feel his fingers and his toes, although they didn't hurt at all. He could still move them but they felt strange and not quite joined on.

He told his mum about it.

"Only pins and needles," she had said, "nothing to worry about. They will soon go away, just wiggle your fingers and toes."

But she didn't know about Astroman. She didn't understand the strange funny feeling like Tommy did. The more he thought about it, the more he realised that the feeling in his hands and feet must have been just the same as those that Astroman had felt when he first learned of his new powers.

Tommy knew then that he was going to be just like Astroman, he was going to learn to fly! Tommy couldn't believe his luck; he was so happy!

Try as he did, Tommy couldn't remember just how he came to start actually flying, how he had launched into the air for the very first time.

He had tried the gentle hovering like Astroman had been able to do at the end of the first day but for some reason that hadn't worked. Still, it couldn't all be expected to happen in exactly the same way for both of them, could it? It wouldn't be so surprising if some things had to be just a bit different. Maybe he would miss out the first part and go straight on to the real flying.

He had decided that this must be where he and Astroman were not quite the same. After all wasn't his dad always saying, "history doesn't repeat itself," and, "lightning never strikes twice in the same place."

Tommy knew that he didn't really understand all of what his dad meant but it did seem to explain why his learning to fly was a little bit different to how Astroman had started.

Thinking harder and harder, Tommy could recall that on the day that he first flew he had gone upstairs to his bedroom and put on the Astroman suit that he had had for Christmas. He thought that it must help to be dressed like Astroman if you were going to fly like him.

All he could really remember about the actual event after that was standing on the sill of his bedroom window with one foot on the inside and one foot out. He knew exactly what to do. With one arm outstretched, the palm of the hand downwards, fingers together pointing in the direction you wanted to go he was ready to go. He had studied Astroman carefully and understood how he could change direction in the air by angling the hand gently to the left or the right. He had practised the technique to perfection by running around the garden time and time again until he got it right.

He had launched himself out into the clear cool air just as Astroman had done on the video.

After that, he didn't know why, he remembered that there was a period of pain, not in any one specific place, more of an all-over sort of pain. It made Tommy flinch a little to think of it; it was quite bad at first but it hadn't lasted long and everything was fine now. He thought that perhaps that was how it was the first time and, after all, once the pain had passed he had felt the wonderful sensation of floating gently skywards.

Tommy instantly knew what this must be; this was the first marvellous feeling of release from the ground; of the freedom of the birds; of flight itself.

As he gained height, climbing ever upwards, he could see below him sights that, at first, he had difficulty in recognising. He thought that this was hardly surprising since he had never been able to see places from above before.

He remembered his Uncle Steve who had told him about his travels all over the world to lots of countries, he said that towns and cities that you knew quite well looked quite different from above.

Just think, Uncle Steve had been all over the world to so many places, flying in great big aeroplanes from airport to airport but now he would be able to tell him that he, Tommy, could go wherever he wanted without any help from any flying machines at all. No aeroplanes, no helicopters, no hot air balloons, nothing, just him, on his own, wherever and whenever he wanted to.

He spotted his house, easily recognisable by the four white chairs in the garden and the big red and white umbrella under which was a round white plastic table. He and his dad and Josh had gone to the garden centre together to buy the complete set as a birthday surprise for his mum. Then they had sneaked it into the garden late one evening so that Mum would find it when she drew the curtains in the morning.

He turned and saw the corner shop where he sometimes went with his mum to spend his pocket money on sweets.

He spotted two people, children, coming out of the shop. He recognised them both. One was Michael Jones, a classmate of his, the other his younger brother, Robert. He thought he would take the opportunity to show off his new-found skills. He swooped down low, right in front of Michael.

"What do you think of this, then?" he said.

Much to his surprise, Michael did nothing, nothing at all. Instead of being shocked or amazed by his sudden appearance from above, Michael ignored him, tugged at his brother's sleeve and urged him to move along home.

Tommy was taken aback by Michael's reaction until he remembered last Wednesday at school. Wasn't it Michael who had been so very upset with him over the paint he accidentally spilt all over his new school shirt?

Obviously Michael was still upset with him. No matter how exciting Tommy's news was, Michael was sure to take no notice of him; Tommy hoped he would get over it one day and they would continue to be friends.

He flew on down the street, down the hill, across the main road and up the other side. He kept to about what he thought was head height for a grown-up. He secretly hoped that someone would see him but he was out of luck, the street was deserted.

The big old grey stone church stood at the top of the hill. As he came closer to it, he looked down and to the right to where a group of people were standing around a neatly-cut, oblong-shaped hole cut deep into the ground of the churchyard.

"I wonder what that's all about." he thought as he came to a stop. By now he was hovering just above them.

He was very surprised to see that he knew who the people were. It was very strange. There was his mum and dad, both grandmas, his one granddad (Granddad Johnson had gone to heaven last year), his brother Josh, Uncle Steve and Auntie Jean. There were lots of other people standing there, some of them he knew, some of them he didn't. He did not attempt to further identify any of them, however, because all of his attention was now focused on what was between them.

At one end of the open hole stood a man in a long white cloak. In front of him was a small white box. The box was a funny shape, like an oblong but with a sort of bulge on each side and shiny silver handles.

The man in the long white cloak was saying something, but Tommy couldn't make out all of the words, even most of those he could hear he didn't understand.

He noticed that his mum was crying. His dad was holding her close, with his head resting on hers, but he was crying as well.

Tommy's first thought was to fly down to them and cheer them up. It wasn't right that they should be standing there crying like that. He was sure that if he went to them and told them of the good news about his being able to fly, that would make them feel much better straight away. They would be so pleased to see him!

He attempted to fly down to them but found that he couldn't. He wanted to go to them, he tried and tried, but for some reason that he didn't understand it just wasn't possible.

Then, quite suddenly, he realised that he wasn't alone up there, there was someone else slightly above him. He sensed that the new arrival was looking down at him. His first thought as he looked up was that it might be his hero, Astroman; after all, he didn't know of anybody else that could fly.

The figure was dressed all in white. There was a sort of soft gentle glow all around him. A long cloak seemed to flow from his shoulders down to his feet. It rippled gently in the breeze.

As Tommy stared upwards, slightly blinded by the intensity of the light, the figure stretched out his arm and beckoned for Tommy to join him.

He hesitated at first, but as his eyes became accustomed to the brightness, he recognised who it was.

Tommy smiled at his granddad and flew up to meet him.

END

TWO SILVER BOXES

TWO SILVER BOXES

It was a bright, sunny day and life was good for young research geneticist Amy Brooklyn. As she walked through the park she could feel the warm sun on her face and the grass soft and tingly on her bare feet. And yet at the same time it was almost as if she was not quite in contact with the ground, more floating just above it.

The reason for this feeling of total elation? She had just been to see her course tutor. He had told her that she had passed her second degree with the highest set of marks ever recorded for any degree awarded in the three hundred year history of the University. She had to admit that she felt more than a little surprised at his news; in fact, when she thought about it, she found it almost impossible to take in. There she was, in the year 2108, a hard-working but humble doctor's daughter, with so many famous and distinguished men and women having gone before her and yet she, of all people, had apparently achieved results exceeding all of them, across all those years. It couldn't be true – could it?

Of course, she realised that her success needed to be viewed in context. After all, it was all relative; from one point of view, who was to say that the required level of marks and standards of measurement had not changed over the years. Who could say that she knew more or understood the subject matter any better than any of those who had gone before? On the other hand, it was clear that such had been the pace of scientific advances that only a hundred years ago the science of genetics had been in its infancy; now there seemed so much more to take in and to learn.

Nevertheless, she told herself that it was an achievement, her achievement, and she was rightly proud of it.

Apart from the notification of the results, she had also been offered a research post at the University working under Professor Jones, a highly respected member of his profession and a man who attracted sponsorship and grants from many major industrial concerns. It helped that he had been one of her lecturers in her final year and she felt honoured that he had asked her to stay on, do some research work under his direction and possibly take advantage of the opportunity to work towards her Doctorate. Life was good and she was happy.

* * * * * *

A year or so went by and Amy felt settled and comfortable in her new role. The work with Professor Jones was going well and since she was enjoying a level of income that she had never experienced before, she started to feel that some kind of investment for her future would be a good idea. That wasn't to say that she didn't know how to have fun, she had good friends and regular partying ensured that she kept some balance in her life. Sooner or later though, she felt, it was necessary to invest a little for her future.

She came to the decision that the best course of action was for her to buy herself a house; somewhere of her own that she could call home.

Probably because she had fond memories of her childhood and the house she was brought up in, she had a preference for an older property, one with character and a little history perhaps. Eventually, after a lot of searching, she found the ideal place, not too far from the University and in her price range. It was about a hundred and fifty years old, having been built in the 1960s, had a nice garden and looked solid and dependable. Even though the house was empty she felt very comfortable and somehow completely at ease the first time she went through the front door. It seemed to invite her in and the instant she crossed the threshold she had the feeling that this could be more than just a house; a home.

She told the agent that it was just what she was looking for and within a few weeks the deal was completed and she moved in.

After about eighteen months, having settled into the job, the house and a new routine, Amy decided it was about time that she treated herself to a vacation. Initially there were plans to go away somewhere sunny and warm with four girlfriends from her graduate days at University but, as is the way of things, one of them got pregnant, another had a family bereavement, they couldn't agree on a location and, ultimately, the whole idea fell through.

There had been no men in her life since the long-term relationship with Richard had broken down. That had hurt her badly and she hadn't had the time, the inclination or the opportunity to get involved with another man since. Maybe, she sometimes thought, that was why she had thrown herself into her studies as much as she had in the last year of her degree course.

So, finding herself with no immediate plans or offers, she decided she would do some work on the house. A good clean, a few minor improvements and some decorating would freshen the place up and be therapeutic at the same time.

The previous occupants had kept the property in good order. It was evident at the time of her first viewing it that it had been used as a family home, cared for and lovingly maintained. Each room had been decorated within the past two or three years and two of them had probably been recently refurbished as part of the preparations for the sale. The garden also was well tended, mostly grass lawn with flower borders which she found reasonably easy to maintain.

The house had four good-sized bedrooms and, living on her own as she did, she had always wanted a study, somewhere that she could work, think and relax; a haven where she could get away from things and where she could concentrate on her thoughts. The study that her father had prepared for her and her younger brother years before when they were at school was a fond memory for her. This room had always been considered as theirs ever since she and her brother had used it as a playroom from as far back as either of them could remember. But that was far away now, both in time and distance, and she only saw her parents three or four times a year. She kept in touch with her brother though, and they always made a point of going back to their parent's house for family reunions at Christmas.

The room that she had decided to convert into her study was a large upstairs bedroom. It was light and airy, with a big picture window down one side. It would easily take two work desks, one at each end, and with a little rewiring it would have all the computing and networking links that she needed to maintain contact with the outside world. She thought about including a sofa bed and a table, there was enough space, then she could also use the room for visitors to stay in should the need arise. She discounted this idea, though, this was to be her place and entry to others would be strictly by invitation only.

The only drawback with the room, she decided, was the lighting. There was just the one electric light in the ceiling of the room and, for some inexplicable reason, it was placed quite close to the window. Even by changing the fitting and making the light bulb as powerful as possible, there was no way that this arrangement could provide sufficient light for the whole of the room. The work desks, of course, could have their own separate lights, but she was convinced that either a second ceiling light would be needed, or it would be necessary to move the existing light fitting closer to the centre of the room. She decided on the first option and decided to find a matching pair of new light fittings.

Her level of electrical expertise was such that she would not trust herself to do the job herself and that some outside help would be needed. Father and brother were too far away and she would therefore have to engage the services of a qualified electrician.

She was intrigued, however, to know what the job entailed. As a woman living alone she did not want to be charged an exorbitant amount by some tradesman who might look upon her as an easy touch. She rang her brother who told her the rudiments of the job and explained how the electrician would install the ceiling fitting from below and add the additional wiring from above by gaining access to the loft.

This was the first time it had entered her head that she may even have a loft, she knew that there was one in her parent's house but she had never even considered that there may be one in her own.

Curiosity rose within her and she asked her brother how she could find out. He laughed and gave her instructions over the phone. She eventually found the small door into the loft space and, following his directions, opened it and discovered that there was a retractable ladder fitted behind it. She just had to take a look. Putting on some old clothes and taking a torch from the kitchen drawer, she used a broom to pull down the ladder, extended it and ventured upon the climb into the unknown.

At the top of the ladder was a light switch; when she pushed it two lights came on in the large open roof space. Her thoughts that there may be hidden treasure left behind by previous occupants over many years just waiting to be discovered were dashed when she was faced with the sight of a completely open and empty space except for three large black plastic tanks. These were presumably for water, she surmised, since she could see that they and the adjoining pipes were lagged for insulation against the cold.

The loft clearly been used as additional storage space at some time since it was partly boarded over and it was possible to see areas of light and dark shading in the flooring where once upon a time large boxes had been standing. Where there was no flooring fitted she could see large timbers and below them what she presumed must be the back of the ceiling panels. The whole area was covered in a funny orange matting material which she later found out to be fibre-glass insulation.

Carefully, on her hands and knees, keeping to the wooden boards and joists as her brother had told her, she made her way over to the place where she thought the future second light might be fitted. It was difficult to calculate the distance up there; the open space was a little disorientating when she didn't have the reference point of the walls below to go by.

Having gained newfound confidence from her expedition into the hitherto unknown territory of the loft, she went back down into the bedroom and measured the distance from the existing light to where the new intended fitting should be. Then she went back up the ladder into the loft, noted the location of the existing fitting and estimated where the new one was to go. There was no flooring in that particular area, although the boarding nearby was close enough to kneel on whilst installing the new light fitting. No problem for the electrician, she thought, it seemed a simple enough task. At the very least, she knew enough now not to be taken in by some exorbitant estimate of the costs involved. She felt quite pleased with herself.

Just where the new fitting was to be located she noticed something a little odd. The funny matting stuff was not lying flat on the ceiling. Instead it was raised up a little, as though there was something underneath it. Carefully, she lifted the matting and, sure enough, there was a small wooden box with a faded pink silk ribbon tied around it.

She made the decision not to open the box there and then but, holding it under her arm, she retraced her steps back down into the room below, slid the ladder back into place and closed the ceiling hatch. Then she took the box downstairs into the dining room and, having laid out an old tablecloth, placed it on the large round dining table. She sat down, thinking about what to do next.

Following her scientific training she decided to adopt a somewhat clinical approach. Since she had no way of knowing how long the box had been there or what the contents might be, she decided it would be advisable to take a few precautions before attempting to open it. This led her to make the decision not to attempt the opening there and then but to delay until she had the right protective equipment.

The following evening found her seated once again at the dining room table wearing safety glasses and protective latex gloves that she had brought home that day from the University.

With great care she removed the ribbon and gently raised the lid of the box. There was no clasp and it opened fairly easily. Inside she could see that there was a piece of paper folded around another smaller solid object. She lifted the contents out and placed them on the table, moving the tablecloth slightly back as she did so to make a space.

Unfolding the paper carefully revealed that inside were two small round silver boxes, slightly tarnished by age but still visibly made of silver. As she did so, she also noticed that there was some writing on the inside of the paper.

Moving the boxes to one side, she opened the paper fully, pressed it flat and examined the writing. It was clearly legible and formed a short poem.

> *The passage of time cannot part us, nor distance us separate.*
> *We shall be together always for that was and is our fate.*
> *No love has ever been stronger or friendship so secure,*
> *Death holds no barrier for a love so true and sure.*
>
> *M and G*
> *2002*

She read it several times. It was clearly a declaration of love, but she felt, somehow, that there was a deeper meaning within the verse that she could not understand.

She turned to concentrate on the silver boxes. She could make out that each was engraved with a single letter, one with M, the other with G. It did not escape her notice that these were the two letters at the bottom of the poem.

Further detailed investigation revealed that there was a seam around the centre of each box, with a tiny hinge on one side and a narrow raised lip directly opposite. Pushing on this lip enabled her, with little effort, to open one of the boxes.

She looked inside and could see that, neatly coiled around the inside and secured with cotton thread, there was a single lock of hair.

She repeated the process with the other box and found the contents to be almost identical, although in this box the hair appeared to be slightly lighter in colour.

Her curiosity having been satisfied, she replaced the two locks of hair in their respective boxes, refolded the paper around them, returned them to their wooden box and put the box away in a drawer for safe keeping. She was curious about the box and its contents but further investigation would have to wait, she was busy and there were more pressing matters to attend to.

She put all thoughts about her find to the back of her mind until one day, a couple of weeks later, she was having lunch in one of the University dining rooms when she spotted a friend, John Wilson, a few tables away and a chance conversation with him brought new light to the subject.

John was a lecturer in history that she sometimes lunched with. When she had first taken up her postgraduate appointment, she had managed to embarrass herself by not fastening her briefcase properly and thereby dropping the entire contents all over the main entrance to the University. John had been the chivalrous knight who had leapt to her assistance. Since then they had struck up a friendship and sometimes had lunch together but that was as far as it went.

She moved to his table and sat down next to him. She asked him what he was working on. John always seemed to have a pet project that he was engaged on, more often than not they were interesting; it was what made him fun to talk to.

His current project turned out to be more relevant than they had both could have anticipated. He told her that he had been researching love tokens and keepsakes from the nineteenth and twentieth centuries and described some of the ways in which lovers had declared their feelings for each other when they were about to encounter long periods of separation.

Even in the first half of the twentieth century the only real means of communication over long distances was handwritten letters which had to be transported by land, sea and, latterly, air to their intended recipients.

As she listened to him she started to realise the relevance of her find in the loft. She told him about it and described in detail what her investigation had revealed when she opened the silver boxes. She was fascinated when he told her that he had heard of such things before. He went on to say that for many centuries it had been the custom that lovers exchanged a lock of hair as a keepsake and as a token of their love for each other. In times when lovers had been separated by long distances because the man was going off to war or on a long journey overseas, such exchanges often took place since there were little or no means of communication and, in many cases, a high possibility that the couple would never see each other again.

Even in times such as the late twentieth and early twenty-first centuries, lovers who were kept apart by distance or circumstances carried on the tradition of exchanging locks of hair.

What was unusual, however, was to find a pair of such lovers' keepsake boxes where, by some means, both had been secreted away together and had remained undiscovered for a long period of time. It was only possible to surmise how such an occurrence had come about and who *M* and *G* might have been; John told her that hers was truly a rare find.

During her drive home that evening Amy had a sudden moment of inspiration. The thought entered her mind that she could use the find as a basis for a technical thesis, possibly in support of her Doctorate. It would certainly be feasible to carry out a full scientific investigation of the two locks of hair detailing what genetic information could be gleaned from them. This could lead on to a proposal as to what further potential alternative courses of action were possible to determine more about *M* and

G and their backgrounds and lifestyles. This was, after all, very clean and uncontaminated genetic material from a different era.

As her thoughts developed she became more and more enthusiastic about the proposition; the two things seemed to come together so perfectly that even her scientifically-trained mind started to think that maybe fate was playing a part.

She spent the next week, day and night, writing the outline of her thesis in order that she could submit it to Professor Jones for his detailed scrutiny and comment. She knew that his blessing would only be achieved if she could convince him that her approach was both viable and likely to end in success. Without his support she knew that there was no way forward; her plan would have to cover the subject from all possible directions and take into account all eventualities.

Sure enough, when she did make her presentation to the Professor, he was challenging, somewhat brusque, and questioned her at great length about her proposal.

She didn't think feel he was too critical however; his approach was to challenge her thinking and she didn't mind that. After all, he had to be convinced that her idea was viable. It was true that the questions he asked were fairly deep and searching, but in order to achieve her goal it was better that he was sure not only of her capabilities but also her commitment to the task in hand. She therefore considered his approach as a compliment, he took her proposal seriously and that it, in itself, she felt was of value.

After three hours of intense discussion, he asked her to leave in order that he could consider the matter and deliberate on his decision. He requested that she return at 10 o'clock the following day when he would be in a position to advise her of the outcome.

She didn't sleep much that night; all the alternating positive and negative thoughts imaginable washed in and out of her mind, denying her brain the chance of rest. Eventually dawn came to her rescue. Breakfast was not an option, eating was unthinkable. She couldn't wait for the Professor's decision, and feeling more than a little impatient, she made her way into the University. She arrived very early for the meeting. Professor Jones, on the other hand, was surprisingly punctual and by the time they sat down her whole body was tingling as her mind bounced between anticipation and dread.

Fortunately, the Professor did not prevaricate and put her out of her misery very early on in their conversation.

Rather formally he stated that, after due consideration, he, and thus the University, would be willing to support her in the development and execution of her thesis, this being used as the basis for her Doctorate.

Her heart leapt as the words, those beautiful words, the words that she so wanted to hear, slipped from his mouth. She half-wanted to jump up and hug him but reason and protocol prevailed and her celebration was restricted to her clenching her fists and letting out an unspoken **"Yes!!"** inside. The formal announcement of the sanction having been delivered, he leaned forward slightly, held out his hand to shake hers, smiled and offered his personal congratulations. This time it was too much for her and she threw her arms round him and hugged him warmly.

When she drew back he was still smiling but looked a little sheepish and embarrassed: it was obviously not the normal reaction he got from students, she thought, and she blushed as she avoided his eyes and looked away.

The professor asked her to remain in his office for a while as he wanted to go and collect somebody that he wished to introduce to her. Ten minutes later he returned with a tall well-dressed man who she guessed was in his early fifties. He was introduced to her as Jeremy Lord, the Chief Executive of Genetics Research Incorporated. They shook hands. It was explained to her that he was a benefactor of the University and that his company, normally known by the initials GRI, was a prime sponsor of some of the major scientific research programmes undertaken there. Indeed, the Professor added that much of the money needed to support the small research programme that she was about to embark upon leading to her Doctorate would be provided by GRI.

The three of them took tea together during which the conversation largely related to the worldwide capabilities of GRI, some of the successful research programmes undertaken by the University and her personal aspirations for the future. She only came to realise much later that Jeremy Lord had been protecting his investment by personally checking her out. At the time she may have been offended by this but when she became more experienced in such matters she understood his motives and was more than a little flattered that he took the time and trouble to meet her in person.

She spent the next month mapping out the three-year programme that would eventually lead to her Doctorate. The plan was to conduct a methodical and closely controlled series of experiments on the contents of the two silver boxes from which detailed reports would be written; these reports would include analysis of the results obtained and predicted outcomes of further experimentation. The whole study would then be brought together by a final report detailing all the results achieved, as well as recommending suggested alternatives as to possible ways forward through further experimentation and investigations. The entire work was to be submitted as a basis for her new qualification.

She met with the Professor to confirm that her plan was acceptable, and having incorporated some minor amendments suggested by him, she made preparations to commence the initial stages of the work as soon as possible.

Three weeks later she entered the University research laboratories to begin work on her programme.

* * * * * *

Having decided to commence with G, rather than M, simply on the basis of alphabetical order, she selected a few strands of hair from the appropriate box and commenced her evaluation.

DNA testing, undertaken over a period of some months, together with other more detailed genetic tests indicated that G had been an adult white male, born around the middle of the twentieth century. He had been in good health and the hair sample had been taken when he was in his late forties or early fifties.

With the diagnostic capability of the equipment available to her and by introducing one or two new techniques that she developed herself, Amy found out quite a lot about G. She produced estimated figures of height and weight, as well as more detailed information on diet, living environment and illnesses that G had been subjected to during his life.

Gradually a detailed picture of G, as he had been in his lifetime, began to emerge. His physical attributes, health and lifestyle were revealed as the experiments continued and Amy's knowledge and understanding increased. She could not, however determine anything about the more esoteric elements of his existence such as his visual appearance, senses, feelings or thoughts. These she could only surmise.

In order to help with these aspects of G's existence, she engaged the services of her old friend John, the historian. He took the physical data that she had obtained and superimposed it on his knowledge of the period, the mid-to-late twentieth century. He determined that G had probably been a professional person, employed for his mental ability rather than any of his physical attributes; possibly a doctor, lawyer or professional engineer rather than a manual worker. In addition, he was likely to have worked in a big city environment but lived in a much more rural, probably country, setting.

Amy was in the second year of her work now, she felt that things were going well and that she was in line with her predicted programme. Her diagnostic work was almost complete on G and, with the first part of her report written, she turned her attention to the silver box marked as M.

The full range of tests that had been carried out on G was now repeated using a few sample strands of the hair taken from the box engraved as M.

In this case, the tests conducted produced a quite different set of results and formulated an altogether different picture. M was undoubtedly female, born in the early 1970s, and was in her late twenties or early thirties when the hair sample had been taken.

After further experimentation, Amy ascertained that M had also lived a healthy lifestyle, was free of genetic and hereditary illnesses and had succumbed only to the normal common ailments that were prevalent at the time when she was alive. The primary difference between her and G, her male companion, was that she had given birth to three children; advanced though her equipment was, it was not possible for Amy to determine how many children G may have fathered during his lifetime!

Amy continued with her in-depth investigation of the small amounts of genetic material that she had available to her. She built up a picture, as far as she was able, of the physical attributes of the two individuals, but more and more she found herself wondering about what their lives had been like, their visual appearance and what they really felt about things at the time that they lived and worked. Thinking back to the wooden box in her loft, she allowed her mind to stray into wondering what their relationship had been and how they felt about each other.

Not a very scientific approach, she thought to herself, but perhaps because of the very nature of how she came to find the two locks of hair and remembering what John Wilson had said, she couldn't really help straying into thinking about what might have been. She liked to think, in her more unscientific moments, that maybe *M* and *G* had been true lovers who had wished to leave a memento of their undying and perpetual feelings for each other for someone to discover, by chance, in the future.

She spent the last few months of the programme writing, reading and rewriting her final thesis paper several times. For the most part, she concentrated on the analysis and results provided from the detailed scientific data that had been drawn from her experiments. She struggled over whether to include her thoughts as to the more personal relationship between the two; after all, such thoughts were not based on true factual data and were only founded on her supposition as to how she imagined the couple might have been. Maybe she read too much into the less scientific guidance provided by John Wilson. In the end, however, Amy decided that the location and the manner in which the two silver boxes were found was relevant and she included a whole section in the thesis dedicated to what *M* and *G* may have been like, why they may have left the boxes as they did and what they could tell us if they were alive today, in 2112.

Once she was happy with the final document and she had decided it was as complete and correct as it was ever going to be, she gave it one more final read through and handed it over to the Professor.

He told her that the review and evaluation process would take about two months to complete and advised that she took a complete break from University life until he contacted her. He added that GRI had been particularly generous over recent months and there were sufficient funds available for her to take off the whole two month period, if she wished, with enough cash for a two-week holiday abroad somewhere away from it all. She admitted to herself that now she had completed the complex and difficult programme, which had required her utmost attention and intensity, she felt tired and could do with some time away to relax and recuperate.

She took her well-earned break and was back at home a few weeks later when the Professor called her and asked her to come and see him. He said that he was now in a position to advise her of the outcome of her work and could only discuss the matter face-to-face. They agreed on an appointment time of two o'clock the following afternoon. The formal tone of the Professor's statement took her back to the meeting when he sanctioned the start of her thesis; even now she couldn't read between the lines to guess what he was going to say to her. She spent a somewhat sleepless and listless night.

She approached the meeting with the Professor with some trepidation and more than a little nervousness. When she arrived he invited her into his office, exchanged pleasantries and asked her how she felt after her holiday. She declined his offer of coffee on the basis that she wanted to minimise the time spent until he told her the outcome of his deliberations, one way or the other.

In the event, she had nothing to worry about. He told her that it was a detailed and highly professional piece of work, well thought out and presented. He was pleased to advise her that the review committee had authorised him to notify her that she was to be awarded her Doctorate. He added that there was someone else in an adjoining room that also wanted to congratulate her. He tapped lightly on the door and, within a few seconds, it was opened by Jeremy Lord, the Chief Executive of GRI.

He was very enthusiastic, even gushing, about the work that she had accomplished and the report she had produced. He said that he was particularly interested in what he called the human angle and had been very impressed by the empathy that she seemed to have with the emotional side of the relationship between G and M.

He asked her if she had ever visited GRI, adding that in the field of genetics they considered themselves to be world leaders. She responded that whilst she had, of course, heard of the company and read about some of the research work carried out there, she had never had the opportunity to visit any of their laboratories personally. Immediately he extended his personal invitation to come and be his guest for the day as soon as she could make it.

Arrangements were made and when she arrived at the GRI headquarters she was impressed, almost embarrassed, at the fuss that they made of her. She was introduced to key members of staff and was given presentations on some of the major research projects being undertaken. She had lunch with the Board of Directors and was given the grand tour of the facilities. And what facilities! GRI was clearly a very rich organisation. Some of the equipment that they were using in their laboratories she had only read about and one or two of the more highly specialised advanced items were new even to her. It was clear that their research programme was taking the field of genetics into areas she had only previously dreamt of and that money was no object.

The middle of the afternoon found her back in Jeremy Lord's office preparing to thank him for taking so much trouble over making the day very special for her.

That was when he made her the offer.

How would she feel about continuing with her work at GRI?

She wasn't sure what he really meant at first, but before she could respond he invited her to accompany him and take a look at what he described as a rather special area of the establishment that she had not, as yet, seen.

By operating a switch strategically placed somewhere inside the top drawer of his desk, he made one of the seemingly solid wall panels of his office slide away to reveal a lift entrance. He motioned for her to join him and, by placing his security badge in a slot and placing his hand against a small blue-lit pad on the wall, the lift door opened. As they entered she noticed that there were only two illuminated lift control buttons, both bright yellow against the soft blue interior. He pressed the lower one and the lift began on its journey downwards. It seemed to her that even though it was moving quite quickly the lift still took a few minutes to come to rest at its destination. The doors opened smoothly and quietly.

They stepped into what she could only describe as a small foyer. That was the first time on the visit that she saw the armed military personnel. They were standing either side of a large stainless steel door, the like of which she had only seen in photographs of bank vault doors. Just to the right of the big shiny door was a desk with a third uniformed military man behind it. He acknowledged Jeremy Lord immediately, turned to Amy and surprised her by welcoming her as 'Miss Brooklyn'. Clearly her visit was expected.

There was a short formal briefing during which she was asked to not reveal the whereabouts or very existence of the facility she was about to enter and not to speak of what she would see inside. She was told that she was required to sign a legally binding paper before they could allow her to proceed beyond the large steel door. Somewhat nervously, she read the document through carefully, and then a second time. The penalties for breaking the terms laid down were very severe, she felt, being instant imprisonment for as long as deemed necessary and apparently without trial!

By way of reassuring her, Jeremy told her that there was no real threat to her providing she kept what she was about to see to herself and that, in due course, he felt she would not only understand but be as excited about the work that was undertaken there as he was. He added that he was hoping that she would come and work with them on one particular research project that they could discuss during their tour of the facility.

As was the way with her, curiosity got the better of her and she willingly signed. A few minor formalities followed, she was issued with her own security badge and they stepped forward in front of the shiny steel doors. The two armed guards moved apart to let them pass. As they did so, without a sound, the two doors swung effortlessly away from them to reveal a short steel bridge and a second set of doors. Jeremy explained that this was an airlock and that they would remain on the bridge for a short time, both sets of doors would close while the pressure equalised, then the second set would open and they could proceed.

She didn't much like the feeling of being there, encased in the steel tube of the airlock, but within a relatively short space of time there followed an almost imperceptible hissing noise after which the doors opened effortlessly.

Before her was a corridor, flanked on either side by beige-coloured walls with yellow doors at equal distances from each other, much the same as she had seen elsewhere in the GRI laboratories, which were presumably by now way above their heads somewhere in the main laboratory building. The corridor had nine doors in it, four on each side and one at the end. By the spacing of the doors, the rooms behind each of them were fairly large.

She was not prepared for what Jeremy Lord had to show her.

Each of the rooms contained an experiment which, in some way, was dedicated to the cloning of human beings. There were various body parts in different stages of development and, in the largest room, two complete cadavers, both male but apparently lifeless.

She couldn't believe her eyes; it was true that some body parts for transplant purposes were produced quite successfully and had been for many years but she understood that the attempted generation of a complete body was banned many years previously by International Agreement.

Jeremy noted her surprise and apprehension. He told her that military intelligence had led the government to believe that other nations were flouting the Agreement and proceeding with research of their own. Therefore it had been decided that they must do the same also. However, their programme of research had hit a number of problems that they had been unable to resolve. Since Amy was recognised as one of the new up-and-coming brains in the world of advance genetics, they, GRI, had decided to support her efforts and monitor her progress. She had demonstrated her capabilities and excelled to such an extent that they had decided to offer her a position on their staff to continue with her work.

Jeremy explained that, whilst they had been successful on two occasions in producing a whole body, perfect, as far as they could tell, in every physiological detail, in both cases neither could sustain life for longer than an hour or so. Their current explanation for this was that they had used only recently available material as their DNA model. That being the case, they believed that the initial driver specimens, as they called them, were too recent. In the case of Amy's research, however, she had experimented with more pure samples from a relatively long time ago and the indications were that her results could produce a more favourable outcome.

The financial package that they offered was beyond anything she could have imagined and, given that the possibilities intrigued her, even excited her, she accepted their offer. She knew, of course, that there were strict rules on cloning and that since the International Treaty had been signed it was only allowed for specific organs required in justifiable cases of transplant surgery. She raised this point with Jeremy who reassured her that her medical ethics would not be compromised. Since this was an initiative being carried out in controlled circumstances under military control, specific clearance had been granted for the research programme.

For the reasons he had explained to her the programme had run into difficulties and, he felt, was in need of an injection of new thinking. Her academic progress and success had been monitored and supported, as had been the case with others like her. She had been the most impressive of all of those that GRI had sponsored and consequently now she was being offered the opportunity to participate in the programme and put her undoubted skills to good use.

After only a few moments of consideration Amy decided that she had no option but to accept the offer and agreed a date with Jeremy for her joining GRI.

****

The first six months were spent as a settling in period to her new environment, selecting and establishing her support team and planning the way forward. She revisited all her previous results and assumptions with her new colleagues before agreeing a detailed plan of action. They were ready to start.

It was agreed that they would commence with the male, G, primarily because there was more data available on male regeneration from the previous experiments carried out at GRI even though they had, to date, proved unsuccessful.

The complete process, from the commencement of the initial breakdown of the hair sample to the production of the complete body was scheduled to take only six months, having been aided by recent advances in tissue generation used in transplant surgery pioneered by GRI. The difficult stages, where attempts had failed so often in the past, would come when what was known as the energising and mobility phases were reached. That was when it was intended that the body could start to operate unaided and become partially self-sustaining. One advantage would be that there would be no ageing or development processes, the completed adult body would be the same age as the hair sample that they had started out with.

She was extremely pleased with the progress that they achieved with G. The process of regeneration went better than they could have anticipated. The resulting body was of a white male, complete in every physical detail. He had clearly been of a strong muscular physique and had looked after his health when he was alive. Early indications of nerve and physical responses indicated that the full energising stage had gone well, but they decided to hold back any further activity and wait until the second regeneration process using the female hair sample was carried out and completed.

The same procedure was instigated and duly completed on the sample known as M. Again, the results proved to be very successful and the indications of mental activity and physical responses were good. As in the case of the male, she was white and physically sound with a strikingly well-proportioned body. The one thing that everyone who saw her remarked upon was her facial features and how beautiful she was. There could be no doubt that when she had been alive she would have been considered an extremely attractive woman.

The point in the programme had now been reached where they had to make a decision as to what course of action to take next. Both of the regenerated bodies were apparently strong and healthy but had only been allowed to develop to a certain level of sentient capability – that is, no attempt had been made to bring either of them to a level approaching full consciousness.

Amy and her team spent three weeks discussing all aspects of the possible ways forward including considering the potential consequences, any likely effects and the ethics of allowing further development to continue.

Should they take the next steps and attempt to bring the two individuals to life?

Amy's team discussed whether to continue with the programme. Jeremy Lord was consulted, as was an ethics consultant from the military. Eventually it was agreed that they would proceed, although with some caution. It was decided that they would commence by attempting to raise the level of consciousness of the male, G, first and try to achieve some degree of communication with him.

And so the full programme of rejuvenation commenced.

G was isolated in a room of his own with constant twenty-four hour surveillance. Various methods were used to stimulate brain activity and, slowly but surely, he began to awaken. This process had to be undertaken carefully and under strict laboratory conditions in order that any potentially negative mental reactions would be minimised.

In the event, the resulting reactions from G were better than they had ever experienced before, although he remained largely uncommunicative and displayed a low level of response to mental stimuli. Whilst he definitely could be described as being awake and aware of his surroundings, the team were disappointed to find that he showed little or no thought processes that could be said to emanate directly from him as an individual. There was life but no spark, no reaction other than base reflexes and no communication, either physical or verbal.

Decisions then had to be made as to what course of action would be appropriate to take as a way forward.

After considerable discussion and deliberation Amy's team decided that they should not proceed further with any more concentrated work on G but turn their attentions to finding out what affect the same stimuli had when applied to the other regenerated individual, the female known as M. M was duly placed in another of the isolation and surveillance rooms, on the other side of the corridor from the room occupied by G.

Again the results were pleasing because they were far in advance of those achieved previously, but at the same time disappointing because there was no evidence of any advancement beyond what they could only describe as the automatic response stage. Unlike G, however, with M there was a limited degree of speech but it was monosyllabic and monotonous and could not really be described as an attempt at real communication with those around her.

This meant that they had now reached the same point with each of the two participants. A month went by and the team continued to try different methods of stimulation but there was no perceptible change in the responses from either G or M.

Although the experiment was considered a success and seen as a great step forward, her team made it clear to Amy that they were unsure that there was much more to be gained from the current situation. Undoubtedly much had been learned from the exercise; many new techniques had been tried and advances made but it was felt that there was little to be achieved beyond what they had accomplished to date.

She realised that adopting this course of action would mean the termination of the experiment and with it, ultimately, the death of the two regenerated bodies. She realised that this would be carried out in a humane and respectful manner but, nevertheless, it made her sad to think about it.

She sat quietly at home one evening, listening to music and drinking a glass of wine. Her thoughts turned to the two relatively inert and somewhat lifeless bodies back in the laboratory. As she did so, she heard a soft click. One of the small wall-mounted cupboard doors made a creaking noise and opened slightly. She didn't take much notice at first, this was an old house and things sometimes moved without any apparent reason. Indeed, in some ways such things just helped to make the old place seem more homely.

She got up to pour another glass of wine and moved to push the door shut. As she did so, she spotted a familiar object just inside the cupboard. It was the wooden box in which the two silver boxes were kept. She reached out and took the box in her hand.

She sat down, opened the box and examined the contents just as she had a few years before when she first discovered it in the loft. Unfolding the piece of paper, she came across the poem. Its very existence had almost been forgotten with all the events that had taken place with the experiments on the samples of hair and the subsequent events at the laboratory, but it reminded her that this was the only clue to who G and M actually had been. Indeed, if it hadn't been for the poem they would not have any written reference to G and M at all.

Amy read the words again and again, over and over. They were beautiful. It seemed that they had meaning beyond mere letters written on a page. She now realised the hidden meaning contained within the poem. This was the expression of love, true love, undying love – a relationship between two people so close that it was difficult to imagine, difficult for others to comprehend.

It could have been the mellowing effect of the wine or maybe the words had touched her sentimental side, but as she read them she felt the lump in her throat and the tears well up in her eyes.

She sat back, wiped her eyes and thought about all that had taken place. After a brief period she determined that, for all the technical achievements and advances that they had made, the experiment was a failure. They may have been able to recreate the physical bodies successfully but there was no life, no soul, in either of them. After all, she thought, she and the team had become totally immersed in the aims and objectives of the programme to the exclusion of taking the time to stand back and consider the morality of what they were attempting to do. What right had they, mere research scientists, to try and play God? Shame on them for even considering it!

As she thought things through, it dawned on her that there was one course of action that they had not actually tried. She began to wonder what would happen if they physically brought the two together by some means. Was it likely that there would be any degree of recognition between them or even an acknowledgement from either of them that the other existed? Amy determined that she would raise the concept with her team the following day.

When she consulted the team she was more than a little upset with their response. They clearly felt that, from a purely cold scientific point of view, there was nothing more to be gained from further work with the two specimens. The general feeling was that had learned all they could from them and that the team should move on to something else; a new venture designed to build on and develop further the knowledge base they had gained to date.

Amy was disappointed that her persuasive powers were insufficient to convince the team that they should continue; even a discussion with Jeremy Lord failed. He told her, rather unkindly she thought, that this was pure research and that she should not allow her heart to rule her head. She became extremely frustrated that none of them could see her point of view that the predecessors of their *G* and *M*, the originators of the two silver boxes, may once have been very close. Why could they not see what she could see and agree to continue? Was she the only one who could understand that the inner strength of their relationship shone through from the words contained within the poem?

The day was duly set for the experiment to be terminated and the subsequent disposal of the lifeless bodies. Jeremy Lord told her to take some solace from the fact that many people would benefit from the experiment since, apart from some items to be kept for detailed dissection, most of the major organs and limbs would provide excellent transplant material. Somehow the concept did not provide her with much comfort, she felt, deep inside, that there had to be more.

Two weeks passed and it was the day before the bodies were to be prepared for 'closedown' as it was euphemistically called; the scientists involved tended to avoid any references to death in such cases.

Since Amy held a senior position in GRI, she had a high level of authorisation and security clearance and she was able to come and go as she pleased. Such was the nature of the work she had been engaged upon, it was not considered unusual for her to be working alone in the laboratory late into the evening.

She didn't mention it to any one of her colleagues but she was determined to carry out one act before the experiment was finally over and that was best done when she was alone in the laboratory.

She had a couple of excuses ready by way of explanation but in the event nobody questioned her as to her reasons when she said she would be working late that evening.

The two regenerants, as they were now referred to, were still kept in the separate allocated rooms in the laboratory on opposite sides of the corridor, each lying on a specialised trolley similar to a hospital intensive care bed. They were normally maintained in a state of suspended animation just below full consciousness, similar to a deep sleep. Each of them was connected to an electronic monitoring system responsible for keeping a constant watch on their physical and mental states. In the morning, these machines would be switched off, termination drugs would be administered and G and M would be no more, the experiment would be over.

Carefully, she disconnected G from his set of machines and, holding the two sets of doors open with heavy pieces of equipment, she wheeled the bed, on its trolley, across the corridor and into the room where M lay resting.

She carried out the same disconnection process on M and then set about the task of bringing her back to a state of consciousness. Knowing that this would take about an hour, she turned her attention to *G*. She estimated that, once initiated, it would take slightly longer to awaken him. This suited her since she felt that having to deal with them both simultaneously would potentially be difficult for her to handle on her own.

When *M* was ready, fully conscious and at the maximum but low level of alertness she was normally able to achieve, Amy operated the bed controls so that she came into a sitting position and helped her to sit upright comfortably.

Turning her attention to *G*, as he came round she repeated her actions such that he was in a similar mental state and physical position as *M*.

At this point they could not see each other. Amy hesitated slightly. She could not predict what may happen if she went ahead and took the next step. There may be no reaction, in which case she would feel disappointed. On the other hand, it could be in some way dangerous for them and she would not like to see either of them hurt in any way.

In the event, she decided that they had come this far and that in the morning, the way things stood, there would be no future for them. If she did nothing she would never know what might have occurred and she would have to live with that for ever.

As she stood there, contemplating her next move, *M* let out a long sigh followed by what sounded like a single word – 'Please'.

It made up Amy's mind for her. Quickly she manoeuvred the beds such that *G* and *M* were facing each other although they both remained staring downwards looking disinterestedly at the floor. By a slight movement to raise their heads a little the two would be able to look directly at each other.

There was nothing at first, no reaction at all from either of them.

As she watched them, it crossed Amy's mind that she had been guilty of letting her personal expectations take precedence over her scientifically trained mind. Why should she think that bringing the two of them together would have any effect at all? There was no basis in fact to expect anything. She had built her hopes up on a silly whim, she had failed and rightly so.

Then, as she continued to observe the couple, she came to realise that something was happening between them. Over a period which was probably no more than two minutes but which seemed a lot longer to Amy, both of them raised their heads simultaneously such that they were able to make eye contact. She noticed that there was a change developing in the way that they were looking at each other. There seemed to be, somehow, a flicker of recognition between them. Instead of the somewhat glazed expression that they had displayed when they were kept apart, it was clear that there was now a deeper and more intense feeling in both of their expressions. Their eyes were locked on each other's intently and she could see that now there was some form of mental exchange taking place. She would almost have said that they were in some way communicating telepathically with each other.

As she sat there, transfixed but watching them intently, Amy felt she could sense the intensity of their feelings. The emotion was almost tangible. It brought tears to her eyes.

She continued to observe them; they were oblivious to her presence. The look, which had started deep in their eyes, began to spread across their faces changing both of their expressions like the fresh, warming rays of the morning sun bring new warmth to the land. They seemed to come to life right in front of her and when their mouths moved in the first semblance of a smile, she sensed the wet streaks trickle down her cheek.

Almost simultaneously, for she could not tell who made the first movement, their hands moved towards each other across the white cotton sheets and then slowly reached out across the short gap between the beds. Gently, so gently, their hands touched, there was a slight hesitation and then their fingers entwined.

Amy noticed that for the entire time they maintained eye contact with each other. She would never forget the tenderness and love expressed in those first few moments. They had never met before and yet it was as though they recognised each other. It was all in the eyes.

She did not leave them that night. They sat quietly and peacefully occasionally reaching out to touch or caress each other. Nothing was said, no word was spoken.

They ignored her completely and did not seem disturbed or bothered by her presence. She wasn't even sure whether verbal communication between them was possible but somehow it seemed unnecessary.

* * * * * *

When Amy's team arrived in the morning she ushered them into one of the unoccupied rooms and asked them to wait together. She then took each of them, one at a time, to meet with the newly united *M* and *G*.

To say that they were amazed at what they saw would be an understatement. Some were struck dumb by the experience and could not speak until the enormity of the event had sunk in; others were so mentally moved by what they had seen that they sat down and quietly wept.

It was clear that they had all underestimated what could be achieved with the two newly-generated beings and that Amy's action that night had meant that they had narrowly avoided missing the opportunity altogether. Furthermore, if the course of action suggested by her team had been followed and then carried through as planned, *M* and *G* would be no more and none of the events that she had brought about would have taken place.

Immediately it was decided that new plans were to be drawn up to detail what was to happen next. Each of the specialists in the team was given forty-eight hours to review this new situation, consider their options and submit their recommendations. The original team was now supplemented by additional groups of specialists, comprising mainly of psychologists and psychiatrists that Amy's team had not had the need for previously.

The intent was that a complete programme of activities would be generated, designed to develop the couple to a new, as yet undiscovered, level of both mental and physical consciousness and, at the same time, achieve the maximum degree of learning for the team.

Two days later the newly expanded team came together to agree the way forward for the programme. Jeremy Lord personally chaired the meeting and advised them that he was to take the role of being the final arbiter in the event of any disagreements that required definitive decisions to be made.

The meeting was long and, at some points stormy, as each expert put forward his or her case for what action was to be taken next. Slowly but surely the detailed programme was drawn up. Amy listened to each of the proposals and, by and large, she did not have any problems with the scientific and technical advice being tabled.

However, by the time the middle of the afternoon was reached, she found that some doubts were starting to grow in her mind. It was becoming evident to her that everyone around the table was approaching the matter from a purely clinical and scientific point of view and thus further developments were expressed in terms of either being a new experiment or at the very least an extension of the current ones.

Eventually, a point was reached where she could contain herself no longer and Amy stepped in and very forcibly expressed her feelings regarding *M*, *G* and their joint futures. She told them that the two should no longer be considered as just experimental material to be poked, prodded and investigated. They should now be considered as people, not things to be experimented on but human individuals to be treated with due care and respect. If they around the table had been fortunate enough to witness what she had witnessed in the early hours of that fateful morning, they would realise that what had happened in front of her very eyes was nothing short of a miracle. She could only describe it as watching the spark of life being rekindled within two real living beings and considered herself very privileged to have been present.

So impassioned was her outburst and so vehement her delivery that the whole room fell silent. No response was forthcoming. She sat down quietly, more than a little surprised with herself and unsure whether she should feel embarrassed about speaking out as she did.

Jeremy Lord, however, was impressed by her depth of feeling and immediately took the decision to put her in sole charge of the programme for the way forward. She had his total authority to proceed as she thought fit and only he could countermand any of the decisions that she made on behalf of *M* and *G*. With that statement he closed the meeting and handed the programme over entirely to her.

She decided that the couple, for that is clearly what they were, would be kept together from now on. After detailed consultation with the psychologists in her team and checking on domestic accommodation in the early 21st century, arrangements were made to turn five of the nine laboratory rooms into a self-contained living area. Amy's own house was used as a model. Food preparation, eating, sleeping, bathing and toilet facilities were included together with a large furnished area such that they could spend time with each other. It was determined that, initially, M and G would spend the waking hours together but sleep in separate rooms.

A facility for listening to music was included; it was felt that music could be therapeutic and assist their development. No visual media were provided, however, since it was considered that if there was the slightest possibility that they did retain any memories from their previous existence (nobody knew whether this was a possibility or not), these would not be affected or contaminated by new knowledge of more recent events.

The remaining four laboratory compartments were modified such that they could house the personnel and equipment that would be utilised primarily to monitor and oversee the couple's activities and behaviour in order to assess their physical and mental development.

It was decided that they would not be advisable to introduce them to life in the 22nd century too early, or expose them to all the changes that had taken place in the intervening period since their time on earth. It was thought that this may have been too much for them to absorb and that, consequentially, psychological damage may have ensued.

And so the work began.

One of Amy's primary objectives was to find out more about them, both as individuals and as a couple. She noted that as they became physically stronger their mental faculties also developed and they gradually became more self-sustaining. Their communication skills improved greatly, their conversational capabilities increased and, amazingly, for each of them parts of their previous memory began to return.

One day, about three months into the programme, was always to be remembered by Amy as a significant breakthrough. That was the day that the level of communication reached the point where she heard them speak their names for the first time and M became Mary and G became George.

Over the next few weeks, apart from the steady improvement in their physical and mental capabilities, their memories of life as they had known it and what it was like to live in the 20th century steadily returned to them. Amy, for her part, told them of many of the changes that had occurred over the intervening period. There were books and electronic records of life as they would have known it, of course, but very quickly she decided that her degree of understanding of that period was deeply inadequate.

To assist her she called once again on her friend from the University, the friend who had first told her of the likely origins of the two silver boxes, John Wilson. She suggested that he might like to meet Mary and George.

She had to broach the subject very carefully and vouch personally for his confidentiality but eventually she managed to arrange for him to come to GRI and meet with them.

He was fascinated by what they had to tell him and spent day after day deep in conversation with them. As he said, books and other media can only tell part of the story, there is no substitute for experience and they were able to fill in many of the gaps in the history scholar's knowledge and understanding of those times.

Amy and her team were keen to find out more about them as individuals. In order to achieve this it was necessary to conduct specific tests with each of them in different rooms. When such tests took place, however, it was clear that they were never as alert or forthcoming as they were when they were together. Somehow it seemed to Amy that when they were close to each other they were focussed on a greater aim, some dream far removed from the cold clinical facts that the scientists were seeking to learn from them.

Amy watched them intently as often as she could, sometimes as an observer when others were present and occasionally from one of the independent monitoring suites in secret when she was alone. What she saw fascinated her more and more as time went by. There was a kind of spark between them, it was the only way she could describe it, she felt that no suitable word existed in her scientific vocabulary. Maybe this was something that she had no knowledge or experience of, maybe this was what some people called love.

As time went by, the exchanges of information continued. Almost a year to the day since that fateful evening when Amy had witnessed the mental awakening of Mary and George, they requested to be allowed to leave the laboratory complex to witness for themselves what life was like on the outside.

Much discussion ensued within the team. There were those that agreed and those that did not. Eventually, however, it was agreed that the couple could be taken on an exploratory trip lasting for about eight hours. Part of the time would be in daylight and part in the dark. The couple were asked if there was anything that they would particularly like to see. In order to help them with their selection, they were shown electronic virtual tours of areas within relatively short distances of the GRI facility that it would be fairly easy to get to, thus minimising the actual travel which they had never previously experienced.

It was decided that the time should be split into six hours during daylight with the remaining two hours after dark. They chose to visit open country areas in the daytime, moving into the city for the final hour of daylight and the remaining evening period.

It was stipulated that they would be accompanied at all times by at least four members of the team, plus Amy. They readily agreed to this since they had no wish to be alone in what was to them an alien environment and of which they could have had no experience or knowledge.

The first trip out duly took place one sunny summers day in June and went smoothly as planned. There were many questions, on both sides, and much was learned by all of those involved. Mary and George came back with their minds overflowing with newfound knowledge and full of excitement over what they had seen. They chattered away deep into the night until they fell asleep, exhausted.

The first excursion having been deemed successful; others followed until they were taking place on about monthly intervals. On each occasion both sides found that their knowledge increased and that they learned a little more.

And so it continued, Amy's team gained more understanding from the couple of the lives that they had led in the past whilst Mary and George learned what life was like in what was, to them, the future.

* * * * * * *

In time, however, the purely scientific interest began to wane and Amy's team, believing that they had learned as much as they could, started to consider what they could move on to next. Even Jeremy Lord, whilst accepting that the programme had proved to be a resounding success, had suggested to Amy that her talents may be best suited to one or two new ventures that he was planning.

Then, one day, the question inevitably arose as to what should become of Mary and George. They had now developed to quite a high level of intellectual ability and were easily capable of looking after themselves. There was even one school of thought that held the belief that they were, in some ways, potentially mentally superior to their 22nd century counterparts.

From the purely clinical point of view, some of the GRI people thought that the experiment should now be considered over and that termination and disposal, as they coldly put it, was the only option. Others believed that a permanent home should be built somewhere on the site so that the couple could live out their days in peace; they argued that should any as yet unknown long-term physical or mental effects arise in the future, they could be observed, monitored and then dealt with quickly and efficiently.

Because of the potential sensitivity of these discussions if they were overheard by Mary or George, they took place well away from the underground laboratory complex in another part of the GRI site.

In the event, it was agreed that each of the possible options as to what course of action could be taken would be submitted to Jeremy Lord. Within a week five written papers were produced, each covering the problem, and possible solutions, from a different perspective. These were to be included as part of the formal presentations to be made to him in order that he could consider all sides before reaching his final decision.

Two days before the presentations, Mary and George asked Amy if they could speak with her alone in private. This was a little unusual; normal policy was for there to always be at least two of Amy's team present at any dealings with the couple. This was, in part, a legacy from the early days when the team were dealing with the unknown; at that time consideration had been given to the possibility that physical protection may be needed. Now it had become a rule adopted more with the aim of achieving consistency in scientific measurements and observations. In this case, however, Amy could see no reason for any such restrictions and readily agreed.

She was not prepared for what they had to tell her.

Mary started the explanation with George adding comments to assist and support her. She said that they realised that the regeneration process had been even more successful than anybody in the GRI team, including Amy, could have realised. Not only did each of them remember themselves as they had been before, but in some ways their capabilities, particularly when they were together as a couple, had been enhanced.

They quoted two examples. Firstly, they could recall intimate details of how they had met, specific places and events they had been to together and how strong their love for each other had been in the time before. She told Amy that they had been determined that their love would not die when their bodies eventually failed, somehow their love was greater than that and it would, they knew, live on.

They told Amy how they had come to put each other's locks of hair in the two silver boxes and then place them in the small wooden box which she had found in the loft of the house where they used to live. What a miracle of fate it was that she, of all people, a person with her background, capabilities and knowledge, was destined to find them.

If the first revelation brought tears to her eyes, the second stunned her completely.

Mary went on to say that in their previous existence they had been, to a limited extent, telepathic. Such was the apparent level of attunement between their minds that they found they could communicate with each other solely through the power of their thoughts. So powerful was it at times that they knew instantly when one was thinking of the other, regardless of the distance between them or what activity each of them was undertaking at the time.

They were convinced that this ability could not apply only to them, it must have existed in humans many thousands of years before but had been lost as speech and, more recently, mechanical and electronic methods of communication came into use. Each of them had, during their lives, met others that they were able to make contact with in this way but it was always to a much lesser degree and never in any way as powerful and as complete as theirs.

Since they had been regenerated as physical beings, however, this telepathic capability had not only returned but had increased greatly. They had discovered now that not only could they communicate with each other at will, they could also understand the thoughts of others, especially when the brain activity of the individual person increased as a result of a concentration of thought activity, for example, when they were focussed on a specific subject or event.

George commented that they found that some minds were easier to read than others and Amy had proved to be a particularly easy candidate, given the intensity of her feelings on certain subjects that she felt strongly about.

To clarify what they meant, they told her that Mary had been able to detect what course of action had been planned for them when they did not react well in the early stages of their mental rejuvenation. This had been confirmed when Amy came to visit them, alone, late one night. They were not fully awake or aware at that stage but they realised collectively that something had to be done or they would not be allowed to continue with their new existence. Hence Mary's extreme effort to gather all her strength and utter the one word of communication so that Amy would understand that there was more if only they could be allowed to live on. Amy had responded just as they had both wished, she took action and consequently ensured that they both survived. The rest was history.

George went on to say that they were fully aware of the discussions regarding their futures that had taken place over the last few days. It didn't matter how far away such discussions were held, as soon as the participants returned to the laboratory, their thoughts gave them away. They told Amy that they had a plan of their own to discuss and that they felt that she was the only one they could really trust.

George said that what they wanted to do was leave the laboratory, leave GRI, leave the country and set up home, just the two of them, and see out their days together in some quiet location overseas away from it all. It would be like a second chance to them, an opportunity to be together all over again, just as they had been all those years before. They would give any guarantees that were required and accede to any request made of them; all they wanted to do was to disappear into the distance and be left to enjoy each other's company for the rest of their natural lives.

Amy told them that this was likely to be a very difficult proposition to get people to agree to. She said that she felt there would be many objections raised and strong reasons put forward as to why this course of action would be unacceptable. She added that she did not want to raise their hopes too far but could understand why they were feeling as they did and why they wanted to take this course of action.

The only promise she could make to them at that time was that she would do her best for them and that the first step she would take would be to go and see Jeremy Lord and make personal appeal to him on their behalf. She went on to say that she thought that with his sanction it might just be possible; without his agreement it most definitely would not. If she could not persuade him on her own, then she would ask him to come and speak with them.

Her discussion with Jeremy Lord did not go exactly as she planned, he was not convinced that allowing the couple to 'vanish overseas', as he put it, was the best course of action to take. There were, in his eyes, too many risks involved. Had she considered that any problems that may arise with the couple, now or in the future, could bounce back on GRI and, ultimately, on him personally? He did, however, eventually, agree to her request to come and talk things over with the couple.

Amy was amazed to find that after a conversation between the four of them lasting about an hour, Jeremy Lord agreed, subject to certain conditions, to accede to their request and to help them achieve their aims. He had been so adamant in his meeting with her, why had he changed his mind? It was almost a complete turnaround from what he had said before. She had assumed that he agreed to the meeting with Mary and George to listen to their point of view and then tell them that he could not agree to their request but, in the event, he had apparently had a complete change of mind.

The outcome was indeed surprising to Amy although she was intrigued when George looked straight into her eyes at a time when Mary was deep in conversation with Jeremy Lord and winked at her. It only then crossed her mind later that the couple may have even more mental powers than she had ever thought possible.

So that was how it came about that the couple were allowed to leave GRI forever.

Mary and George made a commitment to abide by the conditions imposed by the organisation and the military. They would be given false identities and all the necessary accompanying paperwork including birth certificates, passports and identity cards. In return they would not reveal to any source at any time the truth behind their existence and how they came to be. GRI would provide finances via money transfer and credit card systems until such time as both of them ceased, for whatever reason, to make withdrawals. It would then be assumed that they had died naturally. GRI would make no attempt to trace them wherever in the world they chose to live. For their part the couple agreed that contact with any descendants of either of their families was out of the question since it could introduce both complex and difficult questions as well as have potentially serious mental repercussions for both parties.

Finally, Jeremy stated that only certain highly-trusted individuals in GRI, together with some particularly security sensitive parts of the military establishment, even knew of the programme that had brought them into being. Only a handful of people were aware of the successes that had been achieved within the laboratories and thus he believed he could say that their very existence would remain a secret.

False identities and papers were drawn up for the couple and, very early one cold December morning, they were ready to depart.

It was a touching moment; all three of them shed tears as Amy said her goodbyes and then with only a brief look back from the couple their car disappeared into the early morning mist.

* * * * * *

Amy found that she had no heart for the work at GRI. She tried to engage herself in other research programmes but somehow everything she turned to held no challenge, no excitement for her.

She was quite pleased, therefore, when, out of the blue one day, she received a call from Professor Jones at the University. He had not been well and was considering early retirement. After some discussion with Jeremy Lord with regard to her release from GRI, he had decided to offer her the position as his Deputy with the provision that she was to take over from him after six months. He added that, although he did not know what research programme she had been engaged upon, she must have carried out some significant work at GRI since it had been proposed that her faculty be fully funded by them in recognition of her achievements.

It was the offer of a new challenge and, in some ways, the opening of a new chapter in her life.

She accepted the position without hesitation.

* * * * * *

A year later Amy was sitting in the University communal dining room having lunch with some students when one if the administration staff came in. She looked around for Amy and waved to her as she made her way between the tables.

She handed Amy the brown paper package she was carrying, telling her that that it had arrived in the University office earlier that day. Since it was clearly marked as 'Confidential – Hand Carry to Addressee' she thought that it had better be delivered to Amy straight away.

Amy pulled back the layers of brown paper and packaging to reveal a small wooden box with a pale blue ribbon tied around it. Undoing the ribbon and opening the wooden box revealed a single round shiny metal box made, she guessed, of silver.

She eased the lid of the silver box open and gently lifted out the contents.

In the palm of her hand she held two locks of hair, each slightly different in colour, that had been carefully woven together in the form of a tiny plait secured at each end by yellow cotton.

She understood instantly.

One of the students looked over her shoulder and asked what she was holding and what did it mean?

Amy smiled but did not reply.

END

DISTANT CALLER

DISTANT CALLER

He didn't mean it to end that way. He didn't mean her to do that. He didn't mean her to react like that; no sensible, rational person would do that, would they?

* * * * * *

At the time it had seemed so innocent a thing for lovers to do, so right, so natural.

He thought back to the beginning, to how it had all started. He had difficulty recalling just how wonderful things had been between them what was really only months before. It now seemed like an irrevocable uncorrectable lifetime ago.

They had gone away for a weekend together to a little hotel in the Cotswolds, two happy people enjoying life and each other.

It was Saturday and they had been out for most of the day, driving around with no specific destinations in mind, taking in the countryside and stopping as the whim took them to take in the views. On passing through one particularly picturesque village they had come across a typically quaint pub with a thatched roof,

The Golden Lion, he recalled. The convivial and friendly publican and his wife provided them with an excellent lunch.

They found it so relaxing that, on finding that the pub had a couple of rooms, they opted to stay the night. They went for a walk in the local countryside in the afternoon, returning around dusk.

In the evening they changed for dinner and had a very pleasant meal in the hotel restaurant followed by a couple of drinks in the bar chatting to the rather talkative barman. And so to bed.

The room was large with a four-poster bed and an ensuite bathroom. The high ceiling and plain dark walls looked rather sombre against contrasting flowered curtains and bedspread.

She had asked him to get into bed and wait whilst she went into the bathroom to change. She told him that she had a surprise for him, something special just for him.

It was about ten minutes before she called out to him that she was ready and about to enter. They had become ten long minutes for him as the anticipation and excitement arose within him.

What he saw when she stood in the doorway took his breath away and made his heart skip a beat.

She had always been so attractive, beautiful, with long legs and a great figure. Her skin was smooth and silky, with a kind of always-tanned colour. She dressed impeccably with the gift of looking 'just right' for any occasion. She could, as he would say, "wear anything or nothing".

But, even knowing her and loving her as he did, he was totally unprepared for the sight that befell his eyes that night.

Slowly but purposefully she walked into the room, tall and glamorous, upright and confident, saying nothing but challenging him to look at her. He could only gaze back into the dark brown eyes that were looking straight into his.

His mouth fell open as he looked down the full length of her body and back up again, drinking in the sheer pleasure of seeing her like that; understanding, but not really believing, how beautiful she was.

It was one of those perfect moments.

She walked towards him and stood by the bed. She was directly in front of him now, her legs slightly apart with her hands on her hips. He allowed his eyes to wander over her body once again. She was wearing black high heeled shoes and a pure white bra and briefs set the like of which he had never seen before. The material was shiny, glossy even, it seemed to sparkle as the light caught it, and yet it was gossamer-thin and almost completely transparent. The bra was low but hugged and accentuated the delicate curves of her breasts. The briefs were high-cut and highlighted the line of her long shapely legs.

He had a feeling of breathlessness, with his heart pounding against the wall of his chest.

She rotated slowly and gracefully in front of him, allowing his eyes to roam over the whole of her taut and sensuous body. Then, quite unexpectedly, there was a further surprise awaiting his already overstretched senses. As she turned he saw that the shimmering white briefs were almost completely backless, with the thinnest possible strip of material from the lowest point up to where it spread slightly to meet the narrow waistband. She clenched her bottom slightly, knowing that he liked it and in full realisation of the effect that it would have.

For his part, he felt that his heart was about to stop; but at least if it did, this was as close to heaven as any man could imagine himself to be.

An idea came into his mind. He wanted to say something but he hesitated. Should he mention the thought to her or let it pass into oblivion?

But she was too quick for him and knew him too well to allow the fleeting moment to pass without comment. She asked him what he was thinking.

At first he tried to keep it from her and deflect her question, but she pressed him and he found he could not lie to her; he had no choice but to own up.

He asked her if he could photograph her just as she was in that oh-so-perfect moment when she first entered, the moment that was a single point in time that could never be repeated, so breathtaking that he wanted to try and capture it forever.

She was uncertain at first and hesitant in her response. But then she relented. After all, it wouldn't be for anyone else's eyes, only for the two of them, a present from him to her and a symbol of their love and trust for each other.

She looked deep into his eyes, she saw both expectation and then, as she delayed in answering him, a hint of disappointment as he anticipated that her response would be negative. His look turned to joy when she whispered her consent although he found himself unable to utter a single word.

He took just four photographs and then the camera was left on the dressing table.

They cuddled up on the bed, held each other close and kissed long and hard, with passion and fervour, their bodies gently moving together as skin caressed skin. Before long they made love, deeply and intensely.

* * * * * *

Three days after they returned from their weekend away, true to his word, he had shown her the two sets of developed prints, one for him and one for her. As a gesture he gave her the negatives so that she would know that they wouldn't, by some chance, get into the wrong hands.

* * * * * *

Their friends had always thought them to be the perfect couple. It was assumed that they would marry one day, settle down and live happily ever after. But such is the contrariness of life that this wasn't to be.

About six months after their blissful weekend away, their relationship started to go wrong. Slowly at first, almost imperceptibly to the outsider, but the cracks began to appear and an irretrievable crumbling process was underway.

After less than a year they had gone their separate ways.

From a career point of view, she went from strength to strength. She took a chance on a slight change of direction and achieved a good position in a promotions and advertising company. In the relatively short space of time since they had parted, she had risen to junior executive level. She was confident, capable and destined for greater things.

He, by comparison, had two or three attempts at different jobs without much success until he found a sort of niche for himself as a travelling salesman. The job consisted largely of driving around the region selling soft toys, sweets and chocolates to retailers large and small. Along with it came all the trappings; company car, mobile phone, answering machine and expense account.

He was relatively successful but not rich and on occasions his expenditure was inclined to exceed his income. He found it difficult to resist the temptations that came along with trying to live a lifestyle that he could not really afford.

The first step on the disastrous road that was to follow came about quite innocently, it seemed, when he allowed a friend to stay in his flat whilst he was away on holiday. There were advantages on both sides, the friend needed a place to stay in town for a couple of weeks and the flat would be lived in and looked after, not a bad thing considering the recent spate of burglaries in the area.

On his return the friend had told him of how he had lost something of vital importance in the flat one day and of having to turn the place 'upside down' in order to find it.

He didn't know whether to believe what he was being told or not. Was it true or was the friend not the friend he thought he was? Was it just an excuse to justify going through his belongings? Was telling him preparation against the possibility of detection and retribution at some point in the future?

However it came about, he was in no way ready for the comment that the so-called friend made next.

"I could get you a good price for those photographs that you've got in the wardrobe," he had said, "there's always a market for those girl-next-door type of poses. Very nice!"

He was taken aback by the remark. He was both annoyed that his home and private life had been violated and deeply upset that this apparent friend had betrayed his trust so badly. There was also the thought that lurked inside him that maybe it could be in some way partly his fault for misjudging the so-called friend.

His immediate response was, of course, an unequivocal and rather angry rejection, spoken in such a way that there could be no doubts as to his meaning.

The subject was dropped and not raised again. The friend left and went on his way the following week.

* * * * * *

Over the next few weeks nothing went right at work, nobody seemed to be buying and the performance figures went from bad to worse. A large part of his income was made up of commission and consequently the money in his pocket began to suffer.

To cap it all, he was involved in a minor car accident and although a replacement car was provided he lost three days on the road. During this period he was called into Head Office and his boss had told him in no uncertain terms that the situation could not be allowed to continue indefinitely and if things did not improve his position in the firm would be in jeopardy.

Things had gone from bad to worse when he bumped into the friend in a pub some three months later. Late into the evening when several drinks had been downed the subject of the photographs came up again. The difference on this occasion was that it was he, and not the friend, who raised the subject.

The friend had said to him, somewhat sarcastically, that he thought that he would come to his senses when he had had time to consider things in more detail. He had replied that sense had nothing to do with it when you couldn't pay the rent.

They discussed how much the photographs were likely to be worth. He was surprised to hear that the friend already had a price in mind and that the amount involved was considerably higher than he ever thought it would be.

He asked who could possibly be willing to pay so much for four sexy but not that revealing pictures. His friend told him to stop worrying, there was no reason for him to be concerned in any way, he should accept the money offered and be grateful.

And so he agreed, the photographs were duly handed over and the money paid in cash and in full.

* * * * * *

Three weeks later his world fell apart.

He was awoken by a call at 10 o'clock on a Sunday morning. As he came round he realised that it was her, out of the blue and after all this time, he thought sleepily.

"You bastard! You utter, utter bastard!" were the only words she shouted down the phone before she slammed the receiver down.

After he got over the initial shock, he searched around for her telephone number. He tried to call her.

He heard the distant ring of her telephone. It stopped abruptly in mid-ring as it was answered. Within a split second he was cut off. There was no time for him to speak. He tried a couple more times but all he heard was the steady bleep of the engaged tone. He gave up trying and got ready to go out for his usual Sunday lunchtime drink at the local pub.

Two of his friends were already in the bar when he arrived. Almost the first thing one of them said to him was "Well, what about your old girlfriend then?" When he responded by saying that he didn't know what the friend was talking about, the other one produced one of the Sunday tabloid newspapers from his jacket pocket, adding "She's a bit of all right if you ask me!"

His mouth fell open as he unfolded the paper and saw a reproduction of one of the photographs he had taken of her. He read the headline.

'ADVERTISING AGENCY ROCKED BY SEX SCANDAL'

Underneath, there was a second supporting line in large heavy print.

'Employees offer sexual favours to win clients over'

There was little of the article on the front page, the reader was urged to turn to pages six and seven for more of the story. He did so and there, taking up a full half page in colour was another of the photographs. On the right hand side of the open pages was a third and underneath this one her name was printed.

He was shocked, shaken to the very core of his soul. Unable to speak, he left the pub immediately without a word to anyone. As he walked home alone his mind stuttered over what had happened. Emotions of disbelief, anger and utter sadness raged and tumbled inside his head.

When he got back to his flat he tried to call her again but now the only response was the steady monotonous 'number unobtainable' tone.

* * * * * *

Two days after she had called him, on the Tuesday, he took a call on his mobile phone whilst travelling between appointments. He was asked to immediately make his way to the nearest police station; all his remaining planned visits that day had been postponed and rescheduled.

He remembered that he had been asked to wait in an interview room for a particular Police Inspector to arrive; no one could tell him the reason for him being there until then.

The news was broken to him gently but officially, her body had been found in her fume-filled car, parked in her own garage, that morning. A neighbour, being suspicious, had broken in and found her; she had been rushed to hospital but it had all been in vain and they were unable to save her.

She had written a note and left it on the passenger seat saying that there was no alternative, that this was her only way out, that it was all his fault and giving his name, address and mobile phone number.

At the bottom of the note, written in red were the words "You bastard, I will hate you forever".

Slowly the Inspector explained that she had a self-inflicted wound on her left forearm from which it appeared that she had drawn blood, filled her fountain pen and used this to write the damning note. They couldn't be absolutely sure of the train of events but that was how it looked and forensic tests would probably provide confirmation in a few days' time.

He was conscious that the Inspector was watching him carefully and intently. Probably in order to gauge his reaction as the sickening tale was told to him.

Several hours of questioning followed during which all the events leading up to the tragic day were raised and revisited over and over again in microscopic detail. At the end of this seemingly interminable period the Inspector told him that he was free to go, there were no charges to answer. As he left the police station, however, he was left in no doubt as to the contempt in which the officers held him. It was as though each of them that he passed on the way out seemed to be eyeing him with deep disgust.

* * * * * *

It was the following Monday when the first call came.

He had taken a few days' vacation to try and get over the shock of what had happened but the pressure of being on his own and constantly thinking about her only served to take him to the very depths of depression. On the third day he couldn't stand it anymore and so he had decided it would be better to go back to work.

It was, as he remembered, about mid-morning and he had just completed his second call of the day at a busy high street newsagents. As he was leaving the shop a call came through on his mobile phone. He stopped, took it out of his pocket and pressed the answer button.

A female voice at the other end responded to his greeting in a slow, steady tone.

"Watch the woman in the red coat across the road."

He looked up and there was indeed a woman walking rather briskly down the pavement towards him but on the other side of the road. As she reached a point directly opposite him, for no apparent reason and quite suddenly without looking she turned and walked straight into the road directly into the path of an oncoming car.

The driver attempted to stop in time but couldn't avoid hitting her. She was knocked down and fell backwards, the contents of her shopping bag spilling out onto the road. After a few seconds of lying motionless, she attempted to get up and did not appear to be seriously hurt. An ambulance and the police had been called, however, and she was taken to hospital.

It was only when the ambulance was pulling away that his total concentration on the scene that had unfolded in front of him was disturbed by the sound of the siren. He then realised that he still had the phone to his ear. There was no voice now, no sound at all from the caller.

He thought long and hard about the tone and sound of the voice and what it had said. If he hadn't known better, he might have thought it was her's but of course, that couldn't be. The whole event confused him immensely.

Nothing untoward happened for three or four weeks after the high street incident. Although the occurrence had unnerved him at the time and he couldn't explain it, it had been relegated to the back of his mind as other more pressing events had taken over.

The next event occurred as he was working, travelling to visit a customer. At the time he was driving, cruising on a motorway at about eighty miles an hour in the middle lane. The traffic wasn't too heavy and he was having a good day. He recalled that he was just about to overtake a rather large articulated truck. The phone rang, he answered it.

"Pull over, please. Pull over now," said the female voice urgently but firmly.

His first immediate thought was that the voice was somehow not the phone but that there had been some sort of weird crossover with a radio programme.

"Pull over, please. Pull over now," said the female voice once again.

He was now really confused. Was this some new police gadget that he had not heard of? If so, could they prosecute him for speeding, there seemed to be no police car anywhere around him.

In any case, such was the tone of the voice that he decided to comply and do as he was told. He braked, moved in behind the truck, slowed and rolled to a halt on the hard shoulder.

As he did so, the cars in the outside lane suddenly braked very hard, followed by all the vehicles in the other two lanes. Some of them seemed to touch each other, almost gently at first, as though in slow motion, but with disastrous results.

Whatever the initial cause of the accident, the final scene was one of complete carnage. As each driver struggled to keep control, cars and lorries, coaches and vans swerved to avoid each other, resulting in them performing a kind of crazy ballet across the carriageways. Collisions were unavoidable and within minutes the entire road was blocked by a tangled mess of twisted metal.

It was made worse when one of the vans caught fire and he could see that the driver, who appeared to be semi-conscious, was about to be burnt alive

He was shocked and dumbstruck by the awful sight that unfolded in front of him. He jumped out of his car and ran away from the scene, pausing only to look back in terror. Eventually he was found sitting sobbing profusely in a field alongside the road by a paramedic. He was taken to hospital suffering from shock, treated and released some hours later.

He learned later that five people had been killed in the accident and twenty injured, some seriously. It was five hours before the road was finally reopened.

Worst of all, for him, he now realised that he recognised the voice and knew that it was her that had called him. The voice was unmistakeable. How it had come about he couldn't comprehend but it was definitely her.

The third call, only two days later, came as he was shopping in a large local do-it-yourself store.

His mobile phone rang and, unthinkingly, he answered it. The phone display read 'caller unknown' but he answered it anyway. He wasn't expecting to hear her. Her message was brief and to the point as on the previous occasions.

"Go and look at the nice plants."

Intrigued, he did as he was instructed and made his way to the garden section. He walked along the aisle, looking at the rows and rows of potted plants and flowers. He stopped to look closely at some particularly colourful bright yellow and red begonias.

Without warning, a large bag of compost that had been stored on shelves high up above the plants came crashing down, narrowly missing him. The bag split wide open, spilling its contents over a wide area.

A second bag fell and then a third. Bag after bag continued to rain down one after another. Although he managed to avoid some, such was the torrent that fell from above, he was hit several times. Each bag split open as it struck either him or the ground and he was liberally covered in dark brown compost mixture before he managed to make good his escape.

The store was, of course, full of apologies for the incident. It was all blamed on a careless storeman and his inability to control a fork-lift truck as he restocked the shelves from the other side. But he knew better and the recent train of events was starting to make him very uneasy indeed.

During the incident in the store the mobile phone was damaged having been dropped in his haste to escape the falling sacks of compost. As a result of this, he had an idea. He would replace the phone and have the number changed at the same time. If, as he suspected, it was all an elaborate hoax being played out by one of her friends who probably blamed him for her death, then that would put a stop to it all. He reproached himself for not thinking of it sooner.

Thus when the fourth call came on the new phone with its new number, it was particularly devastating for him.

On this occasion the message was short, clear and curt. It chilled him to the very core of his soul.

It was her, she spoke, simply, firmly and clearly.

"I am in control now."

His head began to swim and he passed out.

* * * * * *

There have been about twenty calls now; I lost exact count some time ago. After the eighth or ninth I threw the mobile in a drawer in the bedroom. I left it switched on so that the battery would run down. It was my assumption that by hiding away the means of communication she would no longer be able to make contact with me. To make doubly sure I disconnected the flat phone at the socket on the wall

The next call was less than ten minutes after, this time on the ordinary fixed phone in the flat. Her voice told me that she could not be shut out as easily as that. As if to prove this, the call on the following day was on the uncharged mobile, but the more recent calls have come through on either phone. There is no pattern.

The events that accompany the calls have become less severe than in the earlier ones, but now the fear is in the effect of the call upon my mind rather than the physical manifestation that she used at first to demonstrate to me the power that she has over me.

I don't go out at all now. I cannot concentrate on anything anymore and for weeks I have been unable to leave the flat, let alone do my job. The final letter from the company arrived this morning, my job is no more.

I do not answer either phone now; I will never answer another phone in case she is there.

I know now that I cannot escape her. It is useless to try; her revenge is complete.

I have a shotgun in my hand; it is pointed at my head; it is loaded and cocked; the safety catch is off.

The next time the phone rings I shall pull the trigger.

My guess is she knows that already.

END

THE GIRL IN THE PARK

THE GIRL IN THE PARK

I'm an engineer. Not the most exciting of occupations, you might think, but, like all jobs, I suppose it has its moments. The work that I currently do involves quite a lot of travelling around the country testing and commissioning various types of equipment. On one of our current contracts this means that I have to spend around four to six weeks each year in Plymouth, usually during June and July.

It was on one such visit two years ago that the events that I am about to relate actually took place.

I had a preference for one particular hotel. It was located not far from the city centre and, as such, close to many of the amenities the city had to offer as well as being reasonably near to the location of the job. City centre hotels can be bland with rooms that have a strong resemblance to carpeted boxes, but this one was older and known for its friendly staff and good restaurant. That reputation was how I came to stay there in the first place, about three years before, and I had never had any reason to change.

The hotel was situated in a reasonably prominent position, immediately adjacent to a large traffic intersection at the centre of which was an island covered mostly with grass and some small shaped flowerbeds.

Two sides of the hotel looked out over the roads that were part of the junction, the third over the roof of a large supermarket. Only the fourth had anything like what could be described as a view, and that was of a small park which was accessed via a tunnel which, in turn, joined with a series of interconnecting pedestrian walkways under the roadways.

Luckily, being aware of the location and the layout of the hotel and also something of a 'regular', on checking in I could request the best side. In addition, knowing that some rooms were larger than others, if I asked politely in advance then I could, to a certain extent, take my pick. Which was how I came to be in Room Two-Eleven, overlooking the park.

It was my habit to have a meal in the hotel at around eight o'clock, sometimes in the room but more often than not in the restaurant, after which I would take a walk around the vicinity, varying the route to both learn about the area and also to provide a little variety.

On the Tuesday of the second week, which is when my story really starts, I recall that after eating in the restaurant I did not make my way to the hotel entrance to go out but returned to my room. The main reason was that it had been raining heavily for most of the day and when I had returned that evening and parked my car, there was certainly no indication of it being likely to let up for several hours to come.

I looked out through the rain-spattered window down which the occasional water rivulet slowly ran its meandering course down to the sill below. It wasn't raining particularly hard, but it was a dark overcast evening, wet and windy although probably warmer than it looked for the time of year.

From my vantage point I could see that the little park was deserted, except for a man with a small terrier-like dog on a long extending lead. The man's head was bent low almost as though he thought the rain would have some corrosive effect upon his skin. His body language said it all, he didn't want to be there, he was miserable and wet, but the dog must have his exercise. I watched him as he hurried the dog along and imagined the cursing that was probably going on under his breath.

But I was wrong; there was another visitor in the park. I didn't see her until she arose from the bench where she had been sitting with her back partly towards me. My first impression was that she was old and very frail. She stood very slowly and with what seemed to be a considerable amount of pain. Her steps, when she took them, were short and laboured. Each pace, if you could call it that, was so small and her progress so slow that it almost hurt you to watch her. She carried no aid to help her, no walking frame or stick. She did not appear to limp as such, but it took her a good ten minutes to reach the next bench only some fifteen yards away, then she paused and rested, leaning against the its wooden back.

Just at that moment I was distracted by the ringing of the room phone. I had to cross to the other side of the room to answer it and although I tried, I could not make the cable stretch far enough for me to continue with my observations. The call took longer than I anticipated and by the time I had returned to the window she had gone.

On the following day, and the Thursday, I had some problems with the job and worked on into the evening. I didn't return to the hotel until very late and so tired that all I wanted to do was fall into bed and sleep soundly until morning.

On the Friday I went home for the weekend; Monday I visited my company's home office to pick up some spare parts, so I did not return to Plymouth, and thus the hotel, until the Tuesday.

I had a nice quiet evening meal and returned to my room, intending to relax and watch a football match on the television.

I looked out of the window, half-hoping to see what I had come to think of as 'that little old lady' again. Curious really, I don't know what it was about her that awakened my interest but I somehow felt the need to see if I could spot her.

My anticipation did not go unrewarded. She was not in her usual place, but sitting on a bench further along the path, overlooking the entrance to the hotel car park. As I watched, very carefully and, it seemed somewhat painfully, she got to her feet. As she stood up she stooped forward slightly and then slowly and gently raised herself to her full height.

She turned, picked up her wooden walking stick and taking small, almost shuffling, steps made her way towards the tunnel under the road.

I don't know why, but there was something about her that intrigued me and I had this urge to see her close up. I slipped on my shoes, quickly donned a pullover, checked that I had my room key, hurriedly put it in my pocket and left the room. Walking quickly down the corridor, I opted for the fire escape stairs (rather than the lift) and made my way down, through the front door and out into the small park.

I took a rather circular route to make my way round the outside edge of the hotel so that I could enter the park and approach in such a way that we would be walking towards each other. That way I would be able to observe her for as long as possible.

I have to admit that as the realisation of what I saw dawned on me I was more than surprised; I suppose the only word to describe how I felt at that moment would be shocked.

I know it is true that illnesses normally associated with the elderly can, in some instances, unexpectedly strike down the young. I can only say that what I had presumed, in my ignorance, was undoubtedly wrong.

I had assumed that the cause of her struggle for mobility was a body racked with the pain of arthritis, rheumatism or plain old age, but as she approached me I could see that the face was not that of a little old lady but that of a young woman in her mid-twenties.

She did not look up, concentrating as she was on the task in hand, but I became aware after a few seconds that I was guilty of staring at her. I wanted to make eye contact with her, if only in order to offer a smile, but it wasn't to be. I passed by, turned the corner at the far end of the park, made my way back to the hotel and so to bed.

I suppose I have to admit that thoughts of her slipped to the back of my mind after that. There were problems with the job and my thoughts were taken up with how to rectify them. The hours I was working were not particularly long but quite erratic. Towards the end of a work period such as the one I was engaged in it was often the case that, as the equipment was brought back into full working order, it was necessary for me to be in attendance at odd hours of the day or night.

That was until that day, I think it was a Wednesday, when, through the events that I am about to relate, I actually came to speak to her for the first time.

I was in my room in the hotel lying on the bed. I had ordered a room service meal, the remains of which were on a trolley by the door, waiting to be collected. I had included a few beers with my order and it was my intention to relax and watch a football match on the television in the room.

It was a warm evening and I had found that in this particular room it was possible to open the window to let in some fresh air. I knew that this could not be done in some rooms, presumably for safety reasons; however, in this room it was possible and I had taken advantage of it. Thinking back, if I hadn't then it is likely that I would never have been presented with the opportunity that subsequently came to pass.

As I settled back to relax, I became aware of a noisy commotion somewhere outside, away from the hotel. At first it was at some distance, but there was no doubt that it was getting closer. The sound was clearly coming from a group of people, of raised, rowdy and loud voices. I could detect both male and female, sometimes calling out as individuals, occasionally chanting in small groups.

I craned my neck to see as far as I could. Across the traffic island I could just see the approaching group. There were about twenty of them, approximately fourteen boys and the rest girls. They appeared to be some of the local youth who, having partaken of a few too many drinks at a local hostelry, were engaged in the sport of student baiting. The area around the hotel and the little park being close to the university, there were, on occasions, disputes between some of the more aggressive members on both sides. It rarely led to any serious trouble but there could be some rather unpleasant confrontations.

Looking down into the park, there were a few students around who I could see were due to become the target of the unruly group once they had entered the subway system and crossed the traffic island.

Then I spotted her, the girl in the park. All my protective instincts suddenly welled up inside me. She was sitting quietly at what I now presumed to be her favourite bench. What chance would she have if she got caught in the midst of some unruly mob where emotions might overflow into violent scuffles, or worse, at any time?

The group was getting closer now. I saw that she looked round, towards the advancing noise. I couldn't see her face but her body language indicated that she was feeling apprehension that I thought might develop into fear. I knew instinctively that I must go to her aid.

As quickly as I could, I put on my shoes, picked up my wallet and the room key and made my way down into the park. Within only couple of minutes I was at her side.

She looked a little alarmed at first; I suppose the manner of my arrival must have taken her by surprise. I didn't mess with the niceties of introductions, my natural English reticence and shyness dispensed with in my haste to rush to her assistance and remove her from potential danger.

I told her not to worry, that I was concerned about the noisy disturbance that was coming our way and that my only aim was to offer her my assistance.

In the event, apart from a good deal of gesturing and shouting, the confrontation passed relatively peacefully. The students did not allow themselves to be intimidated and the local youth went on its way presumably looking for other more responsive targets to goad.

But the episode, innocuous though it turned out to be, did serve to break the ice and we started to talk. She thanked me for coming to her aid, even if it hadn't been necessary. She said that I wasn't to know that when I made my move to help her and she embarrassed me by describing it as a brave action on my part.

That was how I came to meet Gemma, shy, softly spoken Gemma with the dark brown eyes.

For two people who had just met, and in fairly strange circumstances, we very quickly fell into deep and interesting conversation. I found her very easy to talk to and my impression was that she was comfortable talking to me. I remember that we covered some fairly esoteric subjects, even on that first meeting.

Then she raised the topic that turned out to be the first step down a very strange path, a path I certainly could never have foreseen and one which I have sometimes reflected on with more than a little confusion.

She, quite tentatively, asked me if I would do her a favour. I responded quickly and positively, thinking that I would be asked at the very least to help her get up, although I secretly wished that she wanted me to walk with her. I was intrigued to know where she lived, how far she came each day to reach the little park, even did she live on her own or were there other family members at home to which she had, for some reason, not referred?

She said that she would like me to answer a question for her. When she did so, I was to respond honestly and without question. If I agreed, then she would promise to tell me why but only if I could be patient with her.

How could anybody refuse such a request? I didn't understand the riddle, what else could I do but agree, I would have spent the rest of my life wondering what she was talking about if I hadn't responded positively.

She hesitated, took a deep breath as though she was plucking up courage and, after a few seconds went ahead. Her question, when it came, caused me to hesitate and consider my reply carefully.

In the event, her request was quite simple but, I have to say, at first a little surprising.

"What is your room number in the hotel?"

She immediately sensed my initial hesitation and reminded me that, in her condition, she was unlikely to be any kind of threat to me.

Looking me straight in the eye, she said, "Trust me, it's just an experiment, I assure you." and I felt that I was unable to resist her request.

"Two eleven, on the second floor," I blurted out, mesmerised by the depth of feeling in her eyes that belied the physical frailty of her unfortunate body.

She asked me if I would sit with her for a while. She wanted me stay next to her but, whatever happened, not to touch her or talk to her. I was also to make sure that nobody else disturbed her. She wanted fifteen minutes in which she could concentrate all her faculties and, once her task was completed she would explain.

She intrigued me, and at the same time confused me, by saying that dependent upon whether her experiment worked, she may have some surprising news for me.

I did as she requested and she raised her head to a level position, as though staring straight ahead, rested her hands gently on her legs, closed her eyes and went into what I can only describe as a light trance.

She stayed that way for about five minutes. It seemed longer but I happened to glance at my watch just as she drifted away into her dream world, probably because I felt more than a little conspicuous sitting there next to her on the park bench, wondering quite what she was going to do or say.

At the end of this period, during which her body was completely motionless, she stirred gently and, lifting her head slowly, she inhaled deeply, taking a long slow breath. Slowly she opened her eyes, her eyelids fluttering slightly as someone would in the act of waking, sensing the first few rays of the morning sun.

She smiled slightly, turned her head slowly towards me and said, "I think I may have a little surprise for you."

I waited with bated breath. I had not seen even a flicker of a smile cross her face in any of the conversations I had had with her. But this was not just an ordinary smile, there was, in a strange way, something behind her eyes, I can only describe it as though she felt a sense of triumph, of achievement.

She asked me to indulge her, to listen to what she had to say and then comment as I thought appropriate. It sounded a bit formal but I said that if that was what she wanted then, of course, that is what I would do.

She spoke with a quiet but confident voice, "In your room, two-eleven, you have an open suitcase. The suitcase is dark blue in colour and on the top of one half there is a white short-sleeved shirt with a navy blue tie resting on it. On the other half is a beige towel, a hand towel, I think."

I was stunned by what she said. How could she possibly know??

I came to my senses a little. It was likely that the suitcase had lain open like that for most of the day, probably since I had left to go to work that morning. She only had to know someone in the hotel, someone who could have told her.

Then my thoughts changed to looking at what she had said from a completely different angle. I became somewhat cynical about the whole thing. It was unlikely that she had been able to go to my room herself. My mind searched for an explanation; to try and analyse what the purpose of her statements and where they were to lead. Was I to be the unexpecting victim of some sort of confidence trick? Was there an accomplice somewhere and, if so, what was their role likely to be? How alarmed should I be of what this was to lead to?

All the thoughts raced through my mind in a few seconds, but she detected from my face that I had doubts about what she had said, even if these doubts followed on from my initial surprise and amazement.

"I can see that you are unsure how to take what I have said to you,"she said.

"I am rather tired and can do no more today, but I will attempt to explain more tomorrow if you will meet me here at the same time as today."

I agreed to meet with her and we went our separate ways. I offered to walk with her, not least because I was curious about where she lived and how long it took her to get there at the laboriously slow pace at which she walked.

She declined my offer. I made some inane comment about having to get some money from the bank cashpoint and walked off in the direction of the city centre. In my mind I selected a route that would enable me to walk through the streets in such a way that it would bring me back to the underpass, by a different road. By walking quickly it would hopefully be possible to return to the vicinity, see her from a distance and observe which direction she took on her slow journey home.

Looking back, it seems a little underhand, but I was so intrigued to know more about how far she came to pay her apparently regular visits to the park.

In the end, I have to say, my ploy did not work. I managed to work my way back to the large traffic island by coming back up a road on the far side from the hotel. As I approached the steps down into the underpass, I carefully studied each of the areas around the tops of the other sets of steps to see if I could spot her. No luck. Then I went quickly down into the lower part, under the roadways and, as fast as I could, checked each of the staircases leading upwards to the light.

She was nowhere to be seen. I couldn't believe that I had missed her, moving at the interminably slow pace that she did, but somehow I had.

Anyone watching would have thought these the antics of a madman, but I was so intent on my goal I didn't really think of the impression I may have given to others. That realisation came much later.

As we had arranged, I met her the following day at the same place, same time. She was already there when I arrived.

After about ten minutes of talking generalities, she raised the subject of what she described as 'her little experiment' the night before. She said that she could see that I was sceptical and, if I was patient with her, she would try to convince me that there was no trickery or deceit involved. She did not understand how, but she was in the process of developing within her new powers, the extent or depth of which she did not, as yet, comprehend. For the moment, she said that she found it in one way interesting but in another more than a little frightening.

She went on to say that she had a very good reason why she wanted to learn more about what was happening to her and discover the full extent of her powers but that she would have to know me a lot better than she did now to feel comfortable enough with me to explain more fully. I said that I respected her position and did not pursue the matter further.

Her problem, she said, was that she did not know anybody well enough to ask them to help her understand what was going on except for those very close to her who knew her so well that they would probably think that she was going crazy. A curious logic, I thought, but I suppose it makes some sort of sense.

Realising from the expression on my face that I was having difficulty following her somewhat convoluted statements, she added by way of explanation that she needed to prove the phenomenon to herself before she told any of those close to her. The chance meeting with me as a stranger, but nevertheless someone who she felt she could trust, was fate providing the means for her to achieve her aim of achieving a greater understanding of what was happening to her.

She said that she felt strong enough to attempt a further experiment. She was willing to try on the assumption that I had not by now become convinced that she was completely mad in which case I was at liberty to walk away and forget that our discussions had ever taken place.

She asked me to nominate three things in my room of which I knew the precise location. I had to be certain or, she said, or there would be the possibility of some doubt as to the success of the outcome. The only other stipulation was that the objects could not be permanent fixtures or fittings. They must be capable of being moved. The significance of this point would only become evident later. I was to tell her the three items but not their location within the room,

I thought for a few minutes, making my selections. There was my mobile phone which I knew was on the bedside table, a discarded shirt draped across the back of the easy chair and the hairbrushes that I had left alongside the sink in the bathroom.

I told her of my choices, though not for one minute contemplating the purpose of the game we were playing.

She told me that she would have to adopt the same trance-like state as on the previous occasion and asked me to sit with her and look after her as she did so. She rested her hands gently on her legs, took a deep breath and allowed her head to fall forward slowly as she exhaled.

I felt a little self-conscious sitting there with her. It struck me that it would be difficult to explain her condition to any passer-by that stopped to ask after her welfare.

After about fifteen minutes she stirred slightly and raised her head again, taking a deep intake of breath as she did so.

She told me to go back to my room, study carefully what I had told her previously and return to the park bench the following evening where she would be waiting for me. Then we would be able to discuss what I had found.

I wished her goodnight and we parted.

I walked through the park, across to the hotel and up the short flight of steps to the main door of the hotel; taking the lift I must have been back in my room within five minutes of leaving her. I went straight to the window and looked out but she was nowhere to be seen.

I turned away from the glass. Keeping in mind our discussion I did as she had asked and commenced my examination of the room, paying particular attention to the specific items that we had talked about.

I have to admit that I was amazed. To start with, the shirt that I was sure I had left discarded on the back of the armchair was on the bed. Then I noticed that the hairbrushes that had been on the side of the sink in the bathroom were now on top of the television.

The third item was my mobile phone. Where was it? I looked everywhere I could think of, searched the main room, the bathroom, in the wardrobe and even in the drawers. I even started to think that this was some kind of elaborate hoax to steal it; you heard so many stories of mobile phones being stolen and reprogrammed.

It had just crossed my mind that I could use the hotel phone in the room and dial the number of the mobile when I thought I could hear it ringing. It was quite faint but it did seem that it was coming from somewhere in the room. Angling my head slightly so that one ear was directed towards the barely audible sound, I followed my senses and concentrated as hard as I could. I crossed the room slowly, checking at each short pace that I was going in the right direction.

I couldn't believe it. The sound of the telephone, my telephone, was coming from inside the fridge!

Tentatively, I opened the door. Resting carefully on two tins of tonic water was my mobile phone, ringing much louder now that it had been freed from its chilly, albeit temporary, prison. It was crying out to be answered. I picked it up and pressed the answer button.

As I put it to my ear I did not speak. Initially, I suppose, because I was dumbstruck by the whole bizarre event but then because my mind, struggling to make sense of what was going on, did not have the capacity to make my mouth work at the same time.

A voice, her voice, spoke softly.

"I'm so glad you found it."

By the time I came to my senses and rushed to the window I was just in time to see her disappearing into the tunnel under the road. It only came to me later that she did not appear to be holding a phone.

Then the voice said, "See you tomorrow."

The following evening when we met, she was already sitting in the park. As I sat down she looked straight into my eyes and, for what I think was the first time, she smiled. I sensed that she was toying with my emotions a little, preparing to pay me back if I was going to be sceptical; at the same time, however, I could feel that there was a sense of achievement emanating from behind her eyes.

After a short pause, she agreed to let me in on her secret. It was not easy to believe her story but I had, and still have, no better explanation.

She told me that she had once been in a situation where her mind and all her senses had become detached in such a way that she was able to look down at her own body, an event that she later came to understand was described as an out-of-body experience.

It had happened whilst she was in hospital. The first time was when she was in the Accident and Emergency unit at the local hospital. She was able to look down and watch the emergency team working methodically but nevertheless urgently on a patient. She said that initially she was unconcerned, somehow nothing seemed relevant or important to her, she was merely an observer. But when one of the doctors stepped aside and she recognised that it was herself lying there apparently unconscious, she became very confused and frightened.

She told me that she had no way of estimating how long the occurrence had lasted but it ended very abruptly when she seemed to rush back into her head like water being poured from a jug. At the same time she felt a searing jolt of pain right across her body.

She knew that her body had contorted violently and that she had let out an involuntary yelp of pain.

She heard a voice say, "She's back! We've got her back!" before she drifted away into unconsciousness.

Later, in the intensive care unit, she had come round to find herself lying on a firm, flat, lightly cushioned bed wearing only a thin cotton nightshirt and covered by a single sheet. The room was warm and the lighting subdued. She realised that she had sensors attached to her body but the machines that they were connected to were behind her somewhere, out of sight. There was a mask on her face and the air that she was breathing felt dry in the back of her throat. A nurse was tending her and spoke softly to her, telling her that all was well and that she should not worry and relax as much as possible.

Time stood still for her while she was kept in the unit, she had no way of judging how long she was there, although she later learned from one of the nurses that it was four or five days.

During that period, she drifted in and out of consciousness and on at least three occasions she had experienced the feeling of floating outside of her body and being able to look down on herself. As she improved and became a little stronger, she found that she was able to look around at others in the unit. She counted four beds in total, with only two of the other three occupied.

She convinced herself that the whole strange occurrence must be only a dream, probably brought on by the cocktail of drugs she was being given. But in her periods of greater awareness she developed a determination to put herself to the test.

She decided that she would think of something that she could not possibly know, given her condition and location, something that may serve to prove the case, one way or the other.

In the event, the selection was not difficult. The next time she found herself there, hovering above her body, she tried to adjust her position so that she could see the bank of electronic monitoring equipment behind her head. There were four main boxes, each on its own trolley. The middle two were blue in colour and slightly larger than the others. Looking at them the potential source of proof became obvious. Each had what she presumed was an identification number marked on the top edge in large white figures.

She concentrated hard and stored them in a corner of her mind. She would never forget them. 101246 and 101448.

She could hardly wait for the nurse to arrive on her rounds to carry out her routine checks. It could only have been an hour but it seemed like an eternity. She spent some of the time wondering whether it would be better for her to ask the nurse to read out the numbers, if they were there, or for her to say them and ask the nurse to confirm. She decided that the former approach would cause less of a fuss if it proved to be true and whilst it may seem a strange request, the result could be kept as her secret.

At first the nurse hesitated, probably unsure of the request, but she did as she was asked and read out the numbers. As she did so, the initial feelings of elation were overtaken by those of confusion as the enormity of the truth of the situation washed over her.

I interrupted her story, asking how she came to be in hospital, what accident had befallen her. Her eyes changed in an instant, she looked away from me into the distance and her expression hardened. She said nothing for a full two or three minutes, as though gathering her strength, and then she continued.

She told me that she had been introduced to a man at a party given by a mutual friend. They hit it off right from the very first time that their eyes met. Their relationship developed over a period of months; initially as friendship and learning about each other, then into love and on into a wild and torrid affair.

Although they were together as much as possible, his job seemed to involve quite a lot of travelling. He had no permanent home in the area and on his visits he stayed in the hotel, the same hotel that we were sitting outside, the hotel where I stayed. I recall making made a mental note at the time that there seemed to be similarities between his existence and mine.

It wasn't very long before she had realised that he was married; when she confronted him he made no attempt to deny it. But she was in too deep and so was he.

For a while she was happy to continue with the relationship as it was, but as time passed her feelings grew stronger and stronger. There came a time when she knew that she could not share him with another woman and that she would have to raise the issue with him. She would have to press him into making a choice and that his choice would have to be for her.

Initially he agreed; he would leave his wife and set up home with her. As time passed, however, he did nothing to convince her that he would go through with his promise.

One night she decided that she would give him an ultimatum, she would force the situation.

They had a pleasant meal together and returned to the hotel as normal. They had a couple of drinks in the hotel bar by way of a nightcap. Over the drinks she told him that she had something important to discuss with him and they went to his room. Once inside they kissed, but she would not let him go any further until they had discussed what she wanted to discuss.

Taking a deep breath and summoning up all her courage, she told him that she wasn't prepared to continue with their affair in the same way. Things were going to have to change. As far as she was concerned, it was time for him to make a decision; it was time for him to make more of a commitment to their relationship. He must deliver on his promise and leave his wife for her.

She thought that she knew him fairly well, that his reaction would be one of surprise, maybe even shock.

She expected him to try and talk her round, to understand her point of view but aim to convince her that all was well and that the best option was to leave things as they were. In her heart, she thought he might even be successful in talking her round.

She was totally unprepared for his reaction.

Without any warning, he flew into an immediate and violent rage. He started with a stream of invective, an outpouring of verbal abuse which told her that she couldn't possibly understand his problems or the stresses under which he was forced to live. For a full five minutes he ranted at her, partly shouting, occasionally swearing, with his voice at times dropping to a sort of snarl uttered through clenched teeth.

When he eventually stopped to draw breath, his head held low, stooping like a cornered animal, she took her first opportunity to speak. She was hurting and her reaction was to respond, to react, to fight back.

It was a mistake.

He was standing sideways on to her and she didn't see what was coming as he spun around. Before she knew it the back of his hand had crashed into the side of her face. It was almost too sudden to hurt, the impact was undoubtedly there but the initial feeling was one of being partly dazed, mixed with shock. The pain came a few seconds later.

It didn't stop there. Once he had started, the blows continued to rain down on her until eventually she lapsed into unconsciousness. She remembered thinking that she didn't expect to come round; this was probably the end.

There was a long pause in her story before she continued.

"That was eighteen months ago." she said quietly.

I bowed my head, embarrassed that I am a man and this is what men are capable of doing to women. I looked up slowly, intending to meet her eye-to-eye even if I didn't have a clue what I was going to say. Thoughts of whether I should sympathise or apologise went through my mind.

In the event, I didn't have to say anything. As my nervous gaze reached her face it was clear that she was staring intently at something behind me, over my left shoulder. Somehow her expression was more than staring; she was transfixed, not a single muscle in her face or body moved as she concentrated intently on what she could see but I could not.

I turned to look. All I could see was the entrance of the hotel underground car park. Coming out of it were two men each carrying a briefcase and wheeling a small suitcase. They walked the short distance to the hotel main entrance and went inside.

Her whole attitude had changed. Instead of the talkative person she had been, albeit on a very serious subject, I was faced with someone who had withdrawn deep inside herself.

I was at a loss; I didn't know what to say. Should I try and say something funny to lighten the situation, something sympathetic to express my understanding or offer my help and support? In the event, I prevaricated too long, lost my nerve and said nothing.

She muttered her excuses and made ready to walk away. Small painful steps at first until the pain eased a little. I walked along with her. My instincts told me to put my arm around her shoulder, or at the very least to offer her my arm to lean on, but my confidence deserted me and I kept a discreet distance to one side.

After about fifty yards we reached the bottom of a flight of steps which led up to the far side of the big roundabout. She climbed the first step, turned and faced me, her head level with mine. She reached out her hand and gently brushed my cheek. Her touch was tender and caring, her skin warm and soft. She reached inside the collar of her coat and tugged gently at her scarf. As it came free she draped it over my head and, holding on to both ends she slowly but deliberately pulled me towards her. She kissed me full on the lips, a long slow sensuous kiss that started as a gesture of friendship but ended with all my senses racing.

She quietly whispered, "Thank you for all you have done for me." and asked me to leave her. I respected her wishes and made my way back to the hotel and the relative comfort of my room.

The following morning I awoke and got up as usual. I looked out of the hotel window on what was a wet and windy day. I recall thinking another Friday, another week over and home tomorrow. After a shower and a shave I made my way down to breakfast in the restaurant on the ground floor.

As the lift door opened, however, I was confronted by a large policeman blocking my path. He politely asked me who I was and whether I was a guest in the hotel. I responded and showed him the hotel key card which I used as my authority to book bills to my account and my room key.

He seemed satisfied with my response and then advised me that the restaurant and other hotel facilities were closed. He further advised me that I would be allowed to collect my car from the car park and leave the hotel but that I may be stopped and questioned by other police officers along the way. Intrigued by his statements I attempted to quiz him on why and what was going on but he told me that he was not in a position to elaborate in any way.

After going to my room, collecting my briefcase and negotiating another policeman in the foyer of the hotel, I was allowed to go to the underground car park to collect my car. Seeing two policemen standing by a patrol car I decided to have one more go to try and find out what was going on.

I put on my best cheerful friendly face and chatty voice but they were not impressed and I failed miserably to get them to enter into any conversation. Their whole demeanour was dour and serious. Clearly whatever had happened they were all under strict orders to say nothing.

As I drove out of the car park, the road to the hotel was sealed off by two police cars with officers standing by them so that they could stop any traffic that wished to pass. In addition, there were blue and white tapes stretched across the road. As I approached, one of the policemen stepped to one side, lifted the tape and motioned me through.

As I drove to work I turned on the car radio and tuned it in to the local station. Within ten minutes the time pips sounded and news started. I listened intently but there was no mention of the events at the hotel. Immediately following the news came the traffic and travel information and only then was there a mention of congestion in the centre of the city caused by what was described as an 'incident'.

At lunchtime, a late lunch as I remember owing to a particularly busy morning, I went to one of the local shops, a newsagent that sold filled rolls and sandwiches as well as doubling as a small general grocery store. As I entered I noticed that the shopkeeper was already in conversation with an elderly lady. I stood behind her, waiting to be served. She was holding a copy of the local evening paper and talking in a rather animated fashion. I didn't take a lot of notice until I overheard her say two words in quick succession – the name of my hotel and 'murder'.

I turned and, seeing copies of the local paper on the rack behind me, I picked one up. The front page headline leapt out at me –*"MURDER MYSTERY AT CITY*

CENTRE HOTEL" and was accompanied by a picture of the front of my hotel.

I interrupted the old ladies conversation, probably rather rudely, and offered the shopkeeper the money for the paper. I forgot all about my sandwich and left the shop rather hurriedly. Once outside, I stood and studied the front page. There was more information on the inside.

The story unfolded as I avidly read the article. Apparently the police were mystified by what they found at the scene. An as yet unidentified man had been found dead in a hotel room having been beaten to death by a heavy blunt object, probably the bedside lamp which had been found, bloodstained, on the floor by the body. Judging by the amount of blood, it was likely that several blows had been inflicted and that the first had been struck while he was asleep.

The primary cause of concern and confusion for the police was that the hotel door had been locked from the inside. The safety latch and chain had been engaged and the police had been forced to break in, smashing both in their efforts to gain entry.

I wondered why the police had taken such drastic action when it could merely have been a case of someone having overslept. As I read on, however, it was stated that the victim's colleague, who happened to have been in the room next door, had alerted them.

He had been woken by thumping noises coming from the room in the early hours, although he had turned over and gone back to sleep when they had stopped. The two men were due to leave early in the morning to travel to a business meeting in Birmingham but, try as he may, he had been unable to raise his colleague.

The hotel staff had opted to call the police when they could not open the door with their spare keys.

The early, but guarded, statement from the police spokeswoman was that initial indications were that they were dealing with a murder case since the wounds could not have been self-inflicted. She confirmed, however, that the room had sealed non-opening windows and that a forced entry had been necessary to overcome the mechanical latch and chain.

At the end of the day I returned to the hotel and, to all outward appearances, nothing untoward had occurred that day. You would not have believed that a gruesome murder had taken place less than eighteen hours before. Inside the hotel, however, it was somewhat different. As I entered the foyer I was confronted by two uniformed policemen, one of the hotel reception staff and a man and a woman who I did not recognise.

The man stepped forward and introduced himself as a Detective Inspector. He raised his arm and motioned the woman to step forward. As she did so he advised that she was the Detective Sergeant assigned to assist him with the case. He asked me to identify myself and whether I was a guest in the hotel. When I did so, he requested confirmation that what I had said was true from the hotel receptionist.

The pleasantries having been exchanged, he asked me if I would mind answering a few questions regarding the events that had taken place earlier that day. He added that they would like me to make a formal statement, if I didn't have any objections, and that it would not be necessary for me to visit the police station since they had set aside a meeting room in the hotel for that purpose.

The interview was fairly straightforward, they asked me a series of questions about my background, the reason for my visit, who could vouch for me and whether I had heard or seen anything that struck me as untoward or unusual. I answered openly and was sure that whilst eliminating me from their enquiries the information was of little use to them in their investigations.

At the end of the session, when I had agreed to sit with the Detective Sergeant and produce the formal statement document, they said they had one final question.

The Inspector reached inside his jacket and produced two photographs. He laid them on the table so that I could see them and asked me if I recognised anybody. Each photograph depicted a man, head and shoulders only, both were wearing what I would describe a business suits with plain shirts and striped ties.

I recognised them both instantly as the two that had such an effect upon the girl in the park as we sat talking only the night before.

For some unaccountable reason I chose to lie. I told them both that I had never seen either of them in my life before now. But the inspector was clearly trained to watch for any flicker of emotion or response that would give a guilty party away and very experienced in his job. Something in my reaction implanted some seed of doubt in his mind. He questioned me further, probing to confirm if he was right to be concerned or not.

I was ready for him, however, and countered by saying that it was terrible to think that one of these two men was now dead. I went on to say how shocked I was to learn that this terrible crime had taken place in the very hotel in which I was staying and asked which one of them was the unfortunate victim. He seemed to accept my little outburst of deep concern, tapped his finger on one of the photographs, thanked me for my assistance and asked me to go with the sergeant to complete the formal statement.

Once it was done and I made my way back to my room, I couldn't help but wonder about the girl, what she had said to me, the strange demonstration of her apparent powers, the way she had reacted to seeing the man at the hotel and his violent death whilst in a locked hotel room.

I asked myself the same questions over and over again. Was it possible that she had developed her mental powers to such a degree that she could infiltrate his room and physically move solid objects to the extent that she could bludgeon him to death? Could hatred, pain, being near to death and cold revenge awaken such Neanderthal capabilities in a person?

I had no answers.

The following day, the Saturday, I went home. I took the Monday and Tuesday as vacation in order to relax and think things through. I hoped that if I could apply some kind of logic and common sense to my understanding (or lack of understanding) of the bizarre train of events that had occurred, then I may be able to come up with a satisfactory explanation.

I spent all of the weekend trying to come to terms with whole episode but I couldn't come up with any answers. Eventually I came to the conclusion that another course of action was preferable. I decided to go and see a policeman friend of mine who I knew from playing football together in the same local team. I rang him and we agreed to meet in a pub near to his home.

We exchanged pleasantries and, over a couple of drinks, shared reminiscences of our days of playing together and what had happened to each of us since.

When I felt the time was right I broached the subject of what had occurred in Plymouth. I had to go through the whole story, of course, in order to provide him with a full explanation of what had transpired and the dilemma in which I found myself. I asked him to listen and take in what I was saying in its entirety before raising any questions or comments.

Once I had finished I asked him to give me his honest opinion of what my next course of action should be. I waited with some trepidation for his reaction.

Surprisingly enough, he was not as dismissive of my story as I thought at first he might be. Although it must have sounded strange and he could have decided that it was best just to humour me and politely depart, I must have struck some chord of respectability with him.

He asked a few questions and I responded as accurately as I could. We had another drink and after a few minutes consideration he made a suggestion.

He told me that he had a couple of contacts in the Devon and Cornwall Police that he had met on training courses in Scotland, one of which he was sure was currently based in Plymouth. He offered to make a telephone call on my behalf and try to arrange an interview for me. He would endeavour to explain my concerns and point out that I was not a merely some crank trying to make a name for himself.

By a stroke of luck it turned out that his contact had been promoted to Detective Sergeant and knew both the officers that had spoken to me at the hotel. My friend must have been held in some esteem because my previous concerns regarding not being taken seriously were unfounded and I was asked to make my way back with some haste in order that the interview could take place as soon as possible. I agreed to return to Plymouth on the Wednesday and the meeting was duly arranged for the early afternoon of the same day.

I was asked to go to the main Police Station in the city and there I met the same male Detective Inspector and female Detective Sergeant that conducted the original interview at the hotel. I have to say that they were much more sympathetic than I expected them to be.

They were quite open with me. They admitted that their investigations so far had drawn a blank and, despite repeated public appeals, they were fast running out of leads to follow. It was agreed that I would tell them all I knew and, in return, they would reveal some of the details of the case that had not been released to the general public; that is in so far as doing so would not jeopardise any potential prosecution.

As I told them my side of the story, the nature of the interview changed such that it became more of a discussion between us and even at one stage developed into an exchange of views.

What they told me that I didn't know was the history of an earlier case of extreme violence involving a girl at the same hotel. They explained that some eighteen months previously a girl had been found unconscious in one of the hotel rooms by a member of the cleaning staff, having been severely beaten and apparently left for dead.

Despite their best endeavours, however, the case had never been brought to a satisfactory conclusion. Initially the victim was in a coma and close to death for a period of some days. Even when the danger period was passed the extent of the physical damage done was such that there was an extended mental recovery period which meant that the victim could not provide any useful information. A false name had been used to book the room and it had been paid for with cash. In the event, the trail had gone cold and the perpetrator of the crime had never been found.

During the course of our discussions the police told me name of the poor unfortunate victim. The Detective Sergeant mentioned it almost in passing; she must have thought it was of little significance to me. But she was wrong, so wrong. The name stunned me as surely as if I had been struck on the head by a wooden mallet.

It was Gemma, Gemma McVeigh. I couldn't be sure about the surname, we simply had never had cause to use them during our conversations in the park, but I knew, deep down I knew, it had to be her.

I asked what became of her following the terrible attack that took place that night in the hotel. Neither of them knew but they called in a uniformed officer and tasked him with the job of finding out. We carried on discussing the case and exchanging information. It seemed a relatively short space of time before there was a knock on the door and the policeman returned. He asked to speak to one of the detectives outside but the Inspector told him that he could speak openly in front of me. He said, somewhat formally, that the last known location of the victim was at a nursing home about twenty miles away out on Dartmoor.

I asked if it would be possible to pay a visit to the nursing home and meet Gemma personally. They said that they would have no problem with me taking that course of action and would be willing to tell me the name and location of the home but added that they thought it would be advisable for them to accompany me. It could assist them in their investigations and was likely that their presence could help in overcoming any barriers that may be put in my way if I went on my own.

After a short space of time during which the Sergeant was checking the route to be taken, the three of us got in an unmarked police car and set off for Dartmoor and the nursing home.

As the car climbed out of the city and out onto the moor I sat in the back and stared out of the window. In my mind I was wondering what we were going to find; my thoughts came and went as one explanation after another was raised and then dismissed, sooner or later, by the application of inevitable logic.

I noticed that the weather became more and more inclement as the journey progressed. There was a dank depressive mist around the car which seemed to open up slightly to allow us through and then close in behind us as we passed. We passed through Princetown where the sight of the steel grey granite walls of the prison made me think of the stories of escaped prisoners who perished while trying to gain their freedom, only to be found weeks later, their bodies cold and stiff as they tried to take shelter from the ravages of the weather on the moor.

Eventually we turned down a narrow lane and then into a short driveway at the end of which was a house. It was a typical granite house of the area and, at first glance, it appeared to be the size of a large farmhouse, having, I would say, about six bedrooms.

The Sergeant knocked on the door. After a short while it was opened by a woman in her thirties wearing a sort of nurse's uniform. The Inspector introduced himself, then the Sergeant and finally me. It was interesting to hear myself described as someone 'helping us with our enquiries'; I always thought that statement was a euphemism for a person detained at a police station who had not yet been charged.

We were taken inside and introduced to the resident manager of the home, a well-dressed woman of about fifty.

At first, the questions asked were of a general nature about the nursing home, its size and the number of patients. It came to light during these discussions that there was an extension built onto the back of the main building that could not be seen from the front and that there were twelve available rooms in all of which eight were occupied.

It was then that she remarked, quite casually, that we, of course, knew about all this. I was unsure of what she meant and looking at the other two it was clear that they did not understand either. When asked she went on to explain that she had been through similar questions with the other policemen only five days before.

The Inspector told her openly that he didn't understand what she had said and that we were certainly the first people she would have seen regarding the case he was investigating.

What she said next totally floored me. She told us that she had assumed that we had come to talk further about the disappearance of Gemma McVeigh.

The three of us could only look at each other, temporarily stunned by her statement. We must have looked odd to her because I remember her asking us what was wrong.

The questioning changed. More details were requested relating specifically to Gemma. It transpired that she had no immediate family, her parents were both dead and there were no brothers or sisters. She had lived at the nursing home since leaving hospital, having completed the first phase of her recovery after the attack at the hotel.

She was unable to walk any distance and for the first six months of her time at the home she had been confined to her bed although as part of her rehabilitation the nursing staff had gradually been getting her up and dressed. There was a day room in which she had been able to watch television, read and mix with the other patients. She was moved around the home in a wheelchair and as the recovery programme developed she had taken for short trips outside around the gardens.

The staff had been working on gradually introducing her to walking once again, at first with a walking frame and more recently with two lightweight aluminium crutches. She had just reached the stage of being able to move herself around on her own with the aid of these crutches but her progress was laboriously slow and painful. She was unable to walk any distance and often one of the nursing staff had to go and find her and bring her back in the wheelchair.

The sister told them that despite her physical improvement they had recently become concerned over an apparent deterioration in her mental wellbeing. Recently there were reports of her being found deep in concentration in what they could only describe as a trance-like state. This condition had been becoming more prevalent to the extent that the last two or three times it had been difficult to bring her back to reality.

And then, last Thursday, just four days ago, Gemma had disappeared. She had gone to bed as usual, although a little early at about half past seven. A nurse had visited her room to wish her goodnight at around ten o'clock and recalled later that all was well.

The following morning she was gone. There was no sign of any means by which she could have been taken and it was considered unlikely that she would have left of her own accord. The police were called and carried out an investigation. They studied recordings from the various video cameras around the home but they revealed nothing that could lead to any explanation as to her disappearance.

I asked if I could meet with the nurse who apparently was the last to see her. The sister agreed and left the room briefly to ask someone to go and find her. Within what must have been only a few minutes there was a knock on the door and a smartly dressed young nurse entered. She was introduced to me as Melanie. I asked her to take me to Gemma's room. I thought I sensed a little hesitation on her part, but she suggested that I follow her and we left the other three to continue with their discussions.

She led me along a short corridor, opened a door to her right and stepped back to allow me to enter. I went in. I turned to talk to her but she was hanging back and seemed reluctant to cross the threshold into the room.

I forgot about her momentarily and turned my attention to the room and its contents. It was better furnished than I imagined it would be. I suppose I was expecting a typical hospital room, white, clinical and relatively sparse. It was, however, furnished more as a bedsit flat for a student would be. There was a bed, two armchairs, a small table and the room was carpeted. In addition, there was a television, radio and music centre. There were no cooking facilities but through another door, which was slightly ajar, I could see a bathroom.

I turned my attention to Nurse Melanie and asked her to join me. She said that she would rather not but I persisted and asked her to come and sit with me and talk for a while. After a brief hesitation she consented and each of us took an armchair.

She told me that she had been the nurse assigned to Gemma for the duration of her time at the nursing home. She recalled the day when Gemma had arrived in an ambulance from the hospital where she had been taken after the attack in the hotel room. She explained that it was standard practice to assign a dedicated nurse to a patient although there would others with whom they would come into contact with during the course of their recovery and rehabilitation treatment. It also provided a stable contact for the patient to identify and confide in, which was seen as a way of identifying and understanding the mental damage caused. The dedicated nurse was encouraged, in effect, to befriend the patient in her charge. In a case such as a violent assault, as Gemma's case obviously was, this was considered to be a particularly beneficial course of action.

Melanie told me that Gemma's recovery had been, for the most part, in three separate phases. Initially, there was the period when the healing of the physical and mental scars was running concurrently. The visible damage inflicted during the attack was quite serious and this was coupled with the fact that Gemma's mental systems had almost shut down in order to blot out the undeniable pain. It was known that she had come close to death and that, in purely physical terms, she had died on the operating table at least three times during the operation to save her life; an operation that took some five hours to complete.

Then followed the second series of operations carried out at the hospital, followed by the transfer to the nursing home, when Melanie had first become involved with the case, and then the long recovery cycle.

The recovery programme had been considered to be going fairly well until the commencement of the third phase at which time events had occurred which were unexpected and had been the cause of some concern for the both the doctors and the nursing staff monitoring the treatment and its progress,

The primary concern was that Gemma was, on a regular basis, slipping into a semi-conscious, almost trance-like, state. When this happened there were instructions to the nursing staff to check her vital signs which included the connection to heart and brain activity monitoring equipment. After each occurrence tests were carried out to look for any potential detrimental effects but, if anything, she seemed to be gaining in the power of her mental faculties.

The doctors were concerned, and somewhat baffled, by what was going on in Gemma's brain and Melanie was charged with the responsibility of find out as much as she could about her general mental state. This she was to do by concentrating on what the experts called her 'buddy' role. In truth, it wasn't difficult; she had come to like her patient a lot. As well as being professionally responsible for Gemma's recuperation programme, she had come to care for her as a person and was troubled by the apparent deterioration in the progress of her recovery.

Gemma seemed reluctant at first to open up and tell her nurse how she felt mentally, but when she did the effect was to cause Melanie to become even more concerned than she was previously.

Gemma talked about being able to travel in her mind, to leave her body and see herself and others from different perspectives. This she had been able to develop to such an extent that she actually felt she could physically project herself to the extent that she could visit other places. She had the first experience when on the operating table shortly after the original attack and, over the months of recovery, she had developed the capability. As her strength gradually returned, so the power in her mind had increased, enabling her to travel for longer periods over greater distances and feel a stronger physical presence whilst doing so.

Melanie hesitated, paused for a short while and then went on to tell me that she had become really concerned about Gemma's mental state when she had mentioned that she had met someone, a friend who she felt that she could depend upon. When questioned she explained that she had met this person, a man, on her mental travels.

Melanie had questioned what she meant by 'travels' knowing that Gemma had not had any opportunity or capability to leave the nursing home. She was even more perturbed by Gemma's response that 'the mind was capable of more than most people could imagine if you could only harness the power'.

Melanie looked at me and our eyes met, it was not just a glance but a short, brief, intense coming together of our minds and a realisation of a common bond between us.

"That's why you're here, isn't it?"She said. "You knew her, didn't you?"

I didn't know how to respond to her and opted to change the subject. Looking up to a small shelf above the bed, I saw a couple of photographs in brightly coloured frames. I stood up, reached across and picked up the one that had caught my eye.

The photograph was of Gemma, clearly in the early days of her time at the nursing home, sitting in a wheelchair in the grounds with Melanie standing behind her. The one thing that instantly caught my attention was the scarf that Gemma was wearing.

Seeing me peering intently at the print, Melanie asked me the reason for my obvious close interest in the detail. I pointed out the scarf to her and asked if she knew where it had come from and how it came into Gemma's possession.

She commented that it was interesting that I had specifically asked about the scarf because it was the cause of some interest to the police investigating Gemma's disappearance. This was because it was a very special and personal item to her. She had made it herself, with some help from Melanie, during the occupational therapy that was part of her recovery programme.

She had chosen the colours and the material herself and she had been personally responsible for every painstaking stitch. It was a very precious object to her. She never went anywhere without it.

The confusion was caused because it had gone missing the day before she herself had disappeared. When she was asked where it had gone she had replied that she had given it away as a gift to someone who had been very kind to her. But she had had no visitors and it was assumed that she had lost or mislaid it. What was causing confusion amongst the nursing staff was that she did not seem to be distressed in any way about the apparent loss of this item that was so special to her.

When she had finished her explanation, I slowly pulled the scarf that Gemma had given me in the park in Plymouth out of my pocket. As I did so Melanie's mouth fell open and her eyes widened as she stared intently at it.

She spoke with a broken, faltering voice, almost stammering as she did so.

"How did you... I mean... Where did you get... That is it, it's hers, how did you come to have it in... I don't understand... I can't understand... Did you meet her?... Are you the friend?..."

I told her that I couldn't answer her questions but that I would tell her my story. And that is what I did.

Even when I had finished, neither of us had any answers.

* * * * * *

We kept in touch for about a year; I would ring her once a month and we would chat for half an hour or so. We became quite good friends, as much as it is possible to be friends with someone at the end of a telephone.

Then one day she rang me and told me that she had received an offer of a job abroad, an offer too good to miss. We agreed to keep in contact but to date I have not heard from her again.

Nothing has ever been heard of Gemma to this day and the police have no suspects for the murder in the hotel.

And so that is the end of my tale, the mystery remains unsolved as far as I am concerned. I have never heard or seen anything of the girl in the park since that final parting kiss.

All I have is the memories and, of course, the scarf.

END

A SWARM OF BLACK

A SWARM OF BLACK

Bert Jackson and Fred Miller were two friends who shared a passion for gardening. They had known each other for many years but since they had both retired and, sadly, both become widowers, they seemed to spend every waking hour engrossed in their hobby.

There was some variation, however, in their individual interests in that each had opted to concentrate on a different facet of horticulture.

Bert specialised in flowers, in particular large bloom varieties. He had developed his ability to produce chrysanthemums and dahlias to such an extent that he had become known locally as 'The Flower Man'.

Fred had great respect for his friend's capabilities and love of fine blooms, but, in the kindest possible way, described them as 'decorative rather than useful'. He had preferred to direct his attentions towards vegetables, where his first loves were onions and leeks.

Both Bert and Fred were active members of the local horticultural society and had won numerous prizes at flower and vegetable shows all around the district.

Although they did engage in some social activities, they had the reputation in the neighbourhood of having a very limited depth of conversation about any subject except one. It was their habit to visit the local pub, the Coach and Horses, every evening at around nine o'clock, where they would sit and sup a pint of bitter or two, usually deeply engrossed in some specialised gardening topic.

They were, of course, known by most of the other regulars, but their discussions tended to be confined to the one subject to such an extent that they were, for most of the time, left to themselves. That was, unless a specific matter relating to flower or vegetable growing arose, in which case their advice or comment was avidly sought, such was their prowess and reputation.

It was on such an evening in May that Bert raised the subject of ants.

He enquired whether Fred had had any major problems with ants attacking the vegetables in his garden. Fred responded that he would not be inclined to use the term 'attacking', ants were sometimes a bit of a nuisance if in great numbers in the garden but even then they did not do a lot of damage. Red ants could sometimes give a tiny nip if they found their way to a delicate part of the body, but they did not trouble the tough skin of the hands of a regular gardener.

Bert commented that he had always been of the same opinion. Apart from instances where ants assisted and protected colonies of aphids in order that they could milk their eggs, the ants themselves were of little consequence as far as damage to foliage and petals were concerned.

Bert leaned forward in his chair and, in a somewhat furtive way, with a glance to left and right, whispered to his friend that something very unusual was taking place in his garden. He would not say more to clarify or explain his remark further, but suggested that Fred paid him a visit the following morning to take a look for himself.

Fred arrived at about ten o'clock, they shared a pot of tea and then Bert escorted him out into the garden at the rear of the house. The garden was reasonably large, about a third of an acre, and sloped slightly away from the house, down towards an open slatted fence through which it was possible to see into the apple orchard behind.

The first part, close to the house and extending for the first fifty feet was rich green lawn. The remainder was cultivated entirely for flower growing with the exception of five parallel bare earth walkways, one on each side and three in the middle, which allowed access to the areas laid out as flower beds. In addition, there was a small shed for tools, a larger potting shed with an angled glass front and a greenhouse.

Bert bade his friend follow him into the garden, across the lawn and along the centre aisle. About halfway down the pathway, Bert asked Fred to stop and look to their right.

The area in front of them appeared to be a perfectly normal flower bed with twelve neat rows of chrysanthemum plants set about a foot apart from each other. There was nothing exceptional about it, Fred thought, until he noticed a bare patch of dark soil in the middle of the plot in which there were no plants at all. He stared at the barren area which was about eight feet across, almost circular in shape and slightly higher than the general level of the surrounding ground. It was as though someone had shaken very dark brown sugar through a massive cooking sieve from a great height.

Bert asked Fred to wait there for a minute while he went to the potting shed. When he returned a few moments later, he was carrying a plastic flowerpot in which was a healthy looking plant, about a foot in height and with thick green foliage.

He asked his friend to accompany him into the flower bed. When they reached the barren patch, he bent down and made a hole in the dark soil about three feet in from the edge with his hand. Fred, now being closer to the darker area than he had been before, could see that not only was the soil deep brown in colour, it was also much finer in texture, almost like very fine compost. It moved easily as Bert scooped out the small hole and Fred's gardening instincts told him that this earth should be rich and fertile in nature, not bare and lifeless as it seemed to be.

Bert lifted the plant in his hand out of its plastic pot, tapped it lightly in the palm of his hand so that some of the potting compound fell away and gently pushed the roots into the hole that he had made. He then brushed the displaced earth back into the hole and pressed his knuckles into the loose soil to complete the planting exercise.

Bert stood up and took a couple of paces backwards and motioned to Fred to come and stand alongside him. He told his friend to watch the plant closely and observe.

For a few seconds nothing happened. Then Fred noticed that the earth all around the newly interred plant within a radius of about six inches was in motion, undulating gently like water simmering in a hot saucepan.

As he stood, transfixed, hundreds of black ants appeared from beneath the surface of the soil and closed in on the defenceless plant. Within what seemed to be only a few seconds, the plant was a seething mass of black.

Bert produced an empty jam jar from his pocket, bent down and scooped up a few of the ants. By the time he had replaced the lid on the jar and stood up again, the tide of ants was starting to recede. As it did so, Fred could see that the lush young plant that Bert had placed neatly in the ground just a short while before was gone, devoured completely by the marauding black swarm.

Fred's jaw dropped, he was unable to move or utter a sound. His mouth fell open as he stared at the ground with unblinking eyes in sheer disbelief and amazement at what he had just witnessed. Bert suggested that they went back indoors.

Once back inside and having regained a little of his composure, Fred asked what became a blur of questions in quick succession.

When did he first notice that there was a problem? Did he have any idea where they might have come from? How long had it been going on for? Had he taken any steps to eradicate them? Why did they attack plants in that way, apparently so organised and with such voracious appetites? What was he going to do next?

Bert handed his friend a cup of tea and said he would do his best to provide answers to all of his questions.

Firstly, the problem had started, or at least Bert had initially realised that something was amiss, about four weeks ago when he noticed that ants were attacking and apparently devouring the leaves of the plants in the centre of the bare area where he had just conducted the demonstration. He had been fascinated by the systematic way in which they would work on each individual leaf, starting by eating the outside edges and working their way inwards until only the inner stem remained.

Over the period up to the present day, the ants had continued to expand their activity, although as the colony grew and progressed they became even more destructive and consumed all parts of the plants above ground and, on further investigation, below.

Nothing that Bert had tried had stopped the relentless onward progress of the ants for more than a day. He had tried powders, liquid sprays and chemicals injected directly under the surface of the soil, in short, every proprietary brand of ant killer available on the market.

He even tried extreme action such as flooding them out and scorching the topsoil with a blow lamp. No single remedy or combination of remedies proved to be a permanent solution.

He felt that any other, and potentially stronger, chemicals would be so powerful that the soil would be permanently contaminated and thus damaged to such an extent that it would be useless for any further cultivation.

As regards the cause of the problem, Bert had thought long and hard about it. The only factor he could come up with was that he had dressed the soil where the problem had first manifested itself with a particular compost that he had obtained from a rather unusual source. About twenty miles away was an agricultural and horticultural research centre which had been shut down, apparently due to a withdrawal of government funding. They had been selling compost at a knock-down price and he had purchased a pallet of ten bags.

He had used two of these bags to dress the area by spreading the contents on the surface and mixing them with the existing soil before planting the seedlings from his greenhouse.

He couldn't say, of course, whether the ants were introduced with the compost from the research centre, whether some chemical in the compost had had some effect upon the ants normally present in his garden, a combination of both factors, or there was some totally unrelated cause. He did know, however, that he had run out of ideas as to how to halt or even slow down the relentless progress of what he had now come to refer to as 'a swarm of black'.

As regards what to do next, he had decided to seek advice elsewhere. He had contacted the local radio station and spoken to the producer of the Sunday morning *'Your Garden'* programme, this being a two hour phone-in for local people to request comments by an expert on gardening concerns and problems. She had advised him to send a sample to the studio so that the resident gardening expert, Bob Muchmore, could study it and thus give a more considered response.

Bert had got the impression from the way that the producer had spoken to him that this was a fairly standard request made of potential contributors to the programme in order that the resident expert could be given the opportunity to prepare at least some of his answers beforehand. Hence the collection of the sample that Fred had witnessed earlier.

Bert duly sent his sample to the radio station, together with a brief written explanation of his analysis of how the problem may have come about and the situation to date.

On the Sunday morning Fred and Bert met once again. Whilst Bert made the tea, Fred tuned the radio in to listen to the deliberations of the expert and hear his advice as to the recommended course of action to be taken.

When the time came, they were disappointed with both his evaluation and his suggestions. As far as they were concerned, he didn't really address or answer the questions that the devastation being caused by the ants raised. He made all sorts of comments about soil being damaged by fungal infection and the resultant effect upon plants, with a little about insect attack and how best to deal with it. There was nothing specific regarding their particular problem.

Immediately after the programme, however, Bert's telephone rang. It was Bob Muchmore, the gardening expert that they had just been listening to. His tone was almost apologetic. He said that he had done some tests of his own using the ants that Bert had sent in but he had never seen anything to compare with the voracious behaviour of the small black insects.

He asked if Bert could give him more information about the problem and Bert agreed to help in any way that he could.

There followed a series of questions about the variety of plant, the soil, what action had been taken, whether any fertiliser had been used and if there was any history of similar occurrences in the area.

In the middle of Bert's responses, Bob suddenly interrupted him, saying that there was someone in the studio trying to get his attention to take an urgent telephone call. He returned a minute or so later and said, rather agitatedly, that something had come up'. He added that would call back when as soon as he could and immediately hung up the telephone.

Bert stared rather disbelievingly at the telephone in his hand. He turned to Fred and commented on how rude he thought it was to ask him questions, apparently to obtain further information, and then cut across his answers to end the conversation in that way.

Fifteen minutes later, Bob rang back. He apologised for his somewhat abrupt termination of their last conversation and explained that he had been summoned by the producer of the programme to take an urgent telephone call from the retired head of the nearby research centre that had recently closed down. He wanted Bob to ascertain from Bert if any compost from the centre had been used on the garden.

For reasons that he was not prepared to go into in detail, the former head of the research centre had told him that if Bert confirmed that this was indeed the case, the only solution was to remove the topsoil completely to a depth of about eighteen inches and dispose of it in a controlled manner. This action was to be taken with some urgency and over a distance at least a metre beyond the area apparently affected because of the likely activity of the ants beneath the surface. Preferably, the local council environmental health department should be informed and involved in the disposal of the discarded earth. Any remaining unused compost should not be utilised and should be handed over at the same time.

Bert led Fred into the garden and as they walked he updated him on what the radio expert and the head of the research centre had said. When they arrived at the patch of dark soil, Fred was amazed to see that it had doubled in size from the last time he had seen it.

Bert noticed the expression on his friend's face and commented that the strongest insecticides and chemicals that he had used had held the ants progress up for a day or so but then they recovered and pushed on regardless.

Fred noticed a thin ring, light blue in colour, around the outside rim of the dark soil. He pointed it out to Bert and asked if he knew what it was. Bert replied that the blue line was all that remained of the last powder that he had used. He had spread it liberally across the whole of the dark circle as the instructions had stated. Over the space of two nights the powder had gradually disappeared, leaving just the traces of the residue that now could be seen at the extremities of the advancing dark earth.

The two men stood by the patch, discussing the course of action that had been suggested by the radio gardening expert. Bert wasn't entirely convinced that this was the only option open to him, whereas Fred commented that at least it would put an end to the problem once and for all in one fell swoop.

As they stood there, talking it over, the ants came to the surface. This was unusual, primarily because it was now midday on Sunday and the ants seemed to do all of their worst damage in the two hours either side of sunrise and sunset. Watching them continuing their seemingly never ending task of destruction during broad daylight was the last straw, the final act that convinced Bert that he should proceed just as the expert had recommended.

When they met in the pub on Monday evening, Bert told Fred that all the necessary arrangements had been made for the removal of the earth, and hence the disposal of the ants, on the Wednesday. He had been quite surprised at the speed of response of the council to his request. Whatever the reason, they obviously wanted to carry out the work as quickly as possible.

Bert said that it was his impression that he was not the first to have encountered this type of problem. He had contacted the council environmental health department at about ten o'clock in the morning and by two o'clock he and a council official were standing in his garden looking at the affected plot discussing the removal and disposal of the soil.

The plan was that a mechanical digger, supplied by the council at their cost, would strip the topsoil to a depth of approximately twenty-four inches ('to be safe' as the council representative had put it) over the whole of the area to a distance of two metres outside that which was obviously contaminated. Bert emphasised the word 'contaminated' and said that he had questioned the council man on its use, but the he would not comment further, saying only that it was only a 'figure of speech'.

The soil removed would be loaded onto a lorry and taken away for disposal. Any unused sacks of compost were not to be touched and would be removed from Bert's garden in the same manner. All the material taken away would be destroyed, along with any insects contained within it including, of course, the ants.

Furthermore, the council would supply, at no charge, replacement high quality topsoil. The whole exercise would be carried out on the Wednesday of that week and thus the whole episode would be closed and the problem with the ants consigned to history. Then, at least as far as Bert was concerned, things could return to normal.

Bert had also queried the word 'destroyed' and the council official responded by saying that the only known way to completely clear up the problem was to incinerate all the material involved, with that a large enough area being extracted to ensure that any foraging or 'scout' ants were included. Again his statement gave a good indication that the environmental health people had had to deal with this, or if not very similar, problems in the recent past.

Bert told Fred that he had asked a couple of direct questions in an effort to learn more of what the council official knew, but he would not be drawn and flatly refused to say any more on the subject.

It was plainly clear, however, that the council's operation was geared to react swiftly to this type of event when it arose.

Bert invited Fred round on the Wednesday to watch the proceedings and share some lunch.

At nine o'clock on the Wednesday morning, Bert went into the garden to take a general look around and, more specifically, at the area to be cleared. The council workmen responsible for the clearance and replenishment of the soil were due to arrive around eleven o'clock, having collected the new replacement topsoil on the way.

When he arrived at the area which was soon to be removed, a curious sight met his eyes.

Instead of the large flat patch of fine dark soil, the appearance of the whole affected area had undergone a dramatic change. The entire surface now appeared to have the texture of mud, although it did not seem to be wet. It was as though the top surface had recently dried out and taken on a flat matt finish.

Of course, it was still relatively early in the morning and there had been insufficient warm air or sunshine to dry out such a large area of mud. In any case, Bert was at a loss to understand where the mud had come from. Any rain that had fallen on the patch up to now had made no perceptible difference to the surface texture of the dark patch of soil.

In the centre of the ring of dried mud was a round projection similar to those anthills sometimes seen on wildlife programmes about Africa. It was conical in shape and about three feet in height. Although it tapered towards the top, it did not finish in a point. At the very tip was a shiny object which seemed to shimmer and sparkle slightly in the rays of the morning sun, giving off a pale blue light as it did so.

Bert could not make out what it was and he could not comprehend where it may have come from, but its very presence intrigued him. He decided that this odd phenomenon was worthy of closer investigation.

He stepped cautiously towards the surface of dried mud and tentatively jabbed at it with the heel of his left boot. To his initial surprise, it was quite hard, the rubber wellington boot made no impression at all. He kicked a few more times, each time a little harder than the last until eventually he was convinced that the surface was firm enough to take his weight.

Confident now that he could step towards the strange structure at the centre of the patch and reach out for the shimmering blue object, he put all his weight on his left foot and stepped out, taking a somewhat larger pace than usual. One more step and he reached out to grasp the shiny object.

As he did so, stretching out to take his goal, the whole of the surface collapsed and the ground beneath him gave way. He fell forward and was instantly enveloped in a heaving mass of dark brown and black.

* * * * * *

Fred arrived, as arranged, at Bert's house at ten o'clock. He opened the gate into the front garden and as he did so, he caught sight of someone waving to him from the house next door. It was the next door neighbour, Mrs Crabtree, trying to get his attention. As she realised that he had seen her, she made urgent little beckoning gestures for him to come to her.

He paused and turned to go towards her house. Before he reached her front gate, she was already there to meet him.

She seemed agitated and somewhat nervous. She clasped his forearm as she spoke to him in an almost furtive way, the tone of her voice low and deliberate.

She told Fred that she was worried about Bert.

She said that she had been making herself some breakfast just after nine o'clock (the morning news was on the radio) when she heard shouting coming from the direction of Bert's garden. She thought it was Bert's voice but she couldn't be absolutely sure. She had gone to the window and looked across but couldn't see him anywhere.

She had gone upstairs to try and get a better view over Bert's garden but still had been unable to see him, or anyone else for that matter. She had been unsure of what to do next. On one hand, she did not want to interfere or pry; on the other she was a little frightened, although she was not sure quite what she was frightened of.

It had been playing on her mind, so she was quite relieved when Fred had turned up; now he could take a look.

Fred told her not to worry and returned to Bert's house. He entered the garden through the gate, went up the red brick path and knocked on the front door. There was no reply and he could not hear any sound from inside. He tried again but there was no response.

He went round to the side gate and reached over the top to release the bolt. As he did so, he was suddenly startled by a movement behind him that he caught sight of out of the corner of his eye. He looked round quickly, only to see Mrs Crabtree close behind him.

He wasn't sure if she was genuinely concerned or just being nosy, but he gave her the benefit of the doubt and suggested that she follow him.

Fred called out for Bert and proceeded to take a look around the garden. He could see nothing of his friend.

As they came to the area of the dark soil, Fred noted nothing different from what he had seen before, except, as Mrs Crabtree pointed out, there was an upturned wellington boot protruding from the ground. It looked odd, sticking up at a peculiar angle but still embedded in the earth.

Fred called out once more; there was no response of any kind. He walked forward and bent down to pick up the boot. He was quite surprised to find that it was stuck firmer than he thought. He pulled a little harder, with short tugs as he did so, rather like pulling up a stubborn plant root. Still it would not budge.

He altered his position so that he stood astride the boot. He took a firm hold and pulled hard with a side-to-side rocking movement. He felt the restriction suddenly give way but before he could react, the boot came away in his hand and he fell backwards onto the ground.

What he saw when he looked back at the spot where the boot had been made him recoil in horror.

Still there in the ground, was a foot, Bert's foot. The sock, if there ever was a sock, had gone and the exposed skin was white with a sheen like polished marble.

Mrs Crabtree let out a short scream, clasped her hand over her mouth and ran away, half stumbling, back towards the sanctuary of her house. She was sobbing deeply and uttering prayers as she went.

Realising that he was still holding it, Fred threw the boot as far away as he could and let out an involuntary sound of utter revulsion. Every muscle in his body seized as the blood ran cold and froze in his veins. He felt powerless and unable to move.

After a few minutes and overcoming his initial reaction, Fred came to his senses. He shook his head to make sure that this was all really happening and that he wasn't experiencing some terrible dream. His worst fears confirmed as he realised the seriousness of the situation, his mind struggled to decide what to do next.

Frantically, he clawed at the soil in a vain attempt to dig his friend out. The body was stuck fast, he was making little or no progress and he could see that this course of action was futile. He ran back to the house, through the open back door, grabbed the telephone and rang for the police, ambulance and fire brigade.

* * * * * *

The following is the last few paragraphs of the statement made to the police by Fred.

"I tried to dig away the soft, dark brown soil with my bare hands but it was so fine that I was unable to make any impression. In fact, I could not dig fast enough to prevent the earth falling back into the space that I had made.

"It became obvious very quickly that I was making no progress and that I needed help. That was when I ran into the house and rang the emergency services.

"Looking back, I suppose I must have been in shock, my message was probably garbled and, for the most part, unintelligible.

"I went back into the garden and although it seemed an age, the fire brigade, an ambulance paramedic team and then the police arrived, in that order.

"Shortly after, the council earth clearance crew turned up as originally planned. They set to and helped as much as they could but it still took over an hour to extricate Bert's body from the ground.

"In one way I didn't want to watch but in another my instincts seemed to tell me that I had to, out of respect somehow.

"It was very strange, I recall, as the body slid from the pool of dark earth which seemed to be reluctant to release its unfortunate prey. As it came into full view I could see that Bert's body was encased in what seemed to be a layer of liquid mud that had now set hard to form a solid brown shell.

"When one of the firemen tapped at the hardened surface with his gloved hand, it made no impression. The process was repeated more firmly with increasing force but with the same result.

"Eventually it was agreed that gentle use of the fireman's axe was in order. This resulted in the cracking of the shell and the removal of a fairly large section. The hard brown piece was lifted away, exposing poor Bert's thigh.

"The newly-revealed skin had a peculiar appearance. It looked rough, like coarse sandpaper, and was red rather than flesh coloured. I had no wish to look any closer but I recall one of the paramedics moving forward to make his examination. He said that he had never seen anything like it; he could only describe it as having the appearance of thousands of tiny bites.

"The one thing I noticed during the whole of the terrible events of that morning was that there wasn't a single ant to be seen anywhere. Eventually, the removal of Bert's body was completed and the go-ahead given to proceed with the original task of replacing the affected soil. I watched the whole exercise from beginning to end, refusing to go to the hospital for treatment for the effects of shock until after the entire task was finished.

"Whether in the earth on the lorry, in the surrounding areas where the soil had been removed or anywhere else in Bert's garden, I did not see a single ant that day. It was as though the whole colony had packed up and left for good.

"I just wonder where they went… "

END

JAMIE

JAMIE

Back in the day I was working as an on-site representative for an avionics company who were under contract to provide support to the RAF at their base at Kinloss. It was customary that when the long-term representative took annual vacation someone such as me would visit the base to fill in to provide cover. Which was how I came to be spending a couple of weeks at a small hotel in Forres.

The hotel was run by three people, a resident couple, husband and wife, and the owner who was the mother of the husband. The place was run on a daily basis by the husband and wife; she being responsible for the kitchen and dining room and he looking after almost everything else to make the operation run smoothly. It was clearly evident, however, that the mother enjoyed her position as matriarch and, although not making much of a contribution to the day-to-day running of the establishment, she was quite content to make comments on anything of which she disapproved.

I suppose that you could say that the hotel was a cross between a bed and breakfast guest house and a country house hotel. I recall that it had about six or eight rooms; the main advantage for me was that it also provided evening meals and a bar so there was no requirement for me to go out and find somewhere to eat or rest up in the evening. It also afforded an opportunity to meet some of the locals who chose to meet in the bar. The husband, Jim, actively encouraged this, presumably as a way of boosting the takings, particularly in the colder winter months when tourists would be few and far between.

On the Friday of my visit I came upon what proved to be a rather quaint local custom. After the evening meal, as I recall around eight o'clock, I had retired to the bar and was sitting alone in a corner of the room composing my weekly report in order that it could be sent to my home office the following day. I found it convenient to construct the report on the Friday evening, sleep on it and re-read it the following day before forwarding. In this way I could ensure that the report was complete and accurately conveyed what I wished to say.

The hotel bar closed, officially, at 11 o'clock. At 10.30 the matriarch rose from her chair in the bar (where nobody else was allowed to sit) and left by the door that led into the lobby/entrance area.

Surprisingly, to me, the whole of the bar clientele followed her. She then made her way straight up the flight of stairs, stopped at the top and turned round on the open landing so as to address the assembled throng below. She looked down and gave a somewhat regal one-handed wave. She then bid all her audience a very good night, turned and went away to her room to bed.

As she did so, all below reciprocated with the same greeting and as she disappeared from sight the entirety of those assembled turned and went straight back into the bar. Jim locked the doors and we were all in, guests and locals, for as long as we wished to stay.

The customary way to consume alcohol in these parts, as I was advised, was a pint of bitter, called heavy in Scotland as I had come to understand, with a malt whisky chaser. The custom was to drink some of the bitter, consume at least three quarters of the whisky, then pour the remaining whisky into the larger glass with the bitter. I noted that some people actually poured some of the bitter into the whisky glass and then back into the larger glass, thus ensuring that none of the precious whisky was lost in the transaction. By the end of the evening, the resulting drink is rather potent but at the same time extremely satisfying.

Partaking in such rituals with the locals together with complementing them on introducing me to the custom is how I came to be accepted, or as much accepted as a Sassenach could be, by the local fraternity.

This is also how I came to meet with a local celebrity named Old Bart. He had a favourite armchair in the bar that, out of respect, no other local would even consider occupying.

By chance, our eyes made contact and, seeing that I was alone, he beckoned me to come and sit with him. I offered to buy him a drink; he declined the beer but accepted a double whisky. For a split second I thought that this could be his way of financing his evening drinking but in the event I parked my cynicism and sat down at his table.

We hit it off very well, considering he was an older Scottish man with a broad highlands accent and me being a young engineer from the South of England. We talked into the early hours of the morning; this is the story that he told me and that I am about to relate to you now.

******

Old Bart told me that not far from where we were there is a small village in the mountains that borders a loch. It consists only of a few cottages, a chapel and a single shop, which is primarily a bakers but which also sells the things that the locals might need on a daily basis. It incorporates a small tearoom with the aim of attracting passing travellers.

In the village lived a young man about seventeen years old by the name of Jamie McCracken. He lived in a small dwelling adjacent to the shop which was run by a woman whose name Bart couldn't recall but he remembered that she had a daughter named Marie. Jamie was an orphan; he had been taken in by the woman, who had been close friends with his parents who had been killed in a terrible accident on an unmanned railway crossing in Norfolk when Jamie was about five years old.

It was thought that the woman hoped, or maybe planned, that Marie and Jamie would marry and take over the shop as she became older and thus unable to run it. Jamie and Marie were close friends, having been brought up together, and Marie was a typical local village girl who was quite happy with things staying as they were and following through on her mother's plan.

Jamie had other ideas however, he was ambitious and gradually became more and more anxious to move away. Jamie was a bright lad and as he grew older and passed his exams in school in Forres and later in Elgin he became more and more unsettled and, consequently, he and Marie became increasingly quarrelsome. She was content to follow her mother's wishes whilst he yearned for something more from life, even if he wasn't quite sure what that was or where it would take him.

One night, after a particularly heated disagreement with Marie, Jamie took himself off for a long walk along the loch side to calm down, think things through and consider his way forward.

There was a light breeze and the loch water lapping against the pebbles on the shore resulted in a light lather of bubbles as the air engaged with the soft water; water that had a slightly brown tinge to it owing to the dense peat in the water.

The night was cloudless with a full moon that, once his eyes had adjusted to it, illuminated a clear way ahead for him as he followed the path along the loch. As he walked he became aware that he was approaching an area of soft bluish light down by the side of the loch, almost as though it was emanating from the water itself.

His view being slightly obscured by some trees, he made his way down to the loch shore.

In a small clearing he came upon a young girl he judged to be about the same age as him. She was wearing a full white dress with a light blue belt together with matching white shoes. On her head she wore a straw boater-style hat with a light blue ribbon around it. He had seen similar styles of clothing in a history book once and that made him think that her clothes appeared to be quite old-fashioned, rather like those worn around the early 1900s.

As he drew nearer to her she turned and smiled, almost as though she was expecting him. She showed no signs of being surprised but smiled sweetly at him as they made eye contact. There was an instantaneous and deep mental closeness between them as, for a few seconds, their eyes met in a deep and intense gaze. She blushed and lowered her head in a rather shy and somewhat coy manner.

Jamie was the first to speak. He mumbled a rather nervy greeting with a tremble in his voice.

"Hello." she responded accordingly.

From that point on, the first verbal contact having been established, they began a long and varied conversation. It transpired that her name was Amoura and that she lived in a large country house at the far end of the loch. She told him that she had been betrothed to a soldier called Jack but that he had been declared missing presumed dead. Jamie thought it unwise to question her any deeper on this for fear of causing her further distress but he was pleasantly surprised when she said that he was the very image of Jack and, indeed, could have been taken as his twin.

They lay down next to each other between the loch shore and the heather. They talked long into the night and lost all track of time; it was as though they were close friends who had always known each other and could confide in each other unreservedly. At times their conversation waned a little but when it did they spent the time looking up at the clear starlit sky and pointing out the occasional shooting star as it created a momentary golden stripe across the heavens.

In the event they talked through the night and it wasn't until the dawn broke and the sun rose behind the hills, gradually spreading its light over the surface of the water that they parted. Both of them, they agreed, had completely lost track of time as they shared their thoughts and feelings.

Jamie suggested that they meet again and Amoura said that she often visited this part of the loch and would very much like to meet him again.

Jamie, his heart lifted and feeling as though he was floating on air, made his way back home. He was determined to ensure that he met her again.

All the following day he found it difficult to concentrate on his studies. Every time he tried to concentrate on his schoolwork thoughts of Amoura broke into his mind to interrupt his train of thought.

He intended to go to the loch and try and meet with Amoura again that evening but the weather was atrocious and this made walking the path along the loch side extremely treacherous, apart from the fact that he thought it was unlikely that she would be out in such adverse weather conditions.

The next day, after supper, Jamie made his way to the spot where he had first encountered Amoura. His head was filled with a mixture of anticipation and excitement with the thought of seeing her again.

As he approached he could hear a voice but he knew instinctively that all was not as it seemed. The voice he could hear was deeper, a man's voice he thought, softly singing a Scottish lament. This time there was no trace of any shimmering blue light as he had seen before, only the light of the moon to which his eyes had, by now, become accustomed and a single white light near the water's edge.

As he drew closer, Jamie could make out the shape of a lone fisherman who having cast his line far out into the loch was patiently sitting on a fold-out seat waiting to see what, if anything, would bite.

Jamie was by no means quiet as he strode out to make his way to the lone angler and, as he was just a few feet away, the fisherman turned and greeted him. "Hello young fellow, what brings you to these parts on a warm summers evening?"

Jamie was reluctant to reveal the true purpose of his visiting the loch so merely replied that it was a stroll that he regularly took around the loch edge.

"Never seen you here before," said the man, "and I've been coming here for about ten to twelve years, off and on."

As they chatted the angler probed a little further into Jamie's reason for visiting that particular spot and, as Jamie grew to trust him he opened up a little more on his experience of meeting Amoura. This was the first opportunity he had had to speak to anyone on his chance meeting with the girl and he revealed that he really wanted to see her again. The angler asked him to describe the girl that he had seen in as much detail as possible.

As Jamie made his explanation of his encounter with Amoura, the angler's mood became more and more sombre. He began to stare into the distance as though deep in thought and his brow became furrowed.

He said, "There is a tale of the Lady of the Loch that I have heard but of which I have never encountered any real evidence." He went on to expand his story by explaining that many years before, around the start of the First World War, a very well-to-do family lived in the country house at the end of the loch. The young girl of the family, whose name he could not recall but was in her late teens, was known to be deeply in love with a young man of about her own age by the name of Jack. They had been friends since childhood, having met via their respective families; they were engaged and about to be married in 1916. All plans were put on hold when war was declared and Jack took up a commission before going off to France to fight for King and Country.

The story goes that he was lost, presumed killed, and that he never returned. It was possible that he had been taken prisoner but at the end of the war there was no word of him save that many of the men in his regiment had been lost during a particularly heavy artillery bombardment and that many of the bodies were never found.

She, being distraught that her one true love is probably not going to come back and that she may live out her life alone for the rest of her days, decides that she will go to him in the afterlife. With her mind distorted and deranged by her grief, she walked slowly into the cold waters of the loch and drowned. Her body was never found.

The story goes that there are reports of her ghostly form being seen around the loch in the 1940s and again in the 1960s. On the second occasion the unfortunate youth who apparently spoke to her had a nervous breakdown, lost his power of speech, was sectioned and was never mentally the same again.

The angler went on to say that he had been to the loch many times to fish at all times of the day or night but he had never encountered any visions of any such tragic girl or seen any strange lights, only the light of the moon reflected in the still water on a clear night.

Whether he believed the story or not, Jamie thought it unlikely that Amoura would come unless he was alone so he bade the angler a good nights fishing and made his way home.

The following day was a Saturday and Jamie had been invited to go and spend the weekend with his grandfather in Edinburgh. His grandfather was the only link that he still had with his birth family, the other grandparents having died, and Jamie liked to see him whenever possible. They often spoke about his parents and what might have been if the tragedy had not occurred. His grandfather had become a mentor to Jamie and had guided him through some difficult times by offering advice and guidance but by being careful not to instruct him on how to think or act.

Early on the Saturday morning Jamie boarded the train from Elgin for the four hour journey to Edinburgh. His grandfather met him at the station and they went for an early lunch after which the grandfather suggested that they went for a drive in his car. He wanted to show Jamie something.

They drove out of the city and took the road towards Dunfermline and on the way took the turn towards South Queensferry. When they arrived the grandfather parked the car and asked Jamie to walk with him to look up at the old original Forth Bridge. He explained that it had been opened in 1890 to enable the railway link between Edinburgh and London. Grandfather, having been a civil and structural engineer before retiring, explained in great detail how the bridge was designed and constructed all those years ago.

Jamie looked up at the massive structure in awe and wonderment. He thought about all the many people and the different roles that they played in the construction of the bridge. It was at that point that he was inspired to follow in his grandfather's footsteps. He made up his mind to become a civil and structural engineer who would play his part in the making of magnificent structures across the world. He understood that it would be a hard journey which would require him to undertake further education courses in Edinburgh or Glasgow with the likelihood of needing a university degree but he felt in his heart that it was his destiny to follow in his grandfather's footsteps.

He thought about it a lot on the journey home on Sunday but as he did so he became even more committed to the idea of his following personal way forward. Any negative thoughts were raised, considered and rejected as being outweighed by the positive aspects. Jamie would follow his destiny come what may.

Early on Sunday evening he went to the spot where he first met Amoura. He stood with the loch water gently lapping at his shoes and called out her name as loudly as he could. There was no response of any kind, not even a hint that she could hear him. Then, after about fifteen minutes, he gave up and turned to take the path back home.

He took only two short paces when a soft voice behind him said, "Jamie, I am here." He knew instantly that it was her and he turned around. It didn't occur to him that she came out of nowhere but now that he could see her she was standing in the loch water where he had been, her bare feet where he had stood and bathed in a haze of bluish light.

He blurted out the events of the weekend and told her of his decision. He tried to talk her into coming with him to the big city, either Edinburgh or Glasgow, where his grandfather was willing to sponsor him in his endeavours. He was sure that when the grandfather met her he would agree to setting them up with money and accommodation and that he would sponsor their way forward. There was, after all, the money left in trust for him by his parents that would easily be enough to cover any venture that they embarked upon.

Initially her response was, "I cannot come, I cannot leave the loch. You are so like my Jack that I am sorely tempted, but I know it cannot be. You must make your journey alone."

But Jamie was not listening; he knew with all his heart that they must be together. Even though they had spent relatively little time together he knew that they were soul mates and that, as far as he was concerned, they had to be together. It didn't really matter where or when, he told her, it was simply the way things had to be, there was no alternative.

He didn't really give Amoura any options; he had considered all the potential negative possibilities and he felt that they could all be dealt with and overcome.

She said, "Unfortunately it can never be but come to me here at midnight and I promise you that I can make you understand. Go now, my love, and return to me as I have asked."

Jamie did as she requested and, probably in his anticipation and excitement, arrived at their spot half an hour early. There was no sign of her, all was still and quiet, the water was calm and the reflection of the moonlight on the surface of the loch cast shadows all around him.

At midnight Jamie could control his emotions no longer; he stood at the water's edge and called out her name. Waiting a few seconds, he called again and then a third time.

Looking out across the water, he perceived that he could make out an area of blue light emanating from just below the surface but growing stronger and wider. His jaw dropped as Amoura appeared from beneath the water, walking slowly towards him and rising up as she approached him.

She was dressed in a long gown, white with full sleeves, a low neckline and made of some kind of diaphanous material. Pearls of water that shimmered in the moonlight only served to emphasise how sheer and translucent it was; every contour of her body was revealed as she rose steadily from the water.

Jamie was stunned and speechless by the vision that moved sensuously towards him, walking slowly with her eyes fixated on his.

She spoke, "Now you see me as I really am. I am yours and you are mine. You are my Jack reincarnated and

I have been waiting for you. Now we can be together forever. You have come to me and you must stay with me. I cannot come with you."

They embraced, a long, lingering and close embrace; two bodies becoming as one.

Gradually her words sunk into his mind and he realised at long last what she was saying to him. He told her that theirs was a deep and intense love that could not diminish but could only be enhanced over the passage of time.

At that moment Jamie gave up all thoughts of leaving her alone again. Inevitably, their lips met in a long and passionate kiss. Initially she resisted a little but then gave herself to him willingly. They paused and she said that she was a little nervous after all the time that had passed in her search for him and was frightened that there may be consequences for both of them.

Jamie responded, "We are together now and nothing can change that. We will be as one for all time and I promise to love and protect you forever."

They continued their embrace for several minutes, their kisses becoming more intense, the spaces between unbroken by speech; they looked deeper and deeper into each other's eyes oblivious to everything around them.

Jamie then scooped Amoura into his arms and carried her into the loch, just as a man would carry his new wife over the threshold. He walked on until they could be seen no more and both disappeared under the surface of the water.

Neither Jamie nor Amoura have ever been seen again to this very day.

* * * * * *

Old Bart sat back in his chair and let out a long sigh. He glanced downwards at his empty whisky glass, the one that I had replenished several times during the course of his storytelling, and I motioned to our host that another refill would be required.

This was the point where I first thought that I had been taken in by an old traditional piece of local folklore. It was possible that this was how Old Bart financed his Friday evening drinks, by telling apocryphal tales to gullible Sassenach visitors to the area.

"I can see from the look in your eyes, young fellow, that you have your doubts about my tale," said Old Bart, "let me continue on a little further and it is possible you may change your mind."

He went on.

"At the inquest into Jamie's disappearance Marie, Marie's mother, his grandfather and the angler were all called to give evidence. Marie and her mother spoke of their intention for Jamie to marry and stay in the village;

his grandfather told of the visit to Edinburgh and Jamie's future career prospects.

"When it came to the angler, however, the tone of the inquest changed completely. He spoke of meeting with Jamie and recounting the old tale of the lady of the loch. Unsurprisingly, maybe, his evidence was rejected out of hand, even mocked, until he revealed that he was fishing at the loch side the very night when Jamie disappeared. Although he was some distance away on an outcrop of rock, he recalled that the moonlight that night was particularly bright and that he could see Jamie with a girl in a white dress. It was clear to him that they only had eyes for each other and were oblivious to anything around them, whether near or far. He further recounted that Jamie had swept the girl off her feet and, cradling her in his arms, had walked slowly and purposefully into the waters of the loch until such time as both of them were no longer visible.

"He added that there was a strange blue aura of light around them which dissipated across the loch as they gradually disappeared beneath the surface of the water.

"Following the angler's testimony at the behest of the Procurator Fiscal a programme to attempt to find Jamie McCracken's body was instigated. There was much dragging of the loch and many searches were conducted by police and military divers. But Jamie's body was never found."

Old Bart sat back in his chair and took another drink. He licked his lips, took a breath then continued.

"The whole event is a matter of record both officially in the Procurator Fiscal's files and also in the local newspapers of the day. To this day nothing of the tragic couple has ever been found.

"On the loch side at the spot where they were last seen there is a memorial stone with a plaque on it which reads:

> *'To the memory of Jamie McCracken who found his true love but lost his future'*

"Reputedly, it was paid for by the lone angler."

He paused, took a sip from his drink followed by a deep breath and let out a long audible sigh.

"We have all been young once and many of us live our lives without finding the one person that we wish to spend the rest of our life with. When two people come together who feel the same as strongly as I think Jamie and Amoura did, nothing can get in the way of their love for each other. Their story may have been a little embellished in the telling, shall we say, over the passing of time but I tell you that all the signs were that their love was as timeless as the loch and that they were as much in love as it is possible for two souls to be."

Old Bart reached into the inside pocket of his old tweed jacket, opened his wallet, leant forward and offered me an old newspaper cutting to read. As I did so, he said softly:

"Oh, and one more thing, young fellow, you will see from the records of the day that, I, Old Bart, was the angler out catching fish that day... "

END

THE VISIT

THE VISIT

Geraldine was feeling wistful. She stood there, her hands gently, but rather mechanically, kneading the delicate pieces of material under the lukewarm soapy water.

As far as she was concerned, washing underwear by hand in the kitchen sink was not the household chore most likely to challenge the brain. Not even as exciting as hunting down a spider with the vacuum cleaner or attempting to solve one of life's most imponderable mysteries – what happens to the missing half of so many single socks and stockings that accumulate in airing cupboards and drawers?

Not a very exciting way to spend a day off from the office, she thought, and so she allowed her mind to wander, her thoughts many and varied.

In general, she was not unhappy with her lot, she felt that she was as intelligent as the next person and, if circumstances had been different, who knows how things may have worked out, what may have happened or where she may have ended up?

She liked to keep her mind active during the time spent doing the more mundane tasks around the house and one of the ways she accomplished this was by playing a game she called 'What if… ?'

The game consisted of considering one specific time in her life and a particular occurrence, good or bad, and applying the question,'What if the event had not taken place or the outcome had been different in some way?' It was her way of going back in time, changing history and guessing the effect such a change would have had on her world as it is now.

She realised, of course, that some resulting outcomes would have been an improvement and some not, some good and some bad.

She considered that no matter how bad some occurrences may have seemed at the time, if you could have changed them, not all the subsequent events may have taken place. That was all part of the game, all part of exercising the mind. Just changing one event could have a multitude of other effects to be taken into consideration. As she put it herself, there is good and bad in all things as the old wives are reputed to have said, whoever they may have been.

She got bored with the game and turned on the radio. It was coming up to ten o'clock. She didn't much like the early morning presenter on the local station but the one after ten had a brighter format with phone-ins and competitions that she liked to listen to. She tuned in and the local news programme was about halfway through.

As she listened her concentration was interrupted momentarily by what seemed to be a deep rumbling sound in the distance. There followed a brief interruption in the radio transmission, then it continued on as if nothing had happened.

She thought, although she couldn't be entirely sure, that shortly after the building shook slightly. She didn't pay lot of attention to it, sometimes it did move in very high winds or thunderstorms, being sixteen stories high. Often they could feel some movement there on the ninth floor.

It was not possible for her to look outside from where she was standing, that could only be accomplished by taking a couple of paces across to the other side of the room.

She had always thought that the architect who designed the building must have been a man; surely no woman would have designed a kitchen such that there was no window over the sink. Then at least there would have been a view of some sort to look at when carrying out the mundane household chores.

She moved towards the window with the intent of looking out, to see if she could find out what the sound was or where it had come from, when she was distracted by a ring on the doorbell.

She went to the door, opened it, and there stood Charles.

"Charles, what are you doing here?" she said with more than a little surprise in her voice.

"I came to see you," he replied.

"What do you want?" she asked, a little more tersely than perhaps she intended, but nevertheless standing aside so that he could enter.

"I know I shouldn't come but I just felt that I had to see you," he said.

"Well, Bob's away in Manchester on business and I gave up worrying about the neighbours and their gossiping a long time ago. You shouldn't really come round during the day but I suppose that now you're here you might as well come in and join me for a coffee."

Although there was a slight hint of her chastising him in her voice, secretly she was pleased to see him. She always was.

As far as each of them was concerned, they were good friends, real friends and always enjoyed each other's company.

They had met one day, twelve years previously, quite by chance, in the factory where they both worked. He was a trainee engineer with a part-time college course sponsored by the company, she a typist trying to better herself by undertaking a secretarial course at evening class.

She had been carrying a pile of papers to the Works Manager's office on the shop floor when her foot slipped and catapulted each and every piece of paper from her arms onto to the dirty workshop floor. She had tried her best to catch them but it only seemed to make matters worse.

The men working on the machines adjacent to the walkway had made her already embarrassing situation worse, initially with their unsympathetic laughing and cheering, followed by them calling out remarks, each one progressively more rude than the last.

Charles had been the only one to leave his post and come to her assistance. The fact that not only did he help her but that he ignored the others, whose remarks were now directed at him also; he gently and carefully escorted her away from what was now a nightmare situation for her. He personally had guided her back to the safe haven of her office and the other girls.

This single act of compassion and caring was the seed from which their friendship had grown. Slowly at first, for both of them were unsure and a little nervous, neither being in a position to know or predict how such a relationship would develop. Although she was already married and he had a steady girlfriend they realised that the feelings that were kindled between them were somehow different.

Since that first meeting some twelve years before their friendship had developed, matured and grown.

In other ways they had both lived their separate lives. She had carried on through a somewhat rocky and childless marriage and was now Secretary to the Managing

Director. He had completed his training, left the company to gain more experience and returned three years ago to take up the position of Manager of the Test Laboratory. He had married his childhood sweetheart and now had three children.

They could, as they had on many occasions, talk openly about their respective spouses, Bob and Melissa. In some ways each of them was content with their marriages and their lives as a whole. They both felt, however, that neither of their partners could possibly understand the depth of their relationship. For this reason they kept their friendship to themselves, they had never sought to introduce their partners to each other or make up any kind of foursome socially.

By keeping in contact, meeting occasionally and sometimes, albeit rarely, managing to create situations where they could spend a few hours together, they had grown very close. Nobody else was involved in their relationship and that was the way they both wanted it.

Over the years, their relationship had become very caring, very loving and very understanding although, perhaps strangely, not sexual in nature. It would have been easy for them to take the next step after a hug or a cuddle or a lingering kiss.

One Christmas Eve in the early times, probably the first or second Christmas, after a couple of drinks at an office party, a situation did arise which caused them to stop and think about their relationship and how it might develop.

They found themselves, probably not entirely by chance, in a darkened office, alone, away from all the others. They had kissed long and hard, yet tenderly and lovingly. The intensity and power of the feelings that were released were an indication to each of them as to how easy it would be for them to go further.

It would have been so simple and maybe so enjoyable to allow emotions to take over and events take their natural course but they had not done so.

They had discussed this on numerous occasions but both of them felt that their relationship may be irrevocably changed by opting to take the fateful step. They valued their friendship so much; it was too precious to both of them to take the risk of changing their feelings towards each other for the sake of a few minutes pleasure, wonderful though it may have seemed at the time.

He spoke again.

"I know it's not right for me to come here. I can only tell you that deep down inside me I felt that I had to come. I needed to see you, needed to speak to you, so here I am."

She responded immediately and without hesitation.

"Well, we always said that if one of us really needed the other then all we had to do was call so carry on. What can I do to help?"

"I really came to say thank you."

"For anything in particular?" she asked, hoping it didn't sound quite as abrupt to him as it did to her. "I didn't mean that to sound as... "

"Don't apologise, and please don't be too angry with me. Just understand and trust me, I need to say it, I need you to listen. Thank you for being you, for loving me in our special way, for being there, for being all the things you are to me and most of all, for us."

"You didn't need to say any of that. You know that I feel the same. It isn't necessary for you to say it; you really don't have to."

"I know, but for some reason I felt compelled to come and tell you. Don't get me wrong, please, it isn't that I have any doubts, quite the opposite, I can only repeat that deep down inside I just know that now is one of those times when I must tell you how I feel."

She knew and understood that this was one of his little ways; she knew him well enough to know that sometimes he needed a little reassuring. It was nice of him really to look her in the eyes and tell her how he felt. She looked upon it as a compliment; it told her that her thoughts and feelings mattered to him, that he cared about her and valued their friendship so much. She felt the same towards him and she hoped he realised it, even if she had to remind him sometimes.

When times were bad, it was his loving, caring nature that kept her going, just thinking about what he might say or how he might react to a problem could help her through. Whatever else happened, they could rely on each other and even if they didn't have the opportunity to get together for a few weeks, or even months, it did not affect the depth of their feelings for each other.

They were good friends, real friends. As far as they were concerned, their friendship was on a different plane, very few people could ever understand such a relationship, even fewer would be lucky enough to experience one.

"Now don't you go all insecure on me," she chided him, although her expression broke into a gentle smile as she said it, "I need you."

"I will always be here for you," he said.

"Well maybe not always, but as long as we are around," she responded, trying to make her reply light-hearted but not so that it would make fun of him.

"Always," he repeated, looking straight into her eyes. The depth and intensity of his expression concerned her a little.

"I know," she said, reaching out for his hand and touching it lightly.

It seemed cold to her touch, but then it crossed her mind that she had not yet ventured out that day, it must be colder than she thought.

"I love you," he said.

"I love you," she responded, "In our special way."

She could feel the tenderness between them and see the reaction to her remark in his eyes. The previous serious and somewhat earnest look was diffused into a softer expression. There was a hint of a tear in his eye which caused a similar reaction in hers.

Will you do something for me, my friend?" he asked.

She sensed that his question was in some way very important to him, so she answered unhesitatingly and without any qualifying or flippant remarks.

"Yes."

"My request is a little unusual and I ask you not to question my reasons but if you say no, then you say no, and I will understand.

"Sounds intriguing, I hope it's not too naughty," she joked. "I trust you, you know that, the answer is still yes, whatever."

"Will you go and put on your white dress for me?"

She paused before answering him.

"It's a bit early in the morning, I am not really at my best," she said, a little defensively.

"Please, for me."

"All right, just for you, would you like a cup of coffee while I am away?"

"No, thank you, I will just sit here quietly and wait for you to return. Don't be too long, I am so looking forward to seeing you in it."

"Cheeky!" she said as she disappeared into the bedroom and pushed the door behind her. She did not bother to close it completely.

There was a story behind the white dress.

Some years ago, she had mentioned in conversation that she didn't know what to wear to the company Christmas Dinner and Dance. It was a chance remark and not intended as any sort of a hint. He had invited her out to lunch; an event that they only undertook when they felt that there was a suitable convenient excuse.

Since they were both on the dance organising committee and raffle prizes had to be purchased, they had volunteered to go out one lunchtime and buy them. They could then, quite justifiably, spend some time together.

On the day, it didn't take too long to complete the necessary shopping and Geraldine had assumed that they would go to a pub and have lunch together. Instead, Charles had told her that he had a surprise for her.

He took her to a large department store and then up to the second floor; ladies fashion. Once there, he led her to a particular display the centrepiece of which was the white dress. He told her that he would like to buy it for her as a Christmas present

Instinctively, she had declined his offer but he had talked her into accepting. She had to admit that it hadn't been too difficult to convince her, the dress was truly amazing to behold.

As always, she had to agree that he had impeccable taste and she had remarked as much to him, which had embarrassed him a little. There was no doubt about it, it was a beautiful dress. He had to admit that she looked breathtaking when she tried it on in the store and sought his approval by modelling it for him.

On the night of the dinner and dance they managed to create one opportunity to dance with each other. He had told her how beautiful she looked that night and she had admitted that she felt on top of the world. That dance became one of their extra-special times together, one of their best memories to look back on.

The song that was being played as they danced became their song. The words seemed to fit their feelings for each other, the special nature of their relationship and the deep friendship that existed between them.

The words lingered in the air:

"How could they ever understand?
The feelings that exist between us
Your smile, the touch of your hand
Is all I need.

This love we have is deep within
It lives on though we may be apart
We know, as no others can
The way we feel."

From that day forward, whenever or wherever either of them heard the words of the song, they had a profound effect upon them, whether together or apart.

Just then, she called out to him.

"Ready or not, here I come."

She emerged from the bedroom and stood for a moment in the doorway so that he could look at her. She did it just for him; she knew that he would like it. She moved across the room and stood in front of him. As she did so, he rose to greet her.

He held out his arms towards her and she willingly succumbed to his embrace. Their arms around each other, they hugged tightly, with additional little squeezes with their fingertips as an extra show of affection.

As she ran her hands over his back, she thought his skin to be a little cold under the cotton shirt, but there was nothing cool about his embrace or the depth of his feelings and so she decided not to mention it.

As they stood there, locked in each other's arms, the radio suddenly seemed to get louder; either that or it was the significance of the song being played that struck her.

They were playing that song, their song.

She closed her eyes and melted into his arms. Their bodies were in complete unison, they moved as one, gently swaying together to the rhythm of the music. For a few minutes, time seemed to stand still.

Eventually, inevitably, the song ended and the time came for her to move slightly away from him. She pulled slowly back in order that she could look up into his eyes.

As her face came into line with his, however, he was not looking back at her but somewhere over her shoulder. She was a little surprised at this, if not offended.

"What are you looking at?" she asked.

He did not reply. He continued to stare into the distance.

He seemed to be looking at something at some distance away, outside the flat, beyond the window.

"What is it?" she said. Again he said nothing.

"Oh well, I suppose I shall just have to take a look for myself."

She moved away from him to the window, drew back the lace curtain and looked out.

She was looking but not really seeing, her mind on other things, affected by the closeness of their bodies and the intimacy of their contact. Thoughts were flashing through her brain of her life with Bob; what was and what might have been with Charles.

Her head turned and her eyes looked lazily towards the factory in the distance. What she saw instantaneously shocked her back into reality.

The factory was ablaze, with a huge column of thick black smoke reaching up into the sky. As she watched, spellbound, her mouth half open, a jet of searing fire shot up into the air, followed by two short bursts of white, then black smoke. She flinched and turned her head away. Even though it was some distance away, the force of the explosion frightened her.

The rumble that followed was not as strong as the one that she had felt earlier, but now she faced the awful realisation of what that first sound must have been. The sound that had interrupted her just before Charles had arrived.

"Charles, come and look! There's a fire at the factory. It looks a real mess; I wonder if anyone's been... "

As she spoke, she turned to urge him to come and look.

But he had gone, she was alone.

Just then the radio crackled loudly and the programme being transmitted stopped abruptly in the middle of a song, their song. After a short pause, an announcer spoke.

"We interrupt this programme to bring you a news bulletin. There has been a serious explosion and fire today at the works of Clark Aviation Fuel Systems in Woolley Road. We take you over now to our reporter, Sally Johnson, at the scene."

"Thank you, John. The explosion, the cause of which is unknown, ripped through the equipment testing laboratory of Clark Aviation Fuel Systems about forty minutes ago, just after ten o'clock this morning. There has been a serious fire followed, less than a minute ago, by several smaller, lesser explosions.

Police advise that detailed casualty figures are not yet known, but that one man is known to have been killed in the initial blast.

The man has been named as a Mr Charles Hollingsworth, the Manager of the Equipment Testing… "

She turned and looked back towards the window, but Geraldine heard no more. Her mind became a confusion of events and emotions, her legs buckled and her head whirled as she slowly sank to the floor.

END

THE QUEXADO

THE QUEXADO

Chapter One
The background to my story

My father was a great storyteller. I would sit at his feet and listen to him telling me about his exploits during his twenty-six years in the Royal Navy.

His stories were all about the good times and, every Christmas his ex-Navy mates would come to visit, drink rum and share their own experiences. It was a real 'coming of age' moment for me when I was allowed to join them; no 100 percent proof rum for me, of course, but just to be with them with a glass of Tizer was reward enough. There was little or no talk of war and its bad experiences, the sights and sounds of conflict, destruction and death were consigned to the history files in their respective minds; comradeship and supporting each other in times of great adversity were the order of the day.

It is impossible for those of us who have not experienced such events to imagine what it must be like to be battened down in a watertight metal prison for days, weeks and possibly months on end with the knowledge that an enemy's sole aim is to nullify you and cancel out the threat that you, and all of your shipmates, present.

One of these stories was the seed behind the events that were about to unfold and eventually make my fortune. The tale relates to an ordinary seaman, a gunner I believe, named 'Chalky' White. It seemed to me that certain surnames in the Navy always carried a nickname as a first name. Nobody ever referred to anybody with the surname of White to anything other than Chalky.

Chalky was always known to be a jolly 'happy-go-lucky' fellow as, apparently, naval gunners often are given their profession, the times spent working under great stress and their vulnerability during attack by the enemy.

Even in wartime crews were given leave when operations allowed and when the ship was docked temporarily in Rosyth, Scotland, for five days whilst undertaking repairs and revictualling, the crew took the opportunity to take shore leave. Unfortunately, given the distance to their home port of Portsmouth and the difficulties of travelling in wartime, it was not possible for members of the crew with family to visit their families and loved ones down south in the bases at Portsmouth, Chatham or Plymouth. Consequently a lot of time (and money) was spent in the pubs around Dunfermline and Edinburgh.

When the crew members reassembled on the ship four days later to get the ship ready for sailing, it came as a surprise to the others when Chalky White joined them. His demeanour had completely changed. Gone was the bouncy, joking, good natured soul that they had come to know. It was replaced by a man who appeared to be carrying a heavy load mentally. Physically there was little change, although some commented privately that he held his head low and that this caused him to stoop slightly.

He looked a broken man. Such were the occurrences and tragedies of war that it was commonplace not to raise any issues with any individual in Chalky's situation. He would open up and tell them when he was ready. It was not that they didn't care for their shipmate; it was just the way that things were handled then; all understood and followed the unwritten rules of the service. The first night back with the ship still alongside in Rosyth and preparations underway for departure, the crew were awoken by Chalky's screaming. Initially as he awoke, apparently from some nightmare, he was seen to be staring straight ahead, his eyes bulging in their sockets. He was sweating profusely, so much so that his face, neck and even his hair were soaking wet. Try as they may, his shipmates could not calm him down and one of their number was sent to get the medical officer.

Before he arrived, however, Chalky had fought his way free from those attempting to constrain him and he rushed through the bulkhead door. Following him, although not being able to get a complete grip on him owing to the confines of the ship's walkways, his fellow crew members tried to hold him back. He ran forwards to his gun which was towards the bow but ran straight on without any hesitation and over the side of the ship. The side where he jumped was close to the dockside and those that saw him leap the guard rail said that he hit the concrete dock wall before being catapulted into the water. They also remarked that he dived, headfirst, without any chance to protect himself as though he had no thought other than to end it all.

When the body was recovered later that day it was clear from the head injuries sustained that death had been instantaneous upon him hitting the side of the dock. Those that were involved remarked on his staring eyes, as though fixated upon some horror in his mind. My father was one of the sailors charged with the responsibility of moving poor Chalky's body and preparing it before the civilian authorities came on board to collect it. It was customary to, whenever possible, send the uniform of the deceased to their relatives if they so wished. By way of preparation, my father was charged with the overseeing of the removal of the outer uniform in order that it could be forwarded to them. In Chalky's case this was trousers, shirt, belt and shoes, the other items of his uniform being still in his locker on board. On removing items from the pockets of the trousers my father came upon a screwed up piece of paper, strangely still dry, on which was written *'Beware the curse of the book'*.

Detailed post-mortems were often not carried out during wartime and Chalky's death was put down to stress caused by fear of combat which was not uncommon in those dark days but rarely spoken of because of the potential negative effect on morale.

My father admitted to me before he died many years later that he kept the piece of paper that he had found and did not reveal at the time that it even existed. He also told me that it included the true name of the book, what that name was and that I was never to speak of it to anyone for fear that a similar fate may be met by me or my descendants.

For reasons which will become evident, I have never revealed the true name of the book to another living soul but have only referred to it by a made-up name which I chose to be '*The Quexado*'.

Chapter Two
The Offering of the Book

Having completed the business of the day I came out of the office I had been visiting in Piccadilly only to be confronted by a dark dank London evening. There must have been about ten taxis that passed me with no 'available' light on. Since I had the right clothing on, including my trusty wet weather coat, I opted to give up on any means of public transport and walk to my hotel.

I figured that it would take me around thirty minutes to walk, via the back streets, across Oxford Street and up the Edgeware Road where my hotel was located close to the Marylebone flyover.

Cutting through the back streets I recall being on the approach to Oxford Street where, looking through the gloom I could make out the trail of buses going to and fro. The intensity of the drizzle increased and, the wind being in my face, I put my head down and strode forward against the weather.

I recall that the shops on my right as I walked were kind of arty, each with one or two pictures in the window to entice customers to enter and further study the goods inside.

As I walked on, stooping slightly with my head down against the increasing shower, I could see, out of the corner of my eye, a figure in what appeared to be a long cape and a large-brimmed hat, standing close to a doorway and looking out into the street. As I passed him he offered me a greeting of, "Good evening, Sir".

Given the weather and my disinclination to speak with anybody, particularly a stranger in the street in London on a wet and dismal evening, I ignored his call and attempted to proceed on my way.

What he said next stopped me in my tracks and caused me to turn and look back at him.

"I understand you may be interested in a copy of the Quexado." (Although he used the full name of the book as my father had told me many years before.)

He stood to one side and raised an arm horizontally in a gesture, motioning towards an open doorway and apparently inviting me to enter.

At first I was unsure but since he had stunned me to the core by what he said, and I was, by that time, feeling increasingly wet and becoming more than a little miserable, what did I have to lose?

I entered the doorway, passed a large green door and into a short passageway of about ten paces as I recall. The end of the corridor opened out into a smallish dimly-lit room in which I could see a large desk behind which was a high-backed armchair panelled in green leather with a smaller similarly upholstered chair in front placed at a slight angle.

To my left was a large open fronted bookcase which reached from floor to ceiling. There was a slightly odd odour in the room that I could not place but, looking up to my right I could sense that it may be coming from two wall lights which flickered a little and I realised could possibly be gaslights.

I stopped and he passed by me, removing his hat as he did so and hanging it on a wooden hook on the back wall. In the half-light I could make out that he had long hair and a slightly pointed beard coupled with a wide waxed moustache, rather in the style of pictures I had seen of Charles Dickens from the Victorian period. I judged him to be between forty and fifty years of age.

He motioned me to sit in the smaller of the two chairs, then he took his place at the desk.

"How did you come to hear of the book?" he asked.

I told him of the story my father had told of the demise of Chalky White,

"I should be clear and precise in my words before we proceed. There are rules which you must understand, obey and adhere to before we take the matter any further. The infringement of any of the rules at any time you are in possession of the book will, you must understand, lead only to disaster, heartache and, quite possibly, death."

"You will never reveal the name of the book to another living soul unless they state it first. Then, and only then, will you know that they are privileged to know of the book, its contents, its secrets and its power". My suggestion would be that you make up your own name for that title of the book and always use it, then you will be unlikely to reveal its true title.

You must never sell or pass the book to another party. It is only loaned to you and you will keep it in safe custody until he or she who is designated to take it from you comes to collect it. This may or may not be me but they will make themselves known to you when the time comes to collect it. If you adhere to the rules then you will be the holder of the book for a period of twelve months.

You must never, under any circumstances, disclose the contents of the book whilst it is in your possession. Although not mandatory, you are advised that it will be best to wait for a period in excess of five years after you're returning the book before revealing what benefits it may have brought to you and even then not reveal the true name.

If you agree to these conditions, I can release the book to your safe custody; there is nothing to sign and no written receipt. Only your stated verbal acknowledgement of the rules as advised to you in this conversation and your confirmation that you have been made aware of the likely consequences should you not adhere fully to the rules as so advised.

He paused.

An avalanche of questions fell through my mind but I remained silent. I, after some thought, took a deep breath and asked him what the book could do for me. Even given all that had happened and all that he had said I still had no idea of the actual contents of the book.

"Before we go any further I need your agreement and total concurrence with the rules regarding the book. The book will then be delivered to you at midnight tonight."

So I thought a little more, decided that it was worth the risk, took a deep breath and told him of my total, unequivocal, agreement.

"Now we can continue," he said.

"It will seem strange but you must make the initial selection and then let the book lead you to your conclusion. You will be able to open the book at the initial contents page where the possible options will be listed. To achieve this you must firstly place a drop of your blood in the centre of the front cover. Then, and only then, will the book accept you and allow you to continue. If the book opens and you decide to proceed then the book will be your guide."

He leaned forward slightly and stared intently into my eyes and went on to say;

"My strong recommendation to you is that you follow the mantra:

Think carefully
Consider fully
Choose wisely

"Above all, take time to consider, once chosen the path is set and cannot be changed."

He hesitated slightly, looking directly into my eyes as though to emphasise his point and ensure that I had taken it in. He then continued:

"Once you have selected, open the book once again at the contents and identify your choice by the application of a drop of your blood placed in the circle adjacent to your choice. Then you must request the approval of your selection by the book.

"In order to achieve this you must place both hands on the book, pressing firmly down with both palms for two full minutes. You will then raise your hands; the book will then open slightly at the predetermined page. Slide your hand carefully in the gap between the pages and your acceptance will have been confirmed. If the book does not accept your request then the book will not open, the process may be considered over and your chance will be gone forever. If you are accepted, however, you can note the page and return to it whenever you so wish; all of the other pages in the book will appear as an indecipherable code and, although visible, will not be readable or translatable by you.

I repeat, you must remember, once selected there is no way to reselect your choice if you change your mind, once chosen there is no way to change your selection.

"In completion, I must emphasise to you for the final time that crossing the book whilst it is in your possession by showing it to another living soul or stating, by any means, the true name of the book will bring about a terrible penalty. All of the demons in your mind will be released and you will undergo unimaginable suffering from inside that will only be quenched by your death."

He went on to say something that stunned me to my core.

"Recall the ramifications of not following these rules as witnessed by your father."

He continued, "Whilst I have warned you of the penalty of revealing the true name of the book, the burden of what happens if you proceed with what it can provide you with and the mental challenge of maintaining the secrecy of what has happened to you becomes too heavy, you may feel the need to share what has come about with others and thus ease your mind. Providing that you never reveal the true name of the book the dire consequences of which I have warned you will not come about since the sceptics and doubters of the world, and there are many of them, will merely think of you as a dreamer or a simpleton and pay no heed to your words."

Chapter Three
Verification

It transpired that, quite by chance, I found myself having to go to London for a business meeting some three weeks later. It entered my head that I would take the same route as I had done previously to get to my hotel even thought it was, admittedly, a little out of my way. This time, the weather was clear and it was a somewhat cool but dry evening. As I walked down the street and approached the series of shopfronts incorporating the doorway that I had been invited to enter before, I was astounded to see that the doorway was not there! Not only was it not there, the existing premises looked as though they had been there forevermore, there was no evidence that the doorway that I had entered had ever existed.

I stopped and stared for a few moments, staring at the shop facades from the other side of the street, trying to take things in and make sense of what was in front of me. After what seemed to be an hour, but was probably only a few minutes, I made the decision to go into the shop premises to the left of where I thought the door should be.

As I entered I could see that the premises were being used as a gallery for paintings and objets d'art. There were paintings, sculptures and a number of antique items displayed tastefully inside.

A man approached me and asked if he could assist me in any way. My initial response to him was that I was only browsing for a gift.

I showed some interest in a couple of the more expensive items, both landscapes, and having got into conversation, he offered me a cup of tea which I accepted.

Without providing him with any details of the background as to how I came to enter his showroom (although I recall that he preferred to refer to it as a gallery). I managed to steer him around to the origins of the premises and he told me that he actually had a photograph of the shop as it had been in the 1920s left by a previous owner. He disappeared into a back office and returned with an old sepia print. Upon closer examination I found an inscription on the reverse of the photograph which stated in beautiful copperplate handwriting:

'Mr. Jellicoe's emporium shewing the newly installed full shop front facade by Joshua Johnson 15th April 1921'.

Unfortunately, he said, he had no evidence as to how the building looked prior Joshua Johnson's work being carried out.

However the he did go on to say that business had been good recently and he was looking to expand. He had engaged the services of a surveyor to advise what was possible, feasible and affordable. He went on to tell me that during his examination the surveyor had told him that there was a hollow area in the wall on one side at the rear of the premises. Thinking on my feet and, I have to admit, lying to him for my own purposes, I told him that I too had been a surveyor in an earlier employment and was interested in the origin and development of old buildings. Since I also expressed a potential further interest in the two landscapes, he suggested that I could possibly come back when his surveyor was due to return, with a builder, to carefully strip the wallpaper and examine the wall behind.

We agreed to this and he committed to contact me when the surveyor's visit was to take place.

True to his word, he called me three weeks later and advised me of the appointed date. I duly arrived at the showroom as we planned and was introduced to the surveyor and his builder colleague. The surveyor marked the area out that he considered to be hollow, the builder laid out dust sheets and set to work on the wall, having been given permission to start work by the gallery owner.

Once the layers of paper and paint that had been applied over the years were removed, it could be seen that a panel had been inserted to block an entranceway, possibly into an area behind. The builder estimated that, given the workmanship and the number of coatings on the wall, the work to section off the area behind had taken place some years previously, probably in the 1910s or 1920s. I noted, to myself, that this would coincide with the building renovations as depicted in the photograph that the owner had shown me.

Permission was granted for the builder to break through and investigate what lay behind the panel. This was duly done and a hole created of a size that a man could get through. Both the builder and the surveyor picked up torches and carefully stepped into the space behind. It turned out to be big enough for both of them to disappear completely inside.

When they came out they invited us to enter, pointing out that there we would find a small room which was dark and dusty but in surprisingly good condition since it had likely been walled up for many years.

What I saw as I entered took my breath away. The room was undoubtedly the room that I had been in only a few weeks before. The furniture was the same, the bookcase was the same and, most shocking of all for me, the green leather chair was exactly as I remembered it had been, albeit with a thin layer of fine dust.

Chapter Four
The Delivering/Reading of the Book

Departing from the gallery, my head still spinning slightly, I made my way to my hotel. I tended to use the same hotel when visiting London, it was easy to reach, consistently good and with friendly staff, some of which had started to recognise me, presumably from my frequent stays. I checked in and made my way to my room.

I had dinner in my room but afterwards did not get ready for bed but watched television and enjoyed a few drinks that I had ordered with the meal.

True to what I had been told there was a knock at the door of my hotel room door at midnight. When I opened it there stood a man, I would guess between forty and fifty years old, dressed in a dark blue suit, white shirt, no tie and brown shoes. In short, he had the appearance of a typical businessman that you would see in around the city. In his hand he held a package about the size of a cereal box, wrapped in brown paper and tied up with string.

He held out his hand and the package was duly handed over. He spoke just to identify that this was indeed the book by its true title. Not another word was spoken by either of us and he turned and walked away down the corridor without any further gesture or looking back.

I closed the door and turned back into my room. I put the package down onto one of the two shelves that served as a desk, pulled off the string and unfolded the brown paper to reveal the contents; the book.

It was about the 11 inches in height, eight inches wide, about the size of an A4 sheet of paper, and I would say around two inches thick. It was quite heavy, being bound in green leather with embossed gold borders on the front and back cover with corresponding gold bands on the spine. The front cover had additional sold embossed diagonals that culminated, where they crossed in a circle shape about one inch in diameter. It occurred to me that the colour of the leather was identical to the chair in the back room of the gallery.

I did as I had been told, pricked my finger and squeezed it slightly in order to produce a drop of blood which I duly dripped gently onto the circle at centre of the front cover. The red liquid disappeared instantly as it was absorbed into the green leather. As I moved my hand away there was no trace or mark left on the front of the book. I then held my hand, palm downwards, on the book and uttered the incantation as I had been instructed. As I released the pressure, the top of the book sprang open slightly releasing the first three or four pages only and revealing a cream-coloured envelope with a red ribbon around it. Written across the front of the envelope was a single word in old-fashioned copperplate script – *'Read'*.

Firstly, I turned to the envelope, removed the red ribbon and opened it. Inside was a single sheet of parchment-type paper with the following statement.

> *"The book can only respond a further three times, each time with a drop of blood only from you. You must learn all you need to know in three openings or your chance will be lost forever.*
> > *Think carefully*
> > *Consider fully*
> > *Choose wisely"*

The first page of the book was blank, as would be expected, but its thickness and texture led me to think that this was old, probably hand-made, paper. Turning the page, I came upon the frontispiece which appeared to be an old geometric print with the title of the book printed across it with a font that can only be described as very old in appearance and probably hand-drawn.

The third page contained the index in the same font but smaller so as to fit the page and accommodate an ornate border. There were no page numbers and the listing consisted of nine headings:

> *The ability to fly*
> *A period of invisibility*
> *To be able to breathe underwater*
> *Limited time travel*
> *To be able to read the minds of others*
> *Temporary metamorphosis*
> *Improvement in looks or appearance*
> *Eternal youth*
> *To choose how to die*

I closed the book, having noted down the headings using pencil and paper just in case there was any restriction on my being able to open it again until I was prepared to make my selection for real.

I went to bed and slept a fitful disturbed night, going over and over what had happened and attempting to make some sense of it. I was, however, comforted by the fact that I had been told that I would hold the book for twelve months and, as such, any plans to be made could be thought over with care and consideration.

Chapter Five
Deliberation and Selection

It struck me that the listing was a little like the menu in a restaurant that you were visiting for the first time. When faced with such a document, one tended to consider the main course first and pay little heed to the starters or desserts on offer. It could be that there were several options that one would like and that choosing was difficult but, on the other hand, it could be that nothing on the menu tempted the palate and that one was left with the 'least worse' option which made it even more difficult to decide.

I felt that the list of options stated in the contents was probably best to be considered fully, as there was no supporting information to expand or explain what the individual single lines meant.

I thought back to the advice given by the man in the green chair:

Think carefully
Consider fully
Choose wisely

And I decided to think each item through to better understand their meaning.

The ability to fly

A simple enough meaning, I thought, presumably the possibility of taking to the air without any mechanical aids and thus to be able to travel freely from one place to another. Although we do require mechanical means to undertake our aviation, there is nothing surprising to us today in taking to the air whereas there may well have been over the life of the book.

A period of invisibility

I felt that there may be opportunities here, although I noted that there may be some risks involved. How long was the likely period to be, did invisibility imply only the body or clothing as well and could one be truly invisible to all persons and non-human creatures alike? One would surely still generate sounds and odours which would potentially give away one's presence to human or animal. Not being seen may present as many challenges, I thought, as it would provide opportunities to gain knowledge or wealth.

To be able to breathe underwater

This may have been miraculous at some time over the eons that the book had probably been in existence but not so fantastic a capability in today's world of breathing apparatus and underwater equipment. Thus it could be discounted.

Limited time travel

An interesting concept, I thought, but what was meant by the term 'limited' and could one go back or forwards in time? I had always understood that any change in the past could lead to paradoxes that would affect the way forward and potentially have an effect upon the present day which would only become evident when one returned. As regards travelling forwards into the future, what would be the benefit in that other than to learn something that could be financially profitable, presumably by investing in future successes or betting on occurrences such as sporting events which were yet to take place?

To be able to read the minds of others

I have to say that I struggled to perceive any instance in which this would be advantageous in the modern day. I cannot see that this ability would help in any business dealings to any great extent. No negotiations would be greatly assisted by understanding the opposing person's point of view or methodology. In personal circumstances I would think that this could be of considerable hindrance, given that we often wish to hide behind our own individual private cloak of security.

Temporary metamorphosis

I must admit that I became a little unsure of what this actually meant, both when considering the context of today or, indeed, at any time in the past. Did it mean the ability to change into another being, as the metamorphosis that takes place between the caterpillar and the butterfly or did it mean the taking on the appearance of another human being and thus masquerading as them? Was this meant to convey the phenomenon of what we would know today as shapeshifting?

Improvement in looks or appearance

I do not consider myself to be a vain individual and, as such, this topic does not hold any interest for me, I can understand that some people would like to change some aspect of their appearance. However, the heading did not seem to imply that such a change would be solely a temporary improvement as could be said of some of the other options so maybe some would be tempted to select it. I can also understand that in the past such afflictions as disease, a poor diet or malnutrition could inflict terrible disfigurement and thus this option could have been seen as a godsend to some whereas today we seem merely to prioritise bodily enhancements driven by the fashions of the day.

Eternal youth

Who in their right mind would want eternal youth? Although undoubtedly at first glance some would argue for the option of staying in the moment and living forever, imagine the mental turmoil of seeing others coming, living their lives and then departing as nature intended whilst not being able to move forward in life with all its challenges and opportunities. I am afraid that I could only view this option as a curse rather than something to aspire to.

To choose how to die

Somewhat gruesome, one would have thought. I suppose that there may have been some advantages in olden times, given the illnesses that prevailed and the severe nature of sentences that were meted out for crimes that we would think insignificant by our modern standards. There was, as far as I could tell from the title, no potential to prolong one's existence and I consider that I am perfectly prepared to meet my maker by any means that fate had in mind for me.

So my issue became, given the broad nature of the headings and no further enhancement or detailed description, a selection based largely on conjecture and guesswork.

I discounted most and came to the decision to focus on two –*A period of invisibility and a brief period of time travel.*

I came to the conclusion, rightly or wrongly, that my main aim was to be to gain some personal wealth from the exercise, to use the ability offered to enhance my financial situation somewhat; not necessarily to make a vast fortune but to at least improve my bank balance to provide me with a comfortable existence going forward.

Now having decided on my aims, I addressed the two subjects further. I would need to make some assumptions and consider potential risks involved with each of the tasks. This is how I went about it.

Firstly, the period of invisibility. I surmised that this was likely to be 24 to 48 hours, certainly not as long as a week.

I could have decided upon clandestine visits to places that one would normally be barred from entering.

I mused on what such places might be for a while but decided to drop this train of thought on the basis that while it may provide some interesting scenarios it was unlikely to contribute to my primary financial objective.

I developed a programme in my head which involved staying in a big London hotel, commencing the process of invisibility and thus on leaving my room I would be able to move about unseen. Presumably once I had decided on that path the book would have provided more details as to the length of time the condition would last and how it could be controlled.

Although I spent weeks thinking about this option whenever I had the time, either during the day or when the conundrum kept me awake at night, I became ever more concerned over the issues that I perceived may arise.

The prospect of invisibility could lead to access to places that I normally couldn't go. This would mean interesting places or meetings, more salacious locations, or opportunities to make financial gain. Possibly financial gain would enable me to go where I wished to anyway.

I have to say that it is not in my nature to be a thief and so I struggled to decide how I would achieve any monetary gains. I did test the notion over a lunch with some friends, not in specific detail, you understand, but more as a question – "What would you do if you could be invisible for, say, two days?" – usually raised after a couple of bottles of wine had been consumed.

The conversation just served to raise more potential pitfalls in my mind such as: Would the invisibility reach to clothing? The question of nakedness could be vitally important in selecting the time of year and the weather. Even a simple thing like rain could become an issue.

How to transport any material goods? Although I may be invisible, surely they would not which severely impacted upon the choice of their size and how I could secrete them. If I held things in my hand or inside my body would they still be visible? Could I, for example, put things, small things of value, in my mouth and them be cloaked by my own invisibility in some way?

How to travel around? There was the obvious issue of transport. How would one travel around using public transport, for example? Surely there could be issues with bumping into other people or, worse, vehicles. Remember, whether people or modes of transport, if they can't see you, you are not in their path.

Would my prescience be traceable after the event? Even if I were not visible would I still leave traces behind such as fingerprints or DNA for others to detect?

Given my doubts I decided to embark on a test which I would call 'The Hatton Garden Conundrum'. I based my deliberations on the assumption (whether correct or not) that whilst anything held in my hand may be visible, things secreted within my mouth would not be. Thus I judged that if I could hide small high-value items in that manner I could successfully carry them away to my personal benefit.

I estimated that I could steal approximately twelve high value rings, probably diamond rings, using this method so I took myself off on a visit to Hatton Garden in London to test out the feasibility of this modus operandi.

I travelled by underground to make the journey from my selected hotel to Hatton Garden. As I did so I tried to consider the pitfalls of using public transport such as this to make my way through the city. It became evident very quickly that whilst I had assumed that being invisible would be a bonus, the opposite was likely to be the case. Primarily the issue was that I would have to be much more aware of my surroundings and my proximity to other members of the general public. Because they would be unable to see me, they would not make any adjustments in their movements to take account of my presence. There was undoubtedly the possibility of their bumping into me as they went on their way undertaking their respective journeys. To remain undetected the onus would be on me and I would have to be aware of and compensate for their actions as well as my own.

When I arrived at Hatton Garden another of my potential concerns was realised. It was raining, only a light drizzle but enough to make my coat wet as I walked along the street. As an additional point, I noted that it was possible to make out my footprints as I walked and, more importantly, I left wet footmarks if I ventured closer into the shop doorways to examine the goods therein in greater detail. Presumably this would also be the case if I ventured inside, at least for the first few paces.

I then came upon three further issues that I had not really taken account of before.

Firstly, was there really sufficient value in the goods that were on display to make the whole venture worthwhile? It is true that there may be other items within some of the shops of greater value but there would always be increased risk, reduced opportunity and a further risk of detection in a more confined environment. It became evident that it would be difficult, if not impossible, to lift them and secrete them within my mouth or elsewhere on my person in order to facilitate the removal of enough really high value items to make me a life-changing amount of money. This was further compounded by the fact that I had not really given a great deal of thought on how I was going to turn my ill-gotten gains into real usable money. In essence, I had not considered sufficiently how to dispose of the goods afterwards and turn them into hard cash.

Furthermore, it was evident that although Hatton Garden had the appearance of a relatively open shopping environment, security was taken seriously and looking around I could see that there were several strong-arm individuals around in the area. Admittedly, they would have difficulty in apprehending me but one slip on my part and the whole exercise could be doomed.

Additionally, there was the issue of whether I would leave behind any traces of my criminal activity such as fingerprints or traces of my DNA? How could I avoid this? The use of gloves would clearly be a non-starter. Whilst I consider that, being a generally law-abiding individual, it was unlikely that any samples of either traceable factors would be in the hands of any law enforcement agency this still added a further risk which I had not previously taken into account.

So the conclusion that I gained from the trial run that I chose to call 'The Hatton Garden Conundrum' was that the whole operation was not for me. It was not in my nature to be a thief; my upbringing had taught me that I should not take things for my own use that would be to the detriment of others. I had no experience of how to steal things that did not belong to me and thus it was plainly evident that there were too many imponderables for me to deal with. Not only that, even with all the foresight and planning that I could muster, I simply did not have the knowledge or experience to carry the venture through and so I decided to review other options that the book offered in greater detail.

I walked, somewhat dejectedly, to Chancery Lane underground station and made my way home.

And so to my second option: *A brief period of time travel*. My concern here was that I didn't know what was meant by 'brief' or whether the travel would be forward or back in time. My decision was hampered by the fact that I couldn't know the entirety of this option until I took the plunge but given that this had become the favoured option (by dint of rejecting all the others) I decided to go with it and to address the book to ascertain how to proceed.

Having now made my ultimate decision, it was time to consult the book once more as to the way forward.

I opened the book once again to reveal the options listing. I knew from the instructions given by the old man in the gallery, together with the note in the mysterious envelope, that I was required to provide a drop of blood to confirm my selection. I duly did this by pricking my finger and allowing a drop of the red fluid to fall on the circle shape adjacent to the head of my selected option. Instantly the globule of red disappeared as it was absorbed into the page. After a couple of seconds the booked moved as it opened almost imperceptibly about three quarters down from the front, thus allowing me to open the book fully at that point.

The book stated that I could move forwards or backwards in time by up to a hundred years for a period of no longer than fourteen days and that the book would only enable one episode to occur.

In addition there was a strong warning that causing any changes, however small, in occurrences whilst visiting back in time could, over a period, cause unimaginable ramifications. This was particularly true when going back and potentially altering or influencing any event which was yet to happen. Even the slightest change could bring about a knock-on resultant impact elsewhere that was unforeseen with dire and potentially catastrophic consequences. At all costs, a time-generated paradox must be avoided.

Chapter Six
Realisation

.

After some deliberation I thought that the best course of action for me was to go forward two weeks for a period of two hours and then return. In doing this, I could ascertain, hopefully, previous national lottery numbers for the intervening period such that I could return to my original time and purchase tickets that I would win me big prize money when claimed.

Thinking the whole exercise through I realised that for the period of time that I chose, it was probable that I would exist twice, once when I leapt forward and again when I 'caught up' on the second occasion. Once I realised this, two things became evident. Firstly I could have no contact with any other individual and secondly I could not come face-to-face with myself. Both instances may cause a time paradox which could have unintended but far-reaching consequences as the book had warned.

This was the course of action that I took.

I waited for about a month in case anything came to mind that would cause me to think that my approach was flawed. When I decided that all possible risks had been evaluated and dismissed, I made the first step.

This was to make two bookings at the large London hotel that I was very familiar with having stayed there on business many times. Both bookings were for a Saturday night/Sunday morning two weeks apart. I stipulated that I must have exactly the same twin double bedded room on both occasions. I duly received confirmation from the hotel that both bookings were made and that my requirements would be adhered to unconditionally.

On the first Saturday I arrived at the hotel around mid-afternoon, checked in and made my way to my room which contained twin double beds as I had requested. I relaxed for an hour or so, watched some television and in the early evening ordered a room service meal. After the meal, having placed the used tray outside the door for collection, I turned my attention to the book.

Having located the selected option in the book that I had chosen, I set about initiating the arrangements which I understood would enable me to undertake the leap in time that I sought. For thethird time this necessitated a drop of my blood onto a circle on the page which, unsurprisingly now, disappeared instantaneously on touch. I cannot go into detail but all the necessary instructions, methods and means by which I could undertake this travelling in time and thus achieve my goal were laid down clearly in the book. I then set about performing the necessary rituals outlined in the book which, I have to say, were not too arduous but of which I cannot tell more.

My selection option of going forward two weeks for a period of two hours had now been refined into determining that those hours were to be four o'clock to six o'clock in the early hours of Sunday morning.

My aim was that during this period I would be able to ascertain the winning lottery numbers from the previous two Saturdays draws, return to my own time and purchase lottery tickets that would secure my financial future.

At around midnight I went to bed, not knowing what would happen, whether this was all real or whether I was merely a pawn in some cruel, callous and rather elaborate hoax. I could not see how I could lose by entering into the game, however, there appeared to be no negative side. Even if it didn't come to pass I would not lose anything, save the cost of the night spent in the hotel.

I had made an outline plan and chose to sleep in the left-hand bed and, although my mind was full of random thoughts about what may or may not happen, I eventually drifted off to sleep, the book on the bedside table beside me.

I don't know how it came to pass but I was awoken by a sudden noise in the room, a dull but resounding thudding sound on the floor. When I looked at the clock it was four o'clock in the morning. The book, heavy though it was, could be seen across the room some distance from the bed and open, apparently lifting itself slightly from the floor and then dropping down to create the sound. It didn't stop until I got up, went across to it and reached out to touch it. On contact with my hand all movement stopped and it was quiet once more.

I checked my phone and my tablet but neither was working, there were only error messages stating that no service was available. I called the operator on the room telephone, made up some story about my having been travelling and had only checked in that day to ask about the date today. She was not at all fazed by my request and calmly informed me that it was indeed two weeks later than when I had checked in.

I rechecked my devices but there clearly was a problem, either with the date or possibly the hotel systems. So I sat on the edge of the bed and pondered what to do next. As I did so I sensed that there was someone else in the room and, more concerning, that they were sleeping in the other, right hand, bed. Then it dawned on me that the other occupant in the room was me! It was me in two weeks' time, two weeks ahead of when I had gone to sleep!

So, what to do next? How to proceed?

I decided that in order to find out the information that I desired would have to rely on means other than electronic devices. My only option, I thought, was to seek the help of others and this led me to the conclusion that could only accomplish his by leaving the room. Given the hour this would mean a trip to the hotel lobby to seek out a member of the hotel staff who would be on duty at that time of night; maybe the duty manager or a night porter?

I had a habit of leaving my important personal items such as my wallet, phone, car keys, home keys, and room keys next to the television. This had been brought about by many years of travelling in my job and numerous health and safety training sessions from companies that I had worked for. The principle was that in the event of a hotel evacuation it was always advisable to be able to locate items of clothing, shoes and important personal items quickly and easily as well as knowing the shortest route to any fire exits, potentially in total darkness. Although I had been fortunate enough never to have been involved in a real hotel fire on several occasions I had been in the position of having to leave the premises quickly because of false alarms and the training advice given had always held me in good stead.

Sure enough, the small folder of room keys was where I always left it so I made my way out of the room and headed down via a lift to the hotel lobby.

I arrived in the hotel reception to find two men at one of the check-in desks. One I recognised as the concierge and another who I took to be the duty manager. They were deep in conversation regarding one of the more important guests and their apparent idiosyncrasies. The concierge broke off to ask whether he could help me. I told him of my dilemma and made up a story that I was travelling for my job and going to the airport for a flight later that morning. However, because of my itinerary and the likely duration of my visit overseas I really wanted to clear up the situation and needed to know the winning numbers for the last weeks Saturday lottery, that is yesterday and the week before.

Initially, he told me that he could not help me owing to the hotel system being unavailable because it was undergoing maintenance and that he did not know for how long it would be unavailable. I attempted flattery, playing to his ego and telling how his reputation was that he was known to be resourceful in the face of adversity. This approach, together with the surreptitious handing over of a £20 note enabled him to call a fellow concierge in another hotel to obtain the information which he duly wrote down on a piece of paper and handed it to me.

It suddenly dawned on me, I know not why, that, given the incentive of the money that he could, if he was inclined to, either make a fake call or that both he and the person he had called could simply make up the numbers in question. After all, I had used the premise that I was due to leave the country later that morning and would not be in a position to challenge him should the information he provided be incorrect. For a few seconds I told myself that he had to be honest given the integrity and responsibility required in his position, then I considered the risk that I was taking and if this information was wrong, all I had been through would have been in vain.

Politely but firmly I asked him to make a further call to a hotel of my choosing and that I would speak to the concierge personally. He raised his eyebrows at my request and said that he was upset that I doubted him. However, a further £20 changed hands and he acceded to my request. I spoke to the person at the end of the phone myself, ensuring myself as much as possible that he was genuine by asking a few pertinent questions. He confirmed the numbers that I had in front of me and I knew that I now had in my hand a piece of paper detailing the results I required and confirmed by a third party. With the piece of paper clutched firmly in my hand, I returned to my room.

It then came into my mind that it was possible that I couldn't simply take the piece of paper back to my own time and use it to register the numbers with the lottery. After all, I would be putting my faith in a piece of paper that hadn't even been written yet since it was only generated in the future when I was back in my own time. I therefore set about memorising the numbers, using various techniques that I had learnt over the years, techniques such as birthdays, memorable numbers and those which had a specific easily remembered significance to me.

Once I was comfortable that I could recall the numbers at will as and when I required to I returned to the left hand bed and went back to sleep, once again making sure that I occupied the left hand bed. Just as I was dropping off I did hear a rustle from the other, right hand, bed in the room but quickly realised that this may just be me two weeks hence and thus I resisted any attempt to speak out or make a sound in any way.

At eight o'clock I awoke. I was alone in the room. I, as when I went to sleep, was in the left hand bed and the other bed was unruffled and untouched. I checked my phone and my tablet and they confirmed that it was Sunday morning, the morning after the day I had arrived.

The difference was the two sets of numbers that I had in my head. As I became further awake and more to my senses I wondered if this had all been a fantastic but nevertheless vivid dream.

Then, as I looked over the side of the bed, there was the Quexado on the floor just where I remembered it had been when it apparently had awoken me in the early hours.

Quickly, I picked up the small hotel notepad and pen by the room telephone and wrote down both sets of numbers as I had remembered them. Folding the piece of paper and placing it in my wallet, I sat down to try and clear the somewhat confused thoughts in my head.

Having showered, shaved and dressed, I packed up my things, checked the room and made my way down to reception where I checked out, picked up my car from the hotel car park and drove home.

On the Monday, I paid a visit to my local supermarket to purchase my lottery tickets. I don't know why but, because of some unknown reasoning on my part, I thought that I needed to conceal what I was doing. Therefore I purchased five entries for each of the following two Saturdays. For the first Saturday's entry I altered one of the six predicted numbers in the sequence supposedly to test my chances of winning. The second week's entry was exactly as predicted with all six numbers as I had remembered.

When the first Saturday came around and the draw was made I have to say that my emotions were that of apprehension and hope tinged with nervousness. In the event I was amazed, but somehow relieved, to find that the five numbers were just as had been foretold and I duly collected my winnings.

I decided that, given the pressures that may come about from the lottery promoters I would make a second entry for the same numbers for the second Saturday. Although one could stipulate no publicity, it was clear that the promoters would wish to advertise winners as much as possible as a means of encouraging future players. I felt, rightly or wrongly, that a split prize won by two winners would attract less attention, even if it transpired that both winners were actually the same person! With this in mind I paid a visit to another supermarket on the other side of town and made the same entry as previously for the second Saturday. I could always say that I had forgotten that I had already entered or mislaid my ticket to explain why I had purchased the same numbers as my entry for a second time.

When the second Saturday came around I left the book at home, for it was closed to me now and its work was done, and made my way back to the hotel, duly arriving around three o'clock as before.

When I attempted to check in I was informed by the hotel reception clerk that there was a problem with my room since the previous guest had overstayed owing to a delayed flight he or she was to catch. I stressed that only this room would suffice. The check-in receptionist offered me a suite at the same price but I stuck to my guns, insisted that the other guest moved and that

I wanted what I booked and what had been agreed. My audible complaining in the hotel reception area brought out the duty manager who clearly was concerned about the effect of the noise on other guests and the disruption being caused by my apparent displeasure. His intervention, coupled with the discreet handing over of a £50 pound note meant that after a short delay of about an hour, the room that I insisted upon having was secured for my use. I presumed that the present incumbent had been offered the suite as an incentive to move.

So I made my way to the room, ordered a room service meal, watched TV and went to bed at around 10 o'clock, making sure that this time I opted for the right hand bed and that I left the small folder containing the room keys, as I normally did, by the television.

I went off to sleep fairly easily and slept well, probably aided by the large glass of wine that I had consumed with the room service meal.

I was awoken in the early hours, I'm not sure of the time, when I thought I thought I heard a sound, someone in the room, potentially someone attempting to access the internet on a device. I perceived that there was a little light coming from one corner of the room. My first instinct was to investigate but then I realised that it was probably me and resolved to stay where I was; making any contact may bring about some time paradox of which the book had forewarned. So I turned over and tried to go back to sleep.

I have to confess that it crossed my mind that I should now be the one going down to the hotel lobby. If I did so, would there then be two of us down there? I decided that such thoughts were too complicated for me so it was best that I stayed put and didn't leave the bed.

I did hear my apparent return from the lobby and I admit that I did turn over in the bed, which I recall is what I heard when I made the leap forward. So all was probably well and, as the room went quiet again, I fell back to sleep.

I recall that shortly after my sleep was slightly disturbed by a strange kind of shudder, that I felt cold and shivered a little.

I awoke at around eight o'clock. As I expected, I was still in my own time and feeling well. The shock came when I realised that, staggeringly, I was in the other bed, not the one that I had initially used the night before but the one that I had awoken in my foray into the future. I had no idea how this had come about but recalled that there was evidence that both beds had been used. I did not bother to contemplate how this could have come about; this, I thought, would prove too difficult for me to comprehend. Trying to think it through would just serve to scramble my brain further.

My first thought was that all that had happened may merely be the explained by a particularly deep and vivid dream. After all, we have all had dreams where our minds have played tricks on us only to find out on becoming fully awake that we have been fooled.

Then, as I looked around the room, I saw the Quexado on the floor by the bed. I reached down and picked it up. It would no longer open and stayed tightly shut, its work being done.

I picked up my tablet, went online, and found the lottery website that confirmed that my numbers were indeed the winning numbers. There was even a comment from the lottery operators stating:

"The jackpot last night was shared between two winners who, by coincidence, live within four miles of each other."

All possible time paradoxes having been avoided, and the lottery results confirmed, I had breakfast in the hotel, checked out, went about my normal business of the day and made preparations to claim and collect my winnings.

Chapter Seven
The Returning

One year on from the delivery of the book, now a much richer and contented man, I checked into the same hotel, now in the best room that they could supply, and waited quietly in my room for the collection of the book.

I sat, fully dressed, in a comfortable chair, sipping a glass of wine and contemplating all that had occurred since that dark dank drizzly night. At midnight there was a gentle but purposeful knock on the door and I arose to open it.

Standing in the corridor was an olive-skinned woman with long brown hair, difficult to judge but aged between 35 and 45 I would say, wearing a three-quarter length grey coat with a fur collar, a red Gucci handbag and matching high heeled shoes. She looked elegant and sophisticated. Our eyes met momentarily and I was instantly smitten.

She spoke, "I have come for the book".

"You must tell me the name to ensure that you are the one," I replied.

She the uttered the correct title quietly, leaning towards me and almost whispering the true name.

I stepped back to allow her to enter the room, she swept past me with a flourish, exuding an air of confidence. Being so close, I could detect the subtle delicate scent of an expensive perfume.

When she saw that I had wrapped the book in brown paper and tied the package up with string, she said, "I must verify that this is the one".

She placed the package on the room table and opened it. Seeing what she needed to see, she re-wrapped it and made towards the door saying only, "Thank you, all is well, I must leave now."

As she left, I had an urge to follow her, I don't really know why although I felt that there were questions that I needed to be answered. Maybe, just maybe, I could offer to buy her a drink in the bar downstairs and thus glean more information about all that had transpired. I turned back and grabbed my room key then made to follow her. By the time I did so she was some fifty feet ahead of me and walking swiftly. She was out of my sight briefly as she turned the corner to the area where there were three lifts down to the hotel lobby.

I hurried along, expecting to meet up with her as she waited for a lift to arrive and possibly travel down with her. When I made it to the lifts, however, there was no sign of her. I couldn't understand where she could have gone, there had been no sound of a lift arriving or of lift doors opening and closing. It then dawned on me that there was also no sound of any movements coming from the lift mechanism. She had, to all intents and purposes, just disappeared into thin air.

Chapter Eight
Completion

So that is my story, from beginning to end, of how initially I made my fortune. True, I have made sound investments based upon good financial advice that I have sought and acted upon wisely. I have all the material goods that I will ever need and contribute to various charities that are near to my heart. I know that most believe that my success is based upon a big lottery win, which I suppose to a point is true but, as I look back and ponder the events that brought about the very comfortable existence that I enjoy, I wonder how many others have had the good luck to have had the same, or similar, experiences as I did and whether others are being given the same opportunities right now to shape their destiny.

I wonder whether such occurrences will carry on into the future and whether other fortunate souls will be offered The Quexado.

END

About the author

Colin Harley has drawn upon his own life experiences to set down in print a collection of short stories.

Born in Portsmouth and having spent much of his life travelling and working both abroad and across the UK he has come across many cultures, customs and beliefs.

When these have been combined with some locally sourced and possibly apocryphal tales that he has recorded and collated over the years, the stories have emerged.

These now form the basis of his writing and having recently retired, he has decided that now is the time to share his experiences with others.